THROUGH THE WALL

Books by Patricia Wentworth

THROUGH THE WALL

PATRICIA WENTWORTH

HarperPerennial

A Division of HarperCollins*Publishers*

HarperCollins books may be purchased for educational, business, or sales promotional use. For information, please call or write: Special Markets Department, HarperCollins Publishers, Inc., 10 East 53rd Street, New York, NY 10022. Telephone: (212) 207-7528; Fax: (212) 207-7222.

First Perennial Library edition published 1989. First HarperPerennial edition published 1992.

LIBRARY OF CONGRESS CATALOG CARD NUMBER 88-45966

ISBN 0-06-092298-2

92 93 94 95 96 WB/MB 10 9 8 7 6 5 4 3 2 1

CHAPTER 1

Mr. Ashton, the senior partner of Ashton & Fenwick, solicitors, looked benevolently across his broad writing-table at Miss Brand. He had no means of knowing whether her extreme restraint of manner was natural or the result of shock. He had just finished explaining to her that under the will of her uncle, Martin Brand, she had succeeded to a very considerable fortune. Since, owing to a family quarrel, she had not up to this moment so much as known that she possessed such a relative, it was not unnatural to suppose that the intelligence had come as a shock. He thought it best to make a pause in the proceedings before handing her the letter entrusted to him by his late client. An eccentric fellow Martin Brand, but not sufficiently eccentric to give the other relations any chance of upsetting the will. He had had a houseful of them on his hands. He hadn't liked any of them very much, and he had left everything to the daughter of the young brother who had flung out of the house and out of the family circle thirty years ago.

And here she was, Marian Brand, very quiet, very self-contained. She was extremely pale. The pallor might be the result of emotion, or it might be natural. There had, at any rate, been no attempt to remedy it. The fine, even skin was untouched by rouge, the well-cut lips were innocent of lipstick. This pallor and the quietness of her manner may have made her seem older than her twenty-seven years. The manner showed breeding. It was quiet, but it was neither nervous nor uncertain. Her voice when she spoke was pleasant and

1

cultivated. He knew that she had been working in a house-agent's office. He considered that she would have been an asset to the firm. She looked—he hesitated for a word and arrived at responsible. Well, she was having responsibility thrust upon her.

He had reached this point, when she spoke.

"Do you mind repeating the last thing you said? I want to be sure about it—about the income."

He leaned back in his chair smiling.

"Well, I can't pretend to give you an exact figure—you will understand that. But by the time all deductions are made—death duties, outstanding accounts, and allowing for income tax and surtax at the present rates—I think you may count on a clear two thousand a year. It may be more—it will, I think, almost certainly be more—but at the most conservative estimate it can hardly be less. Probate will, of course, take some time, but Mr. Brand arranged that a sum of money should be available without delay. You have a banking account?"

Marian Brand said, "No." Then she smiled and added, "Only in the Post Office Savings Bank. I have never had anything but what I earned. I haven't saved very much, I'm afraid—my sister hasn't been strong."

"So Mr. Brand said."

Five pounds a week, and a delicate sister to support, and the delicate sister's work-shy husband. He hoped that most of the money wouldn't just run away down that drain.

He took Martin Brand's letter from a drawer and went out of the office, leaving her to read it alone. She opened it without being able to feel that any of this was really happening. The part of her mind which recognized facts and their relation to other facts, the part which dealt with such things as cause and effect, was in a stunned condition, as completely in abeyance as if the events in which she was taking part were the

2

events of a dream. In a dream nothing astonished you—you no longer expect anything to follow a reasonable course. She turned mechanically to the letter which Mr. Ashton had given her.

The letter was written in a clear and legible hand. She read it with a steady deepening of the feeling that none of it really mattered, because presently she would wake up and find that it had never happened.

My dear Marian,

You will not receive this letter until I am dead and buried. Since we have been strangers in life, there is no need for you to pretend to a sorrow you cannot feel, or to be plunged into the intricacies of family relationships in the morbid atmosphere induced by a funeral. If you decide to meet your relations—and I suppose you may find youself obliged to do so—let it be in circumstances which do not encourage the emotions. I am afraid you must be prepared for these emotions to include hurt feelings, resentment, jealousy, and so forth, but not any personal grief. My relations do not love me any more than I love them. You will naturally ask yourself, since you cannot ask me, why I should have harboured a houseful of them for so many years. The answer is a very simple one. At first the arrangement was one of mutual convenience. I was a helpless widower and a natural prey to the womanly feelings of any unattached female relative. A not sufficiently distant cousin who had become my brother Alfred's widow settled on me with her son. She is Mrs. Alfred Brand, your Aunt Florence, a large woman with small, determined aims. Her son Felix plays the piano. After a year or two the constant visits of Florence's unmarried sister, Cassy Remington, merged into permanent residence at my expense. She also is related to you, and will doubtless make herself quite as unpleasant as if the relationship were a much nearer one.

So much for preliminaries. When I made up my mind that I would rather leave my money to a dogs' home than to anyone in what Florence calls the family circle, I thought that before proceeding to such extremities I would have to look at you and at your sister. I knew where you were, because your father wrote to me during the last week of his life. My reaction at the time was that it was rather late in the day to expect me to be interested. I did, however, instruct my solicitors to make some enquiries, and to furnish me with a quarterly report. I saw no reason why you should not, in the words of the Catechism, learn and labour truly to get your own living, but in a case of extremity I was prepared to intervene. Not to put too fine a point upon it, I considered that I had enough dependent relations and had no wish to add to their number.

I have already indicated the reasons which led me to change my mind. Before taking any steps in the matter of my will I decided to see you. The reports I had received informed me that you were a hardworking, industrious, and well-behaved young woman. I am quite aware that you will consider yourself insulted by this description. Nevertheless you will owe a considerable fortune to these work-a-day qualities. The reports informed me that your sister, on the other hand, was not a suitable beneficiary. She was delicate, easily influenced, and married to a young man too unstable to stick to a humdrum job, and not competent to achieve anything better. I have always greatly disliked incompetence, and see no reason why it should be subsidized.

I am therefore leaving everything to you. Rather a gamble perhaps, but I think I am entitled to amuse myself by taking a risk. When you read this Mr. Ashton will already have explained to you that the Mr. Brook who came down to look at houses and wasted so much of your time without ever really coming to the point was myself in the laudable pursuit of knowledge, not about houses, but with regard to a possible heiress. Speaking as a dead man, I find you very possible indeed. I think you have good looks, good temper, good sense, and good principles. So I am not tying you up too tightly, only I do request you to use the good sense. Do not transfer capital to your sister—it will not benefit her. You will have a power of appointment over half the estate. Mr. Ashton will explain to you what this involves.

Well, I think that is all I have to say, except to wish you well and hope that on the balance what I have done will turn out to be for your happiness. It would seem like a mockery to sign myself yours affectionately, but I believe that I might in other circumstances have come to feel affectionately towards you.

Martin Brand

P.S. If you want to live in the house, it can easily be divided. I do not recommend this, but it may prove difficult to dislodge my dear sister-in-law and her sister.

On reading this over I find that I have not mentioned Penny Halliday—probably because I was dealing with disagreeable relations and neither of these two words is applicable, since she is merely a connection of the Remingtons and has so far shown no signs of taking after them. Pray do not develop a conscience on her account. She is quite reasonably provided for.

Mr. Ashton came back into the room as she finished reading the letter. Some colour had come into her face. There was a look of distress in her eyes. To his "Is anything the matter, Miss Brand?" she responded with more animation than he would have expected.

"He's so bitter—so unhappy!"

"Well, I don't know that I should agree with that. He had a kind of sardonic humour. I think he got a good deal of pleasure out of exercising it."

Her flush was already fading. It had embellished her a good deal. She did not speak. She was folding the letter and putting it away in her bag.

Mr. Ashton said, "Is there anything you would like to ask me?"

She looked up then. He thought she had remarkably fine eyes of an unusual clear grey colour without any trace of blue.

"He says in the letter that I will have a power of appointment over half the estate. Will you tell me what that means?"

Mr. Ashton smiled benevolently.

"It means that you can leave half of it to anyone or anything you like."

"And the rest?"

"Under the will half of the estate is settled. That is to say, if you marry and have children, it will go to them. The other half you can do what you like with. If you die without children, that half which is settled will be divided between the other relations, Mrs. Alfred Brand, her son Felix, and her sister Miss Remington—half of it to Felix, and half between the two sisters. They are his second cousins, besides the connection through Florence's marriage to Alfred Brand. In the last resort, he did not really want the money to go out of the family. You cannot dispose of that part of the estate. It goes to your children, or it goes back to the family. I knew your uncle for thirty years. He might, and did, talk in an embittered manner about his relations, but he would never have allowed family money to go out of the family. You should, of course, consider making a will in the near future."

Marian Brand never knew what made her say what she did. Her mind was in a curious state. She spoke without conscious thought. She said, "What would happen if I didn't make a will—if I was run over on the way home, or something like that?"

Mr. Ashton continued to smile. He said in his pleasant voice,

"A very unlikely contingency, I hope."

She went on looking at him.

"What would happen?"

"The unsettled part would go to your sister. The settled part would be divided as I said."

She took a long sighing breath and said,

"I see—"

Mr. Ashton spoke briskly,

"Now what about that banking account?"

CHAPTER 2

The compartment had been full when they left Victoria. The usual clutter of people who have been up to town for a day's shopping and come piling into third-class carriages with bulging bags and tired feet. If you were one of the early ones you got a seat and had other people more or less standing on you. If you ran it fine you jostled the people who were standing in the narrow strip between the seats, or in the corridor if it was a corridor train.

Marian Brand had been in good time. She had the inside corner seat facing the engine. There was not so much crowding as there often was. Every seat full of course, but only three people standing, and all quite hearty-looking men. They stood as near the window as they could get and exchanged occasional remarks. On Marian's left was one of those women who take up too much room in trains. She bulged and wheezed. She had three shopping-bags which were all quite full.

Marian looked through the glass pane on her other side and saw the corridor going away to a diminishing point, and the row of windows beyond it. It was her eyes that saw the standing men, the stout woman, the flashy girl in the other corner seat, the long receding line of the corridor, but her mind did not really register any of these things. They remained external images which conscious thought rejected because it was far too busy to be concerned with them. A man passed the window, coming up from the end of the corridor. She saw him in the same way that she had seen the other things. His passing meant no more to her than if she had seen a shadow go by.

The man was Richard Cunningham. As he walked along the corridor he saw a woman looking in his direction. There was no reason why he should notice her. The train was full. Each of the corridor windows presented him with a view of people packed like fish—faces pale, flushed, pretty, plain— old, young, middle-aged—a cross section of humanity so closely squeezed together that individuality and interest were lost. There was no reason why he should see one face and remember it. But he saw Marian Brand, checked for a moment, and passed on. When he had reached the first-class compartment which was his aim and had taken the last remaining seat, her face was still there, as vividly present as if it was she who was sitting opposite to him and not the blonde woman who was a little too blonde, a little too waved, a little too lavish in the matter of pearls. Nothing could have presented a more drastic contrast to the face he had seen at the window. He could see it still quite plainly. He contemplated it with an interest which had nothing sentimental about it. He was thirty-five, and though there is no age-limit for folly, he was by many years past an inclination for casual encounters.

He had no idea why this woman's face should catch his attention. She was not beautiful—or was she? That was one of the points which interested him. She was certainly not pretty. Her clothes were the shabby clothes that are chosen for their wearing qualities and must be worn for as long as they can be made to look decent. No indication, therefore, of the character or taste of the woman who wears them, except in so far as the choice of something dark, plain and hardwearing is an indication of character. He dismissed the clothes. She had a good brow—good bones altogether, a certain line from cheek to chin, a certain balance. He put her

9

age at twenty-five, perhaps a year or two more, perhaps a year or two less. She hadn't lived soft. There was no bloom on the smooth, pale skin. But there were no lines either. That would be something to do with the shape of the bones beneath, but a good deal more to a habit of mind. A woman with a face like that didn't fuss about trifles, didn't fuss at all. She would do what she had to do, endure what she had to endure. He thought there had been a fair amount of enduring. She had the look of it in her eyes—patience. It was a look which moved him whenever he encountered it, in a child, in an animal. Sometimes it was the pitiful patience that doesn't hope any longer. This was the other kind, the patience which rests on strength. It endures because in the end it will conquer.

He pulled himself up with half a laugh. Word-spinning! Well, it was his trade. If your brain stopped spinning you stories, you would stop being able to write them. But he couldn't remember being so caught by anything in the way of an external impression for. . . . . He stared back across the years, could find no bridge to the other side. The impression appeared to be unique. It came to him with a shock that the word external was wrong. The whole thing went much deeper than that. He did just know that her hair was dark and her eyes were grey, but all that had nothing to do with his vivid sense of her.

About a quarter of an hour later he got up and went out into the corridor again. It was in his mind to walk slowly past her window to the end of the carriage, wait for a few moments, and then walk back again, but before he had taken more than three or four steps the train swayed, jerked horribly, and left the rails. The whole thing happened with the most appalling suddenness. Everything broke up in a violent cataclysm. A noise like all imaginable noises stunned the ear. The sudden impact of disaster paralysed the senses. The train reared upon itself, buckled, and crashed. A terrible screaming went up. The sliding doors of several of the compartments swung open as the train tilted. Marian Brand was flung from her seat into the corridor. She fell, and was caught in a desperate clutch. And then everything fell together and they went down into blackness.

When she came to, the blackness was still there. It hadn't been dark before the crash, but it was dark now. She shut her eyes. After a minute she opened them again. Thought was beginning. There had been an accident. How long ago? It oughtn't to be so dark. Darkness—burial—the words came to her with the drenching flood. She steadied herself against them, drew on her courage, and got enough to move the other hand. It went out a little way and touched a man's arm. She felt the rough stuff, the hard muscle, and movement. The blessedness of that relief was not to be measured. Movement means life—not to be quite alone in the darkness with the dead. A man's voice said, "I'm here. Don't be afraid."

It was the most beautiful sound she had ever heard. It was, in plain fact, a voice naturally pleasant, but a good deal handicapped by choking dust. She said,

"Where are we?"

"Under what's left of the train. They'll get us out presently. Are you all right?"

She hadn't got as far as thinking about that. She began to think about it now, clutching at his arm, experimenting to see what she could move. After a moment she said,

"I'm all right, I think. Everything moves a little, but I can't lift up or turn—there's something over us."

"Yes—lucky for us. There was a ditch—we went down into it. Fortunately we got there first. A door opened and shot us out before the train came down on us. I was in the corridor just outside your compartment. I grabbed you, and we came down together. We're in the bottom of the ditch.

There's a good deal of stuff over us, and it may take some time to get us out, but we shall be all right.''

As his voice ceased, she began to be aware of sounds which had not come to her before. They must have been there, but they had not reached her—movement, voices, the scrape of metal on metal, a heavy thudding, a sound of groaning, a sound of someone crying, and once, high-pitched and terrible, a scream. It all seemed to be a long way off, not in distance but—removed. The sensation of being withdrawn from her surroundings had not been broken by the accident but intensified. What she thought and felt seemed to come to her from the other side of a misty barrier which made everything unreal.

She drew a long breath. Whether it was heard or felt she did not know. She was still holding to the stuff of his coat. His left hand came over now and took her wrist, feeling for the pulse. Then, releasing that, he took her hand.

"You're all right. We've just got to pass the time. Take your hand away if you want to—but you're a bit cold—I thought perhaps something to hold on to—''

She said, "Yes," and, after a long pause, "Thank you.''

It didn't do to think what it would have been like to be there alone. She was glad when he spoke again.

"Well, we've got the time to put in. By the bye, they know we're here, so you needn't worry about that. I was calling out, and a man came and spoke to me just before you woke up. They can't get this stuff off till the breakdown gang rolls up. Fortunately there's lots of air. What would you like to talk about? My name is Richard Cunningham, and I write—novels, plays, verse, belles lettres.''

He heard her take another of those long breaths, but this time it was quicker.

"You wrote *The Whispering Tree.*''

"Yes.''

12

"I read when I can—there's so little time. My sister reads a lot. She isn't strong—she can't take a job. I've always tried to manage a library subscription for her. She runs through the books so quickly that I can't keep up—there's no time. But I did read *The Whispering Tree*. I loved it."

"Why isn't there time? What do you do?"

"I work in a house-agent's office in Norwood. We live there."

"Who is we?"

"My sister and I, and her husband—when he's there."

He repeated the last words.

"When he's there. Why isn't he there?"

"He's an actor. He gets a part in a touring company—now and then."

"Like that?"

"Yes. They oughtn't to have married. She was eighteen and he was twenty. He was in a bank, but it bored him. He thought he was going to do wonders on the stage. He has a light tenor voice, and he's quite nice-looking. He got small parts easily at first—and then not so easily. Ina isn't strong. There's nothing actually the matter, but she cracks up."

There was a odd inflection in his voice as he said,

"And you are the bread-winner?"

"There isn't anyone else."

There was a curious dream quality about their talk. They lay in the dark—strangers, with clasped hands. Shock and terror had broken down the barrier which convention builds. It was as if their thoughts spoke. It was as if anything could be asked and anything said with a naked truthfulness which needed no excuse. Even looking back upon it afterwards, it all seemed natural to Marian Brand. They had never met before, and they would never meet again. They were on the edge of terror. They lay in the dark and held hands. She said things that she had never said to anyone before. Sometimes

13

there were long pauses. Once or twice there was a faintness, but it cleared. If they were silent for too long, the darkness came too close. Sometimes he asked a question. Whenever that happened she had the feeling that the answer mattered.

When she said in a surprised voice, "But it's all very dull," he laughed a little.

"People aren't dull. They're my trade. What they do and why they do it—it may be horrifying, or humiliating, or surprising, but it's never dull. If it is, it's because you're dull yourself—one of those whose touch turns all to dust brigade." Then, quite abruptly, "So you've got everything on your shoulders. Haven't you any family?"

"We hadn't. My father quarrelled with his people. I suppose you would call him a rolling stone. We went all over the world—France, Italy, Africa, the Argentine, California, New York. Sometimes there was plenty of money, and sometimes there wasn't any at all. We came back to England when I was ten, and my mother died. Ina and I were put in a school at Norwood, and my father went off again."

It didn't come out all at once. There would be a whole sentence, and then three or four words, and then two or three more. The gaps between did not seem to have any relation to the sense, they just happened. The voice would stop, and go on for a bit, and stop again. It was rather like listening to someone talking in her sleep.

It was, perhaps, with some idea of wakening a sleeper that he asked abruptly,

"How old are you now?"

"Twenty-seven. Ina is a year younger."

"I thought you would be about that when I saw you in the train."

She said in that expressionless way,

"Did you—see me?"

"Oh, yes. You were sitting next to the door into the cor-

14

ridor. I saw you, but you didn't see me—you were about a million miles away."

The tone of her voice changed for the first time. It had been grave and level. Now it was touched by a faint shade of something which might have been surprise. She said,

"Not quite so far as that."

"Go on—I interrupted. You and Ina went to school. Were you happy?"

"Ina was. I should have been. But it was the same thing all over again—the money part of it, you know. Sometimes it came, and sometimes it didn't. Just before I was eighteen my father came to England and died. There wasn't any money. I learned to type, and Miss Fisher got me a job. Ina had one too, but—I told you—she married Cyril Felton. There was a lot of worry, and she can't stand worry—it knocks her over. We've just managed to carry on."

"And why were you a million miles away? Something happened. What?"

She said, "How did you know? Yes, something did happen."

"Go on."

She laughed.

"I don't really believe in it, you know—not yet. I haven't told anyone—there hasn't been time. Perhaps if I tell you, it will make it feel real."

"You can always try."

Her hand moved in his, not withdrawing itself, just turning a little. When she spoke there were not quite so many of those pauses.

"It began about six months ago, only I didn't know there was anything in it then. A Mr. Brook came into the office and asked about houses. He was oldish—rather sharp in his manner. He took a long time, going through the particulars of everything we had on our books. He asked a lot of ques-

15

tions—about the neighbourhood—about shops, social things—where did I shop myself—did I belong to a tennis club, a dramatic society. I thought he was asking on account of his own family. Actually, I can see now that he wanted to know how I lived, what I did. I had to tell him about Ina, to explain why I didn't do any of the things he asked about. Of course he must have made other enquiries too—in fact I know he did. He went away without doing anything about a house, and I put him down as one of those people who just go round wasting time."

"And what was he really?"

She said, "You're quick." And then, "He was my father's brother—my uncle, Martin Brand."

"And? What happened next?"

"Nothing for six months. Then yesterday I got a letter from a firm of solicitors—Ashton & Fenwick, Lawton Street. They're big people, quite well known."

"Yes."

"They said to come up and see them—there was something to my advantage. You know, just a stiff lawyer's letter. It didn't tell me anything. I didn't say anything to Ina and Cyril, but I showed it to Mr. Morton where I work, and he was very kind. He gave me the day off, and I went up—today."

"And was there something to your advantage?"

"Yes, there was. Mr. Ashton told me about Mr. Brook being my uncle. He said he was dead and he hadn't wished me to be told until after the funeral. Then he said that he had left me all his money. That's the part that keeps on floating away. I just can't get it to feel real. When I think of it—I don't feel—quite real either."

The hand that was holding hers closed firmly.

"You'll get used to it. It's surprising how soon you can get used to having money. It's much easier than getting used to not having it."

16

There was a long pause, after which she said rather faintly, "It's such a lot—"

He wondered what she would call a lot. What had she been managing on? Five pounds a week? With the delicate sister thrown in, to say nothing of Cyril who almost certainly didn't earn his keep, let alone come anywhere near supporting his wife! He would have liked to know what Martin Brand's pile amounted to, but even at this moment he did not feel quite equal to putting the question. Instead he laughed, found that it hurt him sharply, and wondered if he had a broken a rib, or ribs. Hideously inconvenient if he had.

The train of thought set up by this induced his next remark.

"I'm supposed to be flying to America in ten days' time."

She said in an abstracted voice,

"I liked being there. I'd like to go back. Are you going to stay?"

"Only a month. Business. My mother was an American, and I have a sister married over there—about the only relation I've got."

Her hand moved. He thought the movement was involuntary.

"I've come in for a lot of relations as well as the money. It's rather frightening. My uncle didn't like them. He wrote me—an odd letter. I don't know why he went on living with them if he felt like that."

He began to be quite sure about the rib. It just didn't do to laugh. He said,

"Perhaps they lived with him."

"Oh, yes, they did. There's a house—it sounds big—and they must have expected—they must have thought it would come to them—and the money too. I haven't had time to think about it yet, but I shall have to."

His hand was steady on hers.

"These things have a way of settling themselves. I shouldn't worry about it now."

After a very long silence she said,

"If I'd been killed, Ina would have got some of it, and the relations would have had the rest. It would have saved a lot of trouble. If we don't get out—"

He said quite loudly and firmly,

"Oh, but we're going to get out."

CHAPTER 3

Lying in hospital with a couple of broken ribs, Richard Cunningham was aware of a zest for life which recalled his early twenties. The morning papers had informed him of just how lucky his escape had been—his and Marian Brand's. The smallest of the papers naturally had the largest headlines. TRAPPED UNDER TRAIN—WHAT IT FEELS LIKE TO BE BURIED ALIVE—EXCLUSIVE INTERVIEW WITH RICHARD CUNNINGHAM. That made him laugh, and you really can't afford to laugh with your ribs strapped up. He recalled a reporter buzzing round when first Marian, and then he, had been dragged out from under the partially shifted wreckage. To the best of his recollection, he had replied to a spate of questions as to what it felt like to be buried alive with the single word, "Damnable!" After which he had tried to get on to his own feet instead of being carried like a carcase, and had promptly covered himself with shame by passing out.

He perused the exclusive interview with enjoyment. It was packed with high-toned drama, and it would make a magnificent advertisement for his new book.

He looked across at the long window which framed a view of low cloud and sheeting rain, and found it exceedingly good to be alive and—practically—undamaged. Daylight, even of this suffused and teeming kind, was an uplifting sight. He might have been lying on a mortuary slab, instead of which here he was, in a clean bed, and quite comfortable so long as he didn't move too suddenly. Everything was pretty good.

He began to think about Marian Brand. She hadn't been taken to hospital—a stubborn line of enquiry had elicited that. She had said she was all right and would rather go home. She had been saying that quite perseveringly just before he went tumbling down into his swoon. An idiotic performance on both their parts. If he hadn't been fool enough to faint he would have put it across her. Something on the lines of "Of course I know what it's all about—you think Ina will be frightened. But if you want to terrify her into fits you have only got to loom up looking like death, with your hat stove in, your hair full of cinders and your face smothered in dust and blood."

He frowned when he remembered the blood. Someone had turned a powerful electric torch on her, and she was a messy sight. Of course a little blood goes a long way on a face. He thought it came from a cut somewhere up on the edge of the scalp. He supposed the first-aid people would have cleaned her up before they let her go. Because she had gone. Quite definitely they hadn't managed to get her to the hospital. She had just faded away. Rather an intriguing end to the whole curious experience. Too commonplace really, to meet in this cool antiseptic light of day and compare bandages. He had an idea that she would have one round her head—or perhaps only a bit of strapping. It came to him with a feeling of shock that he wouldn't find her commonplace if they were to meet emptying garbage cans—that being the least romantic occupation he could think of offhand. He called his last view

19

of her to mind. If a feeling of romance can survive a battered hat sliding from dishevelled hair, garments suggestive of the dustbin which his fancy had just called up, a face rendered ghastly by blood and sweat and dirt, its roots must run down deep to the hidden springs of life. The picture came and stayed. Her eyes looked at him out of the reddened grime with which her face was smeared. The feeling of romance survived. He began to wonder what was happening to him.

On the second day he rang up the house-agents and got her address. He remembered that she had said Mr. Morton when she was speaking of her employer. "Mr. Morton was kind—he gave me the day off." The telephone directory did the rest. He persevered until he achieved Mr. Morton himself, and was informed that Miss Brand was not in the office— Miss Brand had been in a railway accident.

Richard Cunningham said,

"Yes, I know. I was in it too. I wanted to be sure that Miss Brand was all right."

Mr. Morton blew his nose and opined that it had been a providential escape. He didn't sound like a live wire, but he did sound kind and concerned. Miss Brand was taking a few days off. The experience had naturally been a shock. He was sorry to say they would be losing her services shortly—a change in her circumstances. "Her address? Well—I really don't know—"

Richard Cunningham said,

"Yes, she told me. We were fellow travellers. My name is Richard Cunningham. I'm in hospital with a couple of broken ribs. I thought I should just like to send Miss Brand some flowers. I don't think she would consider it intrusive."

Mr. Morton read the papers. He knew all about Richard Cunningham. He had even read the exclusive interview. He made no further difficulty about giving the address.

20

CHAPTER 4

In spite of having been cleaned up by an ambulance party, Marian Brand was not able to avoid arousing a good deal of alarm at No. 52 Sandringham Road, where she and Ina and Cyril inhabited two bedrooms and a sitting-room. The house belonged to Mrs. Deane, who was the widow of a deceased partner in the firm of Morton and Fenwick. She was a nice woman but not characterized by any degree of optimism.

By the time that Ina had begun to wonder what on earth was keeping Marian so late Mrs. Deane was able to supply a number of possible reasons, none of which were calculated to restore cheerfulness and calm. They ranged from an encounter with a lunatic in a railway carriage experienced by the friend of a sister-in-law's aunt, to the really moving tale of a cousin's mother-in-law who had been stuck in a lavatory on the Underground and unable to extricate herself until the inspector came round.

"I won't say she wasn't a sharp-tongued woman, and I won't say she wasn't a good deal worked-up after six hours and wondering what her husband was going to say if she wasn't there to cook his supper, and I daresay she said more than she ought. Anyhow he took a high tone with her. Said there wasn't anything wrong with the lock that he could see, and if she'd done the right thing it would have opened easily enough. Well, you can just imagine what she said to that! And he came back with, 'All right, I'll show you.' My dear Mrs. Felton, you won't believe it, but she went back in with him, and when he went to show her—there was the door stuck like glue again and the pair of them trapped, and there they were till the morning!"

Ina stared in horror.

"Oh, Mrs. Deane, why did she go back?"

Mrs. Deane shook a large and rather untidy head. She had a passion for trying new hair styles culled from a page in a weekly paper headed "Why be dowdy?", and they were not always very successful. Her faded hair, well streaked with grey, was at the moment disintegrating from the curls in which it had been set. She gave it a casual pat as she said,

"You may well ask! You wouldn't think anyone would, or him either! But the fact is they'd got each other's backs up, and neither of them thinking anything in the world except proving they were right and the other one wrong."

"How grim! What did they do?"

Mrs. Deane gave the hair another pat.

"Stayed there till morning. Mrs. Pratt said she thought she knew something about swearing—her husband had been at sea, and you know what sailors are—but the language that inspector used was beyond anything she'd ever heard in her life. And you can't really wonder! And after that they had the inspectors go round a lot oftener so it shouldn't happen again—locking the door after the horse was stolen—because once was enough, I'm sure, and not at all the sort of thing you'd expect to have cropping up constantly, though you never can tell."

Ina went back to listening at the window which overlooked the street. She didn't think Marian was locked in a lavatory, and she was quite sure she couldn't be alone in a railway carriage with a lunatic, because the trains were always crowded till much later than this. But Mrs. Deane's anecdotes had not been reassuring. There were a lot of other things that could happen to you besides getting locked in and meeting lunatics. Look at what you read in the papers every day. And

22

it was all very well when it was happening to someone who was just a name in a column of newsprint—you read it, and it made a break in the dull everyday things which were happening all round you. And you didn't mind very much even if it was something rather dreadful, because it didn't seem real unless you knew the people yourself. But if something dreadful was to happen to someone you knew—if something dreadful was to happen to Marian—Her hands and feet were suddenly cold.

And then she was listening and looking out, because the bus had stopped at the end of the road and people were getting off. One of them was a woman, and she was coming this way. She didn't look like Marian. The road was not very brightly lighted. The woman passed into the shadowed stretch between the lampposts. Ina opened the window and leaned out. Now she was coming towards the light again—yellow light, spilled like a pool on the damp pavement. It must have been raining.

The woman came into the pool of light, and Ina drew back, catching her breath. Because it was a stranger. It wasn't anyone she had ever seen before. It wasn't Marian.

She shut the window and turned back into the room. She was really frightened now. It was after nine o'clock. Marian would never be as late as this unless something had happened. Something—the word was like a black curtain behind which all the imaginable and unimaginable terrors crouched. At any moment the curtain might lift or part. She stood there looking at the clock, whilst the cold spread upwards from hands and feet until she was shivering with it.

At eighteen she had been quite unusually pretty, with dark curling hair, eyes like blue flowers—it was Cyril who had made this comparison—and the fine delicate skin which takes such a lovely bloom in health and fades so soon in illness. Ina was not actually ill, but she had lost her bloom. She led a dull, uninteresting life, and she had no energy to do anything about it. By the time she had tidied up their three rooms and walked round to the shops, where she had to stand in a queue for fish, it was as much as she could do to get as far as the library and change her book. She wouldn't have missed doing that for anything in the world. Her fatigue would vanish as she took down book after book from the shelves, dipping here and reading there, fleeting the morning away till it was time to go home and make her lunch of whatever had been left over from supper the night before. Sometimes she didn't even take the trouble to warm it, and then as often as not she would leave it on her plate. Once or twice a week she took a bus at the end of the road and met Marian for lunch at a cheap café, but they couldn't afford to do it very often. Then she would take the bus back again and spend the afternoon lying on the sofa waiting for Marian to come home. It was Marian who cooked whatever Ina had bought for supper. It was Marian who brought in her stories of what had been happening in the office—who was taking what house—young people getting married—old people going to live with a son or daughter—Mrs. Potter who was putting in a second bathroom and turning the flower-room into a kitchenette so that she could divide her house and let off half of it.

"You remember Maureen Potter, Ina—she was in the sixth when we first went to school. She married someone with a lot of money. She came in with her mother. I think dividing the house was her idea really, and she said at once, 'You're Marian Brand, aren't you? Miss Fisher told me you were working here. How do you like it?' And she asked after you, and said how pretty you were, and said something about coming to see us. But I don't suppose she'll have time—she's only here for a few days."

There was never anything more exciting than that. Of

course if Cyril was at home, everything was different. Sometimes he came back with plenty of money, and for a few days life became almost too exciting. He made love to her in an exigent, masterful way, he took her out to lunch, to tea, to dinner. And then either the money ran out or he became bored—Cyril found it terribly easy to be bored—and he would go off again with an airy "Goodbye—I'll be seeing you." It was worse when he came back without any money at all, because that was when Marian put her foot down and kept it there. Cyril could have house-room, and the same meals that she and Ina had, but no more. If he wanted money for drinks or cigarettes, or even for bus fares, he must earn it. Cyril would stick his hands in his pockets and stride dramatically up and down the sitting-room telling Ina just what he thought about the meanness, the callous hard-heartedness of Marian's behaviour. Ina could, of course, see his point. A man must have some money in his pocket—he must be able to buy a packet of cigarettes and stand a friend a drink. But she could see Marian's point of view just as clearly, and sometimes she was tactless enough to say so.

"But, darling, she really hasn't got it. We only just manage as it is."

It didn't go down at all well. Cyril would pause in the current stride and give a sardonic laugh.

"That's what she tells you! She would! And you take her part! You don't care how much I'm humiliated!"

At which point Ina was apt to dissolve into tears. Taking one thing with another, the dullness of the times when Cyril was away was preferable to the strain and exhaustion of the times when he was here.

Tonight Ina could forget everything and feel sick with longing for his presence. When he had been away for some time she could, and did, superimpose the hero of her latest novel upon her recollections of Cyril. It helped a lot. And now, when she was feeling so frightened about Marian, she thought how wonderful it would be to have Cyril's arms round her, and his voice telling her how stupid it was to get the wind up. In the book she had finished at tea-time Pendred Cothelstone had had a very hearty way with feminine fears. The longing she felt was actually a longing for someone who would be hearty about Marian not being in at half past nine after saying she would be back by seven.

Half an hour later it is doubtful whether Pendred himself could have reassured her. Mrs. Deane had been up again with a fresh batch of stories. This time they were about people who had disappeared and were never heard of again.

"There was a gentleman, I forget his name, but he was walking down Victoria Street with his wife—rather a lot of people about and the pavement crowded, so she got a step or two ahead of him, but talking all the time if you see what I mean. Well, presently he didn't answer something she'd said, and she turned round and he wasn't there, and from that day to this there wasn't a word or whisper, or anyone who could say what had happened. Just vanished right there in Victoria Street in the middle of the afternoon. And she never even got to know whether she was a widow or not, poor thing."

"Oh, Mrs. Deane, *don't*!"

"Well, my dear, you can't get away from it, such things do happen, and no good worrying or upsetting yourself. Never meet trouble half way—that's what my poor husband used to say, and I daresay he was right, though, I usen't to agree with him. Better be prepared for the worst, I used to tell him, and then if it turns out all right there's no harm done."

It was half past ten before a taxi stopped at the door and Marian Brand got out. She had had to borrow the money to pay for it, because her bag was still somewhere under the

26

wreckage. She thanked the driver, and he gave her his arm to help her out and up the steps, because now that it was all over she was stiff and aching from head to foot. Her key was in the lost bag, so she had to ring the bell. And then there was Mrs. Deane, opening the door on the chain in the manner of one who expects armed burglars, and Ina running down the stairs to push her aside.

"Oh, Marian—where have you been? I thought something had happened. Oh!"

The "Oh!" came as the door was shut and the passage light showed quite unmistakably that something really had happened. The dust and blood had been washed from Marian's face, but there was a dark bruise on her forehead and a narrow line of strapping above it. There had been so little left of her hat that it had not been worth while to bring it away. The right-hand sleeve of her suit had been wrenched from the armhole, and the skirt was fit for nothing but a rag-bag.

"Marian!"

"Oh, Miss Brand!"

The two horrified faces swam in a haze. Marian heard herself say,

"It's nothing, really. There was an accident—but I'm quite all right."

She groped her way to the foot of the stairs and sat down on the second step.

CHAPTER 5

Cyril Felton came home on the fourth day after the accident. Someone drew his attention to a paragraph in the evening paper, and he took the first train back. Not too pleased to discover that his wife and sister-in-law had gone to London for the day, but Mrs. Deane was in a chatty mood and more than willing to invite him to tea in her sitting-room and tell him all she knew. If it was impossible to regard him as a good husband, she did think him very handsome and romantic, and she derived considerable satisfaction from the fact that she had just done her hair in what her "Why be dowdy?" column called "a queenly style." She began to get out her best tea-set.

"I don't know a thing, Mrs. Deane, except what I saw in the paper."

"Oh, Mr. Felton—fancy their not letting you know!"

"Oh, well, I was moving about. They wouldn't know where to write. But what's happened? All I saw was three or four lines about Marian being in an accident just when she'd heard she had come in for some money."

"Yes, that's right. That's just how it was—on Tuesday. She came home with the clothes pretty well off her back, and a bruise on her forehead. It's gone down nicely now, and you really wouldn't notice it. Mrs. Felton was in a terrible way, but there wasn't any real harm done, and they went off at ten o'clock this morning to do some shopping and to see their uncle's lawyer—something about the house that was left. Down by the sea, it is, and Miss Brand wants to get Mrs.

28

Felton there as soon as possible, the sea air being what they always say would do her good."

Cyril said sharply, "There must be something more than a house."

Mrs. Deane put two spoons of tea in the pot.

"Oh, as to that, I'm sure I couldn't say, Mr. Felton—I'm not one to pry. But no cause to worry, I'm sure. Mrs. Felton's been so excited ever since it happened, you wouldn't know her for the same person—singing all over the house, and quite a colour."

He had time to feel very impatient indeed before his wife and sister-in-law came home.

Ina's eyes were shining like stars. She had had her hair set. She had bought all the sort of things she had never been able to afford for her face—a whole range of vanishing creams, cleansing creams, night creams, lipsticks, two different and enchanting shades of rouge, a face-powder which was a dream, and several different shades of nail-polish. The girl in the beauty-parlour had showed her just what to do, and she was in a state of quivering pleasure. She looked what she used to look like when she was eighteen—no, better than that, because she had never had any of these lovely things before. She felt like the heroine of a novel, she felt romantic and sophisticated. She was wearing new shoes and stockings, and a coat and skirt which had cost more than she had ever paid for anything in all her life. She rushed into Cyril's arms and poured the whole thing out, finishing up with,

"Oh, darling, isn't it marvellous? Just look at me!"

Cyril looked, at first with amazement, then with genuine admiration, and lastly with a good deal of apprehension, because he knew what things cost and he hoped she wasn't putting too much in the shop window. All very well to have everything new and costing the earth—and he wouldn't say Ina didn't pay for dressing; every woman did—but the really

29

important thing was, what did it all amount to in hard cash, and how much of it was going to come his way. In fact Mr. Mantalini had, as it were, taken some very appropriate words out of his mouth a hundred years ago by enquiring "What's the demd total?"

It wasn't, of course, the moment to come out with it as bluntly as that. He had to look and admire, and stand with his arm round Ina while she chattered away nineteen to the dozen, for all the world like she used to when she was a schoolgirl.

"Oh, Cyril, isn't it all simply too marvellous! There's a house—did I tell you there was a house—and it's by the sea—in Ledshire—a place called Farne—and we're going there just as soon as ever we can. I can't believe it, I really can't—we're going to the sea! I have to keep saying it out loud, because it doesn't seem as if it could be true. The house is really two houses, only Uncle Martin's grandfather had such a big family he threw them into one and lived there with all his relations. Rather frightful, but people used to. At least, it would be fun if you liked them, and perhaps you would—"

"Darling, I don't know what you're talking about."

She rubbed her cheek against his.

"That's because it's all so wonderful—it won't get into words. I'm so thrilled about the house. You see, Mr. Ashton says—"

"Who is Mr. Ashton?"

"Uncle Martin's solicitor. We've been seeing him. He says the house can quite easily be made into two again. It would only mean shutting the doors that were cut through, and we could have an electric stove in the old kitchen, and then we shouldn't have to turn the relations out, which he says would be frightfully difficult—and of course rather horrid. I mean, you don't want to *start* with a family row, and then have to

30

live next door to each other for ever and ever—too, too grim!"

He had his arm round her and he called her darling, but his voice had an edge to it.

"I haven't the faintest idea what you're talking about, darling."

Marian had gathered up her parcels and gone into her own room. Like Ina she was wearing a new suit and everything else to match, beautifully cut and very becoming—one of those grey-green shades which are flattering to dark hair and grey eyes. She had said "How do you do?" and taken up her parcels and gone away. At the time he had been pleased, because of course he would get more out of Ina if they were alone. But she didn't come back, and he was beginning to wonder if there wasn't something rather marked about her not joining in. Nobody could say Marian was stupid. She had a head on her shoulders all right, and she must know perfectly well that he would want to hear just what it all amounted to. Ina's enthusiasm was like so much whipped cream—all very fluffy and nice, but nothing you could make a meal off. He wanted to know just what Cyril Felton was going to get out of it.

He didn't listen very attentively whilst Ina told him about the relations.

"Aunt Florence Brand—she's the widow of Uncle Martin's brother Alfred, and of course he was my father's brother too. They both were—Martin and Alfred, I mean—only it seems so funny when we had never heard of them. Alfred married Florence Remington who was some sort of a cousin, and when he died and Uncle Martin's wife died she came and kept house for him. And he hated her. Her sister, Cassy Remington, came and lived there too. And he hated them both. Then there's Felix, who is Aunt Florence's son. He plays the piano—"

Cyril woke up.

31

"Not Felix Brand!"

"Yes, that's his name. Do you know him? Oh, Cyril—how exciting!"

His voice became very cold indeed.

"He's Helen Adrian's accompanist. He's got a foul temper. I don't know him."

Ina gazed at him in an ecstasy.

"I've heard her—on Mrs. Deane's wireless—she was lovely! Do you suppose he was playing for her then? Darling, it's almost too romantic! The secret cousin!"

The arm that had been round her dropped.

"Look here, Ina, stop babbling! I've had a hell of a time—everything going wrong that possibly could. I'm not in the mood for all this talk. I want some plain facts. You've got it all in your head, but I haven't. Nobody tells me anything. I've had nothing but three lines in a paper to go on, and I want to know where we stand."

Ina continued to gaze, but the ecstasy was a little dashed.

"But I've told you. Uncle Martin came down here and called himself Mr. Brook, and pretended he wanted a house, and saw Marian—only of course she didn't know who he was—"

"He didn't see you?"

"Oh, no. He went to the office—he was supposed to be looking for houses. He saw Marian, and he went away and made his will."

"Now we're getting there. He made a will. I want to know what was in it."

"But, darling, I *told* you. He left her everything—just like that."

Ina drew back a little, because he was looking quite frightening. Not really of course—it was just being on the stage—it was just—

"What was in it, damn you!"

32

She drew in a sharp breath. He oughtn't to swear—she hadn't done anything—she *had* told him. She said,

"I did tell you. He left everything to Marian."

"Not to you?"

"No—I keep telling you—to Marian."

"You don't get anything at all?"

"No."

She had gone back another step. He was angry. Of course she could see that it was disappointing for him, but it wasn't her fault.

He was quite pale with anger. His eyes were light and cold. He said in a hard undertone,

"But she'll give you some of it. She's bound to do that in common decency. What has she said about it?"

"She hasn't—said anything—not about sharing."

"What has she said?"

"Cyril—don't!"

"What has she said?"

"She wants me to have—an allowance."

"How much?"

"A hundred a year."

"How much does *she* get?"

"I—don't—know. Mr. Ashton can't be sure—till everything is—settled up."

"He'll have a damned good idea. What will she get?"

Ina said in a faltering voice,

"He wasn't sure—he said—about—two thousand."

"Two thousand clear?"

"That's what he said—after income tax was paid."

"And she'll give you a beggarly hundred! Not much!" He took her in his arms. "Ina, it's marvellous! No wonder you couldn't talk sense! It's—it's unbelievable! But look here, darling, she's got to do the square thing—she's got to give you half. I mean, it's only decent. She can't just put all that money in her pocket and leave us to starve."

It was, perhaps, unfortunate that Marian should open the door in time to hear this last remark. It rang with passionate conviction, but affected her only to the extent of inducing a hope that Cyril really might achieve some success upon the stage. She had changed into an old dress in order to get supper. As she began to lay the table she said in her pleasant voice,

"You won't starve, Cyril. Supper's just about ready. "

He stared, hesitated, and plunged.

"I didn't mean that. Marian—"

She went through into the slip of a room which served as a kitchenette, and he followed her.

"You'll do something for us—it's a lot of money. Ina's your sister."

She had soup on a low gas. She began to pour it off into the plates she had set to warm. She was smiling.

"I'll look after Ina. I always have, haven't I?"

"But Marian—"

She shook her head.

"I'm tired, and the soup will get cold. We'll talk tomorrow."

"Then you'll do something—you will, won't you? You've always been an angel. Don't think I don't know what we owe you, because I do."

She went on smiling.

"There—if you'll just take your plate and Ina's. It's out of a tin, but it's good."

He stood with a smoking soup-plate in either hand.

"You don't know how hard it is to get a footing on the stage—the jealousies—everyone trying to down you. Now if I had a backer I could run my own company and really show what I could do."

Marian wanted to say, "Nonsense!" but she restrained herself. She said with half a laugh,

34

"Oh, my dear Cyril!" And then, "Come along! Ina and I had a sketchy lunch and no tea, and I hate cold soup."

It was no use. You can't push women. He would have to let her have her head, play up to her a bit. Perhaps it was a mistake to have said anything about running a company of his own. He wasn't even sure that he wanted to do it. Too much responsibility, and quite an easy way of losing money. He wasn't sure that he would not do better to stick to his present game—plenty of pickings and very few risks.

He went into the other room and made an excellent supper, maintaining a quite convincing appearance of being interested in Ina's purchases, and in the plans which she produced in rainbow-coloured succession. What he could see was that she had fairly taken the bit between her teeth and was all out on the spending line. And that had got to be stopped. It was for the man to say how the money was to be laid out. He went on smiling carelessly and feeling angrier and more determined every minute.

There were expensive flowers in the room—tulips, narcissus, lilac. When he thought of what they must have cost—money just chucked down the drain! Ina saw him looking at them. She went on talking in that new excited way.

"Aren't they heavenly! And do you know where they came from? Mr. Cunningham sent them—Richard Cunningham— *the* Richard Cunningham! He was in the accident with Marian. They were buried under the piled-up stuff in a ditch for *hours* together. I got so frightened I nearly died, because of course I knew something must have happened, and I thought of all the dreadful things in the world." She shuddered and turned pale under the new make-up. "You can't think how grim it was. And Mr. Cunningham had two ribs broken and had to go to hospital. And he's going to America as soon as they'll let him, but he sent those lovely flowers yesterday, and a copy of *The Whispering Tree*."

35

Cyril maintained his role of careless good humour with increasing difficulty.

It was not until he and Ina were alone at last in their own room with the door shut that the smile came off. Ina, at the dressing-table, saw his face come up out of the shadowed glass like a drowned face coming up out of water. Only the bedside light was on, with its frayed green shade. Cyril had bought it once when he won some money on a horse. He said the glare of the overhead light hurt his eyes, so Ina had the bedside lamp for a birthday present. It gave the room an underwater look. Cyril's face floated up in the glass.

"What a lot of nonsense women talk."

She turned round with a nervous start. His voice was cutting, the smile quite gone.

"Cyril!"

He made an angry sound.

"Don't Cyril me! I've had enough of your chatter! And don't start crying and making a noise for everyone to hear. You've got to make Marian see reason."

"But, Cyril—"

"You've got to make her see reason. I never heard anything so insulting in my life—she comes in for all that money, and she has the nerve to say she's going to keep it for herself!"

"Oh, Cyril!"

"Will you be quiet! Do you want her to hear you? She's going to give you an allowance—one hundred a year out of two thousand! What does that mean? Will it give us a home? Will it give me a job? Will it give me my proper position as your husband? All it does is to keep you under her thumb the way you've always been, and give her the say-so in everything. A nice position, I must say! But I'm not putting up with it. Do you hear——I'm not putting up with it!"

Ina sat leaning against the dressing-table with the tilted oval glass at her back. It reflected her cloudy dark hair, the

36

turn of her shoulder. Her hand with the comb in it had dropped to her lap. She had bought a new one that afternoon, but this was the old broken thing she had used for years. Whether her face was quite drained of colour, or whether it was only the effect of the light, it had an exasperating effect upon Cyril Felton. A man expected to be able to put a few plain facts before his wife without her staring at him like a ghost. He took an angry step to the bedside and tilted the old green shade to clear the light. It struck full on Ina's face and showed it colourless.

"But, Cyril—"

He came over and took her by the wrist.

"Don't keep yapping at me! You've got to talk to Marian— make her see reason. You can do it if you like. You've only got to let her see how you feel about it. After all, it's what's fair. A thousand a year each—what does she want with more than that? She wouldn't know how to spend it."

His tone had moderated. The clasp on her wrist was almost a caress. She relaxed into a sigh and made the most profound remark of her life.

"You can *always* spend money."

He laughed.

"That's right—all we want is to have it to spend! She can't just keep you hanging on like a sort of pensioner—it isn't decent. She'll have to give you your share. Come—you'll have a try—put up a good show for us—try a spot of crying and say you can't live without me. Come, Ina—it's up to you. If it comes off, I'll give you the time of your life."

Ina felt an immense fatigue. She hadn't been tired all day, but the pleasure and the excitement which had kept her up were gone. It sounded all right the way Cyril said it, but deep inside her she knew that Marian wouldn't be moved about the money. Cyril wouldn't get a penny of it, and nothing she could do or say would alter that. She felt so tired that she would have liked to lie down and die—much too tired to be made love to. But by the time that Cyril had talked himself into believing that Marian could be persuaded into handing over a thousand a year he was in the mood for making love.

She was sinking into an exhausted sleep, when his voice broke in upon the beginning of a dream. She heard words, but they didn't seem to mean anything. He repeated them with insistence.

"What's the matter with you? Can't you hear what I'm saying? That money that Marian has come in for—"

Ina blinked and turned. His hand was on her shoulder, shaking her. The words were there. She groped for a meaning.

"Money—"

Cyril swore under his breath.

"Your Uncle Martin's money—if Marian had been killed in that accident, who'd have got it?"

She blinked again, and woke up.

"I should—half of it. The rest would go back—to the relations—if Marian—had been—killed."

He let go of her shoulder with the effect of a jerk. She began to slip back into her dream. Not a very nice dream— rather frightening. Money—if Marian had been—killed. Someone said, "Pity she wasn't." It couldn't be Cyril—Cyril wouldn't say a thing—like that—

She went right down into sleep and lost herself.

CHAPTER 6

"I can't think what Felix will say."

Miss Remington cocked a small birdlike head and looked brightly sideways at her sister. She was a little creature with closely waved grey hair, bright blue eyes, and a complexion of which she was still very proud. If she assisted it a little, it was no one's business but her own, and very discreetly done. It being breakfast time and a chilly morning, she wore an old tweed skirt and a faded lilac jumper and cardigan which she had knitted herself. One bar of an electric fire burned on a hearth which had been built for better things. In front of it, with that air of despising his surroundings which is peculiar to his race, sat the cat Mactavish. He had just completed a meticulous toilet. His orange coat recalled the best Dundee marmalade. He looked down at the electric fire which he despised and waited for Felix or Penny to come and bone a herring for him. He had a passion for herrings, but he did not consider that either of the two older ladies was to be trusted in the matter of bones. A saucer of fish prepared for him by Miss Cassy had already been rejected. He sat with his back to it and waited for Felix to come down.

Behind the tea-things Mrs. Alfred Brand was mountainous in one of those horrible garments to which stout women, unless very determined, find themselves condemned—black, with a pattern suggestive of mud spots and red ink. Florence Brand could be determined, but clothes did not interest her, and she had never had any taste. She bought what fitted her and wore it one year for best, two years for secondary occasions, and as long as it would hold together for housework and gardening. She had a large, smooth, pale face, brown hair with very little grey in it, and those rather prominent brown eyes which give the impression that the eyelids have had to be stretched to make them fit. All her movements were measured and deliberate. She opened a tin of powdered coffee, poured a measured teaspoon into two of the four Minton cups on the tray in front of her, and added boiling water and a modicum of milk. The cups had a blue lattice-work pattern and were about eighty years old. Miss Remington took the one nearest to her, put in two tablets of saccharin, stirred them well, and repeated her remark.

"I can't think what Felix will say."

Florence Brand did not trouble to reply. She sipped her coffee, which she took unsweetened. Since Felix would be down at any moment, it seemed unnecessary to speculate as to what he would say. The two letters lay open in front of his plate at the table, one from Mr. Ashton, and one from Marian Brand. He would probably express himself violently, which would alter nothing. As she thought about what Martin had done to them, the insurmountable barrier set between the living and the dead filled her with resentment. Martin had got away behind it. They couldn't reach him, and that was that. There was nothing to be gained by talking about it.

She took a slice of toast and spread it with home-made marmalade before she put her thought into words.

"It doesn't do any good to talk about it. They will be coming here next week."

Cassy Remington looked up from a tiny sip.

"Rather amusing, don't you think? Perhaps we shall like them very much. Young people make a place lively. We shan't be living together. They needn't interfere with us."

Mrs. Brand said heavily,

"Very simple, I suppose, Cassy. Mr. Ashton seems to think so, and so do you. We keep to this side of the house, lock the connecting doors, and settle down as neighbours. And all the furniture has been left to her. I have a few things of my own, but you have nothing. She can take the bed you sleep on and all the other things. She can take the carpet from the floor and leave you with the bare boards."

Cassy darted one of those sideways glances.

"But she wouldn't."

"Probably not. What matters is that Martin should have left it in her power to do so. Then there is Eliza Cotton. Is she to continue to cook for us or for them? Mr. Ashton informs me that she is actually now in the service of Marian Brand. If she wishes to remain with us, she will have to give her notice."

"She won't like the old kitchen," said Cassy brightly. "You see—she'll stay with us. An electric stove is what she's always said she didn't hold with. She won't go and leave all the things she's accustomed to."

"That remains to be seen."

"And there's Mactavish—she'd never leave Mactavish."

Florence Brand allowed her eyes to rest for a moment upon his magnificent orange back.

"Like everything else, he now belongs to Marian."

"He won't stay on her side of the house if he doesn't want to."

"He'll stay whichever side Eliza stays."

"He won't like not being the same side as Felix and Penny."

Florence Brand said in a gloomy voice,

"Probably not. Thanks to Martin, there will be a great many things which none of us will like."

Cassy Remington had the place by the fire. She turned in her chair and bent to stroke the orange head.

"Mactavish will do just what he chooses—he always does."

What he chose to do at this moment was to give her a look of dignified reproof, lick a paw, and remove the undesired caress. But by this time she had turned back again, her air brightly expectant.

"Here comes Felix."

There was a clatter of feet on the stair, the door was jerked open and Felix Brand came in. A haggard young man in an orange sweater with a good deal of untidy black hair brushed carelessly from his brow. Within five minutes of leaving his room it would be falling into his eyes and being pushed back with the thrust of long nervous fingers, only to fall again and cut the line of a perpetual frown.

Miss Cassy twittered.

"My dear Felix, I'm afraid you won't be pleased. There's a letter from Mr. Ashton, and one from Marian Brand. She's coming down, and the sister too—what's her name—Ina Felton. What a pity she's married. Someone told me she was pretty—I can't think who it could have been. You might have fallen in love with her, and then the whole thing would have been settled."

She might have been talking in an empty room for all the notice anyone took.

Felix came up to the table, bent his dark frowning gaze upon the letters, and read them—Mr. Ashton's first, and then the few lines which had cost Marian Brand a couple of sleepless nights and a good deal of distressed thought, all to no purpose at all, because, whatever she had written, it would have encountered the same implacable resentment.

Cassy Remington had stopped talking. She made little fidgeting movements with her hands. She and her sister both watched Felix, Florence Brand sitting quite still. They might not have been there for all the notice he took of them, until he suddenly looked up and said in a quiet, deadly voice,

42

"She can't come next week. You must write and say so. Helen is coming."

Cassy twisted her fingers.

"Oh, Felix—I don't think we can. Mr. Ashton—it's her house, you know. Everything belongs to her now. She could turn us right out. It isn't as if we had our own furniture or anything—it's all hers."

He said, "I wasn't speaking to you." He met his mother's stare. "You'd better wire and say the house is full."

Florence Brand's face did not change at all. It was heavy, without any look of youth, but there were no lines on the pale, smooth skin.

"Do you think that would be wise?"

"I don't care whether it's wise or not."

Mrs. Brand appeared to consider this. When she spoke it was with great deliberation.

"Eliza Cotton will not want to leave her room. I understand that she is, legally, in Marian's service. There can therefore be no objection to her remaining on that side of the house. That leaves us four bedrooms and the attic on this side."

"Do you propose to put Helen in the attic?"

Her answer was as bland as oil.

"No. I hardly think that would be suitable. I thought perhaps Penny."

His face darkened.

"Why?"

"Well, your room would hardly be suitable—too small and cold. But I could move Penny to the attic, and Miss Adrian could have her room. She would not, in any case, care to be on Marian's side of the house. It would not be pleasant for her to feel that she was being forced upon a stranger—would it?"

Some sort of clash made itself apparent. Miss Cassy darted her birdlike glances at her sister's face, which showed noth-

43

ing, and at her nephew's, which showed too much. There was a malicious sparkle in the bright blue eyes. She discerned the pressure of Florence's formidable will, the resistance with which Felix opposed it, the moment when the resistance broke down. She was even aware of why it broke. Did he really want Helen Adrian on the far side of the house? He was fond of Penny. He didn't like her being sent up to the attic. Penny wouldn't like it either. Not only Cassy's eyes but all her thoughts sparkled as she considered how pleased Penny would be at being sent up to the attic to make room for Helen Adrian. And Felix—dear me, how positively murderous he was looking. Of course he didn't like it either—not at first—not whilst he was thinking about Penny—not until he began to remember that he would have Helen Adrian just across the landing. Ah—he was beginning to think of it now!

She sipped her coffee and watched him over the rim of the Minton cup. He looked away, stared down at the letters, and said angrily,

"Have it your own way! It's all damnable!" Without sitting down he made himself a cup of coffee, gulped it down without milk or sugar, put an apple in his pocket, and went out of the room, banging the door behind him.

He met Penny Halliday on the stairs and turned an accusing frown on her.

"You're late."

"About five minutes later than you, darling. Besides, I've been turning out the attic."

"What for?"

"Well, Eliza will have to come over here, won't she? And do you see her turning it out herself?"

"Did they tell you to do it?"

"Well, yes."

"Which of them?"

44

"Aunt Cassy has been kind of hinting all round it for days, and yesterday Aunt Florence told me to get on with it."

"For Eliza?"

A look of surprise came and went.

"I suppose so."

He said in his most brutal voice,

"It isn't for Eliza, it's for you."

Standing on the step above him, her eyes were almost level with his. They were brown eyes, round and clear. They matched her short brown curls, which she wore in an out-of-date bob. She stood there, small, and slight, and straight, with one hand resting on the banister. She leaned on it and said,

"I don't know what you mean."

"Helen's coming on Monday. They're giving her your room. You're to have the attic."

She had a round childish face and a soft red mouth. Her skin was berry-brown from the tang of the sea air. Sometimes she had a colour that was berry-bright too. She had none now. There was an effect of sternness as she said,

"Why is she coming?"

"Sea air."

"Is her throat better?"

He made an angry gesture.

"I don't know. She doesn't know. She's afraid to try it. They said two months. It's that now. She's coming here. If it's all right, she'll want to practise." The sentence came out in jerks.

She put her hand on his arm.

"Darling, don't worry—she'll be better."

She might have been touching a bit of wood.

"What makes you think so?"

When he said that his arm jerked. She took her hand away. He went on in an exasperated tone.

45

"What's the good of saying that? You don't know a thing about it. Nobody does, with voices. These lovely high ones— you never can tell. I don't know what the specialist said to her. She's frightened. And I'll tell you what, she's got something up her sleeve. There's that man Mount, he follows her round like a shadow. He's filthy with money. If she thought her voice was cracking up she'd take him. What else could she do? She won't have saved a penny. Damn Uncle Martin!"

"Darling!"

He said in a tone of concentrated rage,

"And damn the girl! Why couldn't she have been killed in that train smash? Talk about luck! She gets all the money and comes out from under a crashed train without so much as a scratch! What price seeing whether she'd drown if I push her over the cliff!"

Penny put out her hand, but this time she did not touch him. She said, "My poor lamb—" and all at once he put his head down on her shoulder, holding her so hard that it hurt. She stroked his hair, and said the sort of things she would have said to a child.

"Darling, don't. Don't mind so much. I'm here. It'll be all right. I promise you it will. Only be good, darling, and don't talk nonsense about murdering people, because you'd be very bad at it. Have you had any breakfast?"

He said, "Coffee—" in a choking voice.

"Silly!" She pulled his handkerchief out of his pocket and gave it to him. "Here you are. Now you'll just come down and have some with me, because they'll be on to me like a pack of wolves if I go in alone. You know, darling, I can just bear your being in love with Helen, but I can't bear them twitting me about it, and they will if you don't come and protect me."

He scrubbed his eyes and stuffed the handkerchief into the pocket of his slacks.

46

"Penny—I'm a beast to you."

"Yes, darling, you are rather, but you can study to improve. And I don't mind a bit about the attic—I don't, honestly. Only I think your mother is balmy to leave Eliza in the enemy's camp, because she'll go over. You see if she doesn't."

"She will anyhow. She hates us. Who wouldn't?"

She reached up and kissed him on the point of the chin—a soft, careless kiss, childish and rather sweet.

"You won't feel nearly so hateful when you've had some breakfast," she said.

Neither of them had heard the breakfast-room door open. One of the things which Martin Brand had so greatly disliked was the entirely soundless manner in which both his sister-in-law and her sister moved about the house. One was fat and the other was thin, but it didn't seem to make a pennorth of difference—you never heard them open a door. One moment you were comfortably alone, and the next there was Florence, or it might be Cassy, looming up out of the silence. And he would maintain to the entire British Medical Association that his hearing was one hundred per cent good.

Felix and Penny shared his views. Neither of them had heard a sound, yet on dropping back from that light kiss and giving Felix's sleeve a small persuasive tug Penny was aware of Cassy Remington on the mat at the foot of the stairs, her head cocked, her blue eyes bright and sly. Felix had already seen her. He jerked his arm away and ran down the remaining steps as Cassy said,

"You haven't had any breakfast. I was coming to find you. Eliza will be furious if no one eats her herrings."

Penny came down sedately.

"Felix will eat two, and Mactavish and I will have one between us."

CHAPTER 7

"I've not made up my mind," said Eliza Cotton.

A slant of sunlight came in through the window. The fire burned bright in the range. The cat Mactavish sat in front of it with his chin resting upon the oven trivet, which was pleasantly warm. He was full of fish, and he found it agreeable to listen to the voices of Penny and Eliza.

Penny sat on the kitchen table in what she had begun to call their side of the house and swung her legs. She was wearing grey slacks and an old white sweater which had belonged to Felix in his middle teens and had now shrunk several sizes and turned yellow with washing.

Eliza was tall and as flat as a board. She could never have been handsome, but she had probably always had a very competent look. The bone of her nose was high, and the eyes on either side of it appeared to have two of the qualifications ascribed by Mr. Wordsworth to his perfect woman—they were admirably fitted to warn and to command. The poet, it will be remembered, inserts "to comfort" between these rather formidable attributes, but there was nothing about Eliza's appearance to suggest that this might apply to her. She was mixing something in a basin. She beat hard at a grocer's egg, looked at Penny in a masterful manner, and repeated what she had just said.

"I haven't made up my mind. And sitting on my kitchen table is a thing I don't hold with, so you can just get down."

Penny leaned sideways, picked up a Sultana, and put it in her mouth.

48

"Darling Eliza, don't be cross. When are you going to make it up?"

"When I'm ready. And I'll say now and nobody'll get me from it, it wouldn't take me long if I hadn't given my word to Mr. Brand."

"Did you tell him you'd stay?"

"No I didn't, nor he wouldn't ask me. What'd there be to stay for, with Mr. Felix all set to marry in haste and repent at leisure? And if you were to tell me you'd be here more than five minutes after that, I'd not believe you, not if you took your Bible oath."

Penny shook her head.

"I shouldn't waste a Bible oath on it. I'd go like a flash of lightning. We could go together, darling, and have two rooms, and take in washing or something."

Eliza beat the egg.

"What I promised Mr. Brand was that I'd wait and see. If Miss Marian Brand was to come here, I was to wait and see how we'd get on. He said likely enough she'd be put on if I didn't, and he'd like her to get a fair start."

Penny took another Sultana.

"Electric stoves are all right when you're used to them," she said.

"I don't hold with them. That range on the other side 'ud be all right if it was took in hand."

Penny caught her breath. Eliza was really thinking about staying. The Sultana began to taste good.

"Mactavish likes the kitchen on the other side," she said.

"That's because there's mice there, which there wouldn't be if it was used."

"He might hope they were going to come back."

"There'd be no good his hoping. I don't hold with mice. What he likes or don't like is neither here nor there."

49

Penny let this go. She took another Sultana, and was snapped at.

"If I'm to make a plain cake, better have said so to start with and no pretence made. Are you meeting that train or not?"

Penny nodded.

"I thought someone had better. Rather grim, coming to a new place and nobody wanting you."

"Then you can't go in those clothes, and high time you was changing."

"Eliza, you're a bully."

"You'll put on your brown tweed skirt, and a decent jumper, and your tweed coat. The wind's in the north for all you don't feel it here. Is Felix going?"

"Eliza—*darling!*"

"Saving himself to meet *her!*" said Eliza with a formidable toss of the head.

Penny said, "Of course." Then she jumped down from the table and got behind Eliza, because all of a sudden she had come over all shaky.

"I don't know what everything's coming to," said Eliza grimly. She had beaten the egg until it was pure froth. She now began to dowse it with sugar. "What Felix wants is to keep a hold of himself, or that temper of his'll be getting him into trouble some day. It was bad enough when he was a boy, and he'd ought to have been broken of it, and could have been if it hadn't been for some I could mention that never could leave him alone. If a child's got a fancy for playing the piano, well, why not let him be? It's not my fancy, but it takes all sorts to make a world, as they say, and set on music he is, and always will be. Then what's the sense of nattering after him all the time? 'Felix, you ought to be out on the beach'—or posting a letter, or going on an errand, or anything except what he's doing. And, 'You didn't ought to

50

practise so much,' and, 'Why can't you play something with a nice tune to it?' Enough to spoil any child's temper if you ask me, and done to be aggravating! Puts me in mind of Mactavish with a mouse, and when it's a poor dumb animal you don't blame them, but when it's a yuman being that calls itself a Christian and goes to church regular, then there are things I could say, only I know my place."

Behind her back Penny said in a small soft voice,

"He's so unhappy—"

Eliza jerked.

"He gives away to it. He'll need to watch that temper. Look at the things he's said! Only this morning Mrs. Bell asks me where she shall start, and I told her, 'You take and give the front hall and the stairs a good doing,' and she comes back and tells me she daresn't. And when I ask why, she can tell me that Felix was on the stairs saying damn his Uncle Martin, and damn someone else that he didn't go so far as to name, but easy enough to tell it was Miss Marian Brand, and a pity she hadn't got killed in that railway smash she was in. And, 'What a way to talk!' she said. And I sent her over to do the old kitchen. It's clean enough, for I saw she did it out myself so soon as ever I heard Miss Brand would be coming, but I thought it would get her out of the way, and the men had been in fixing that electric. She went off grumbling—she could see I'd more use for her room than her company. But she's right, it's no way to talk nor to let people hear you doing it, and where you've got a daily help you've got someone that'll fetch and carry with everything that goes on, and put a bit on to it for good measure."

Penny said, "He doesn't mean it."

Eliza turned round sharp and quick.

"Then he didn't ought to say it, and you'd better tell him so! Is it true he went so far as to talk about giving Miss Marian Brand a push over the cliff and see if that'd drown her?"

51

Penny had flushed to the roots of her hair.

"He didn't mean it. He doesn't mean anything at all when he says things like that. It's like screaming out when someone stamps on your foot. The aunts had been stamping about Helen Adrian and—and he can't bear it."

Eliza said, "He isn't the only one. There's plenty of things we've got to bear whether we like it or not. And no call to talk like a murdering lunatic. There's a piano he can go and bang on if that's what he feels like, and no harm done. And if you want to catch that train you'd better run."

Penny ran.

CHAPTER 8

After all, Penny hadn't time to change. She took one look at the clock, snatched her bicycle, and coasted down the hill into Farne, which used to be a fishing village, but managed during the years between the wars to collect a good many rows of small houses, a distressing eruption of bungalows, and a hideous but comfortable hotel. The houses were always cram full. They had been built to let, and let they did at fantastic prices, since the demand was constantly greater than the supply. There was an aerodrome three miles inland, and a consequent run on all possible accommodation within a five-mile radius.

Penny got to the station just half a minute before the train, flung her bicycle against a wall, ducked under a porter's arm, and saw Marian Brand and Ina Felton get out of the third carriage from the engine. She hadn't the slightest doubt as to who they were, because she had seen them both before.

There was a portrait of Ina hanging in the drawing-room at this minute with a Leghorn hat tied on over her dark curls and a white muslin dress, only the name under it was Isabella, not Ina, Brand. And a miniature of Marian had always stood on the top of Uncle Martin's chest of drawers—his mother, painted at the time of her marriage when she was just eighteen. So that was why he had left her the money. Penny thought it was very romantic.

She ran up to them all flushed and friendly and said,

"I'm Penny. You *are* Marian and Ina, aren't you?"

They collected luggage and got everything on to a taxi, including Penny's bicycle, because she wasn't going to pound up that hill and let them arrive alone. They packed in somehow. The friendly glow persisted. Penny chattered.

"I'm not a cousin. I'm something on the Remington side. I hadn't any other relations, so the aunts took me. It was very good of them."

Her tone betrayed that this was dictated by conscience. After that it brightened again.

"Uncle Martin was sweet to me. And Eliza—oh, Marian, what are you going to do about Eliza Cotton? Because you'd better have it all ready and say it straight away. She's a simply angel cook."

Marian said, "Who is Eliza?"

Penny couldn't believe her ears. The life of the house revolved round Eliza—it always had. Her eyes went quite round with surprise, but she could only get hold of the most inadequate words.

"She was Uncle Martin's housekeeper."

Marian looked troubled.

"But your aunts will want her, won't they? I couldn't—"

Penny clutched her with a little brown hand.

"She isn't theirs—she's yours. Mr. Ashton said so. He said she was in your service, and she would have to give you

53

notice if she didn't want to stay. You won't let her, will you?"

"Perhaps she won't want to stay with us."

"She hasn't made up her mind. But she will when she sees you. She adored Uncle Martin, and she wants to stay because of Mactavish, and Felix, and me. Mactavish is the cat—he was Uncle Martin's cat. A Scotch friend of his sent him all the way from Edinburgh in a basket with his name tied around his neck on a label. Eliza adores him. If Mactavish likes you, she will stay. You *will* have her, won't you?" She dropped her voice to a confidential note. "I think she has really practically made up her mind, because she has had the sweep, and the kitchen on your side done out twice, and she says there's nothing wrong with the range except not being used."

"Oh—" Marian looked anxious. "Mr. Ashton said he was arranging about an electric stove."

Penny nodded.

"Yes, that's all right—it's in. But Eliza doesn't hold with electrics. Look here, you'll have to be firm. If Eliza says she'll stay, the aunts will suggest sharing meals, and her cooking for everyone. Well, she'll do it for a day or two, but she won't go on. Just as soon as Eliza has made up her mind, she won't so much as cook a potato for our side of the house."

Marian began to feel appalled.

"But, Penny—I can't—"

"You won't have to. And you needn't feel bad about it either. Eliza wouldn't stay with the aunts if they paid her millions. But she'd like to stay with Mactavish and Felix and me. You see, if she's next door, and you didn't mind frightfully, I could come in and see her and Mactavish. He doesn't really like our side of the house, and I couldn't bear not seeing him. Anyhow, he wouldn't leave Eliza, and he does like the kitchen on your side. Eliza says it's because of mice, but I think he just likes it. She's got rather a mouse complex, you know. Honestly, she'll do you awfully well if she makes up her mind to stay. And you don't need to have a conscience about it, because Mrs. Bell will go on coming to us, and she's got a sister who can cook and who will come in every day except Sunday, so we'll be perfectly all right. Look! Just round this next corner you'll see the house."

They turned the corner, and Marian saw Cove House standing waiting for them. There was a wall of heaped stones between it and the road, and two rough pillars to mark the entrance. A few hard-bitten trees and shrubs were huddled low against the wind. Behind them the straggling white house, two stories high and a slanting attic floor above. There were two front doors painted bright blue, with identical knockers and old-fashioned iron bellpulls. Late narcissus were dying off amongst the wallflower in a narrow bed on either side.

As the taxi stopped, the right-hand door opened and Eliza Cotton loomed up. Marian got out and came forward. That feeling of being in a dream which she had had off and on for more than a month now was strong upon her. Her house— her own house. It didn't seem as if it could be real. Now— now—now it must break round her. But whilst the dream lasts you bear your part in it. She shook hands with Eliza, encountered a strong searching look, said something about the fine day, and turned back to pay the taxi. There was a bustle of luggage coming in. The driver was very obliging.

Penny had a despairing feeling that Felix ought to be there, and that if he were, nothing that she could do or say would be in the least likely to make him behave tolerably. And the aunts would be sharpening every tooth and claw they had.

She followed up the stairs and heard Eliza ahead of her.

"This was Mr. Brand's bedroom. I considered you would wish to have it. And the one next door for Mrs. Felton. They have both got the view of the sea."

55

The room was not large, but very pleasant. Between the windows and on either side old-fashioned shutters were folded back into the walls. They were painted the same bright blue as the front door.

Ina and Marian stood side by side and looked out at an enchanting view. First came the small walled garden. There were fruit trees trained against the walls. A bright pink froth of apple blossom showed here and there on nectarine and peach. Then steps going down to a wide terraced ledge. More steps, another ledge, and another, dropping to the little cove from which the house took its name. It faced south and the cliffs sheltered it on either side. The terraced gardens were full of spring flowers—wallflower and tulip, fruit blossom and early clematis, aubrietia, polyanthus, and arabis. The colours were as bright as jewels under the spring sun. Beyond and below, a long narrow stretch of shingle, and beyond that the sea, as clear and blue as the sky above it. When they turned back into the room it seemed dark. All that colour and brilliance outside, but the plain white walls, the plain old furniture, the short blue and white curtains which matched the bedspread, had a charm of their own. They were simple and restful.

The bathroom was next door, and then Ina's room. It had the same blue shutters and curtains, but there was an old-fashioned wall-paper with pink roses on it, and the ewer and basin on the bow-front marble-topped washstand had a rose pattern instead of the blue and white in Marian's room.

Ina had hardly spoken at all. She said, "Yes," when she was asked if she liked her room, and, "No," when she was asked if she was tired. She had become so pale that the delicately applied colour which had been so becoming when she started now showed up like a patch on the white skin. When they went to see the rest of the house she contrived to remain behind.

Penny went on doing showman.

"The rooms are the same on both sides—four bedrooms on this floor, and an attic room above. And there is a linen-cupboard on each side. It really was two houses to start with. That's the door through to our side—there's one on each floor. Eliza sleeps in your attic, so the other two bedrooms are spare. Then downstairs there are three sitting-rooms, and the kitchen, and things like that—the same both sides. You've got the dining-room, and a little room that hasn't been used much, and Uncle Martin's study, which I think is the nicest room in the house. And on our side there's the breakfast-room, and the drawing-room, and a room the aunts have always had for themselves. No one ever goes into the draw-ing-room except Felix—because of the piano, you know. It's a lovely Bechstein grand. He really does play beautifully. And he composes. He ought to be doing that all the time, instead of going round playing people's accompaniments."

Marian wasn't stupid. There was an emphasis on "peo-ple"—Penny's eyes were bright and her cheeks flushed. She remembered that Felix Brand was Helen Adrian's accompa-nist, and that Helen Adrian was, from her pictures, a very pretty woman. There was no need to say anything. They were coming into the study, and when they were really there all she could do was to draw a long satisfied breath and say, "Oh!"

It was the most comfortable room she had ever seen. All the strangeness went out of her as she looked at it. It wasn't until afterwards that she could notice and admire the pair of Chippendale bookcases with their curved horns and diamond lattice-work, or the writing-table with its pigeon-holes and little drawers, and the brass handles which were the colour of very pale gold. At the time she only knew that it was a beautiful room, and that she loved it.

Penny squeezed her arm and pulled her over to the window. The view was the same as from the bedroom above, but you saw more garden and less cover. There was a narrow bed of forget-me-nots under the three windows, set with May-flowering tulips just coming into bloom, the long pointed buds still green but flushed and streaked with rose, and purple, and scarlet, and yellow. The middle window was a door with two shallow steps going down to a flagged path beyond the flowers. You only had to turn a handle and step out. There was a pink cherry in bloom away to the left.

"It's nice, isn't it?" said Penny. She was still holding Marian's arm. Eliza had vanished. They were alone.

Marian said, "Yes," with a deep sigh of content, and all at once Penny felt that she could say anything. Her hand squeezed harder. The words came tumbling out.

"Marian—you won't want to take the piano, will you? I don't know what Felix would do without it, and it wouldn't be right in here—not a bit. The aunts have been saying you'd want it, and the drawing-room furniture. And of course it's all yours, but you'd hate it really—nasty gilt spindly stuff, and the sort of shiny brocade you can only sit on in your best evening dress. You wouldn't really want to spoil this room with it—would you?"

"I should hate it. And of course I won't take the piano away from Felix."

The door behind them was open. Eliza came through it with a tea-tray. The cat Mactavish followed, walking delicately, like Agag. Having set down the tray, Eliza straightened herself. Penny became aware that the moment was a fateful one. There were persons so uninstructed as to address a princely Persian as "puss." There were ill-mannered vulgarians who attempted to lay an uninvited hand upon him. There were those who knew how to treat him. Eliza was undoubtedly waiting to see into which category Miss Marian Brand would fall. She said,

"I thought you would like a cup of tea after the journey."

And Marian said, "How lovely," and "Thank you," and sat down in front of the table which held the tray.

The critical moment impended. Mactavish advanced, his tail fluffed out to its fullest extent, his topaz eyes wary upon the stranger.

Marian said, "Oh, how beautiful!" on what was felt to be a very proper note, and then, "What is his name?"

Eliza noted the pronoun with approbation. She had a biting contempt for people who alluded to all cats as *her*.

"His name's Mactavish."

Marian gazed admiringly.

"Will he come to me?"

"He'll please himself."

Mactavish pleased himself. The tone of this person's voice satisfied a fastidious ear. He was aware of being admired, not fulsomely, but in a well-bred manner. When the voice addressed him by name he advanced and sniffed at a respectfully extended hand. Considering that it had been an agreeable smell, he rubbed his head against it and permitted himself to be delicately stroked behind the ear. Then, before the astonished eyes of Penny and Eliza, he leaped on to the stranger's lap and settled there.

As the sound of a faint purr became audible, Eliza made up her mind. If anyone had told her that Mactavish would have taken such a fancy, she wouldn't have believed them. Few indeed were the chosen laps upon which he would condescend to sit—Mr. Brand's, Felix's, and Penny's. If lifted up by Mrs. Alfred Brand or Miss Cassy, his eyes flamed with fury and he removed himself with all possible haste. He had been known to kick, to scratch, and even to bite. He always washed himself all over afterwards. And now just to look at him, with his paws doubled under and purring like a teakettle! If that wasn't a sign, Eliza didn't know one. She said,

"My goodness, gracious me!" and went out of the room in a hurry.

Upstairs in her new bedroom Ina was leaning out of the window. It was all lovely, and she was very unhappy. Cyril was behaving very badly indeed. When it happened right under your eyes like that, it was no good going on trying to pretend any longer. He didn't want to work—he never had wanted to work. He wanted all the things you can't get without working for them. He wanted Marian to give him half the money. And she wouldn't. Ina had said whatever Cyril had wanted her to say. And still Marian wouldn't. Deep down inside her there was something which said that Marian was right. Since the last really dreadful row Ina found herself unable to close her thought to that voice. It told her that all Cyril ever wanted with money was to spend it on having a good time, and that when it was spent he would want more, and more, and more. She was finding it impossible to drape this Cyril any longer in the garments of romance. He was beginning to emerge as a selfish, emotional young man who could see no reason why everything should not give way to him. He had not come down with them to Cove House because, after the last row two days ago, he had flung out of the house and banged the door behind him. She didn't know where he was, or when she would see him again.

She didn't want to see him again.

This thought shocked her so much that she felt giddy. She leaned right out, and heard voices from the window next to hers. This window was on the other side of the wall which divided the two houses, but it was only three or four feet away, and it was open. There were two voices—two women's voices. One said, "It would be a good thing if she was dead." And the other said, "People don't die just because you want them to."

60

Ina felt a kind of stinging horror. She drew back, and saw Penny smiling at her from the doorway.

"There's some tea in the study. I expect you're dying for it. Marian couldn't come up for you because Mactavish won't get off her lap."

CHAPTER 9

Miss Silver looked up from her writing-table as a slight sound met her ear. After a pause had convinced her that the client whom she was expecting had not yet arrived, and that the sound must have proceeded from some cause other than the opening and closing of her front door, she sat back in her chair and returned to the letter which she had been reading. It was from her niece, Ethel Burkett, whose husband was a bank manager at Birleton. Her three boys now attended the excellent grammar school in that town. After some preliminaries in which a recent illness of little Josephine's was described—the one cherished girl, a good deal younger than the boys—she wrote:

"When Dr. Anderson said sea air *if possible*, you can just imagine how I felt, because of course I could not see *any* way in which it could be contrived. And then, the next morning, there was Muriel Lester's letter—you may remember I was at school with her. She had heard about Josephine. A cousin of hers has a flat in this building—Muriel wrote to me, and I was able to tell her about it before it got on to house-agents' books, so they have always felt very grateful. Well, Muriel wrote so very kindly and said she and her husband were obliged to go over to the Channel Islands to settle up his mother's estate—quite complicated under the old French law—and she wondered if I would care to occupy their house while they were away. They would not care to let, but would be glad not to leave it empty—really the number of burglaries is quite dreadful. It seemed like a direct answer to prayer, and I wired my grateful acceptance. She rang up last night after seven, and it is all fixed. John's unmarried sister, Mabel, will come in and take full charge here. Josephine and I go south tomorrow.

"Dearest Auntie, can you, *will* you, join us at Farne? It would be so delightful. Could you possibly shut the flat and bring Hannah? I cannot tell you what a comfort it would be. Farne is a small seaside place not very far from Ledstow but farther along the coast. I think you have friends in the neighbourhood . . ."

There followed an address, details of trains, and the request that a reply should be sent by telegram.

Since this had already been done, and an affectionate acceptance indicated, Miss Silver was able to continue her re-reading of Mrs. Burkett's letter without any sense of hurry. When she had finished she put it back in its envelope and bestowed the envelope in a drawer.

Her client had still not arrived. She allowed her gaze to rest with pleasure upon the comfortable sitting-room of her flat in Montague Mansions. As always when her thoughts turned that way, they became penetrated with gratitude to the Providence, which had so blessed her work as to establish her in this modest comfort. When she left school to become a governess at the scanty salary then obtaining, she had had no other expectation than to work hard all her life in other people's houses and in the end retire to some sordid back room. The contrast of this expectation with her pleasant four-roomed flat, served by a convenient lift and kept in spotless order by her faithful Hannah Meadows, never failed to stir her deepest feelings.

She sat there, her neat mousy hair arranged in a deep curled fringe very competently controlled by a net, her small slight person arrayed in a dress of olive-green wool made high to the chin by means of a cream net front with a collar supported by small strips of whalebone after the manner of her Edwardian youth. There was an old-fashioned gold chain about her neck from which depended a sizable locket upon which the initials of her parents, long deceased, were entwined in high relief.

The events which had led her to abandon what she herself called the scholastic profession for the much more lucrative work of private detection had long ago receded into the quite distant past. Her comfortable room was a subject for present gratitude. She considered it, as she always did, with approval. The carpet was getting shabby, but everyone's carpets were shabby now, and the really worn edge was well hidden by the bookcase. The affair of Lady Portington's pearls had enabled her to replace the old peacock-blue curtains which had weathered the war. After much faithful service they had suddenly shown signs of complete disintegration, and she had been most fortunate in finding some stuff of very nearly the same colour in a shop at Ledbury. It really toned in very well indeed with the upholstery of her walnut chairs and with the old carpet. The chairs were Victorian. They had spreading laps and odd-shaped arms and legs with a good deal of yellow carving about them, but they were surprisingly comfortable to sit in.

Miss Silver glanced at the watch which she wore pinned to the left side of her dress by an old-fashioned bar brooch set with small seed pearls. Her client was late.

As the thought passed through her mind, the door opened and Hannah announced, "Miss Adrian—"

63

Helen Adrian brought the scent of violets into the room. Her large blue eyes took in Miss Silver and her surroundings at a glance. With no perceptible pause she smiled and said, "How do you do?" and took the chair on the other side of the writing-table, all with an air of being very completely at her ease.

Miss Silver had not risen. She said, "Good-morning," and she inclined her head. Then she picked up the useful grey stocking which she was making for her niece Ethel Burkett's second boy, Derek, and began to knit, holding the needles in the continental manner, her hands low in her lap and her eyes quite free to observe her visitor.

They told her a good deal. First, and quite obviously, Helen Adrian was a rather spectacularly beautiful young woman. About thirty years old, or perhaps a little less. Or even perhaps a little more. Rather fairer than most fair women, with eyes that were larger and bluer than most blue eyes, and a complexion which may have been originated by nature but had been most exquisitely cultivated by art. It was really impossible to say which of the two owed more to the other. A perfectly tailored black coat and skirt displayed the excellence of Miss Adrian's figure. A glimpse of the ivory tailored silk of the shirt bespoke the excellence of Miss Adrian's taste. A small black hat in the latest mode emphasized the burnished gold of Miss Adrian's hair.

Miss Silver took in all these things and waited for her client to speak. She had not long to wait. In the manner of one who endeavours to put a social inferior at her ease, Miss Adrian said,

"It is very kind of you to see me, but I am afraid I may be just wasting your time. A friend of mine told me that Lady Portington—I don't know her myself, but she is a very intimate friend of my friend's—"

Miss Silver coughed.

"I was able to be of some help to Lady Portington."

Miss Adrian smiled encouragement.

"Oh, you are too modest. The pearls are heirlooms."

Miss Silver knitted for a moment in silence. Then she said,

"I think you did not come here to discuss Lady Portington's pearls. What can I do for you, Miss Adrian?"

Helen Adrian said, "Well, I don't know—" She had the sensation that you have when you find that you have missed a step in the dark. She felt as if she had come down hard on something she didn't know was there. She had been thinking that Miss Silver was a scream, and so was her room, and that she would get a good laugh out of the show if she didn't get anything else. And then, with a cough, a something in her voice, an odd sort of look in those very ordinary greyish eyes, this governessy little old maid was making her feel snubbed, uncertain. She hadn't felt like this since her first term at school. The thought just went through her mind, and was pushed out. She said, "Well, I don't know," and looked down at her immaculately gloved hands. They were holding her bag too tightly. It was Fred Mount's latest present and very expensive—black suede, with ivory fittings. She relaxed her hold on it and looked up, to see that Miss Silver was watching her.

"In what way can I help you, Miss Adrian?"

She was startled into honesty.

"I don't know that you can."

"But you came here to find out, did you not?"

"Well—"

Miss Silver smiled gravely.

"We shall not get very much farther unless you tell me what has brought you here."

The blue eyes looked away, looked down. The lashes which screened them were of really phenomenal length, and had been left to what appeared to be their natural shade, a very beautiful golden brown. The lips pouted for a moment, then took a line of resolve. Helen Adrian said,

"I'm being blackmailed. What do you advise me to do about it?"

Miss Silver's needles clicked briskly.

"The best advice that I or any other responsible person can give you is to go to the police."

"Did you ever know anyone who would take it?"

Miss Silver gave a regretful sigh.

"It is always extremely difficult to induce anyone to accept good advice."

Helen Adrian gave a short hard laugh.

"It's so easy, isn't it? People don't blackmail you unless there's something you don't want everyone to know. It mayn't be anything much, it mayn't be—anything at all. Everyone's got things they'd rather keep to themselves, I suppose. After all, if you're quite well known to the public you *have* got a private life, and it's none of their business, is it? Easy enough to say go to the police. But how can you? Once you've done it you can't go back. If it means bringing a case, you've got to go through with it, and a case means standing up and having mud thrown at you, and whatever you do, and however little there is in it, some of it's going to stick. I can't go to the police, and that's that."

Miss Silver coughed mildly.

"Since that is the case, perhaps you will tell me a little more. You must have had some idea that I should be able to help you, or you would not have come. I think you would do well to make up your mind to be frank with regard to the blackmailing attempt to which you have referred."

The blue eyes dwelt on her in an appraising fashion.

"Well—I don't know. I suppose it would all be—quite in confidence? My friend said I could rely on that."

Miss Silver drew herself up a little. The distance between

her and Miss Adrian appeared to have widened. She spoke across it.

"Certainly you may rely upon that."

"Oh, well, one has to be sure."

Miss Silver was knitting at a high rate of speed.

"If you cannot make up your mind to trust me, I can be of no possible assistance to you." She had recourse to a Victorian poet whom she revered. " 'Trust me not at all or all in all,' as the late Lord Tennyson says."

Helen Adrian stared. She really was a scream! The thought drifted away. Something else took its place—an odd touch of fear—the underlying pressure of necessity.

Miss Silver looked at her very steadily and said,

"It is for you to choose, Miss Adrian."

Helen Adrian made her choice. She had been leaning a little forward. Now she sat back.

"Well, I suppose you're right. Not that there's anything very much to tell—it's just the use that might be made of it. I expect you know my name. Most people do now, and I've worked pretty hard for it. Perhaps you have heard me sing?"

"No, I have not had that pleasure."

"Well, I did a good bit with concert parties at the end of the war—and of course broadcasting. I've had offers to go on the stage—musicals and revues—but—well, the fact is, I'm not much good at the acting part of it. There—you said to be frank, and if that isn't frank, I don't know what is."

Miss Silver coughed.

"You are doubtless wise to confine yourself to what you are sure of doing well."

Miss Adrian nodded in a casual manner.

"Yes—there's that. And then—you wouldn't think it to look at me, but I'm not out of the way strong. I get cold rather easily. I was near having pneumonia in the autumn, and they say I've got to be careful—I've had to rest my voice as it is.

So now we come to what's really at the bottom of the whole thing. I've had to think very seriously of whether it wouldn't be better to play safe. At the best of it, my sort of voice doesn't go on for ever, and why should I knock myself up travelling all over the place in goodness knows what sort of weather, when I could make a comfortable marriage, and have my own car, and nothing to worry about for the rest of my life?"

Miss Silver knitted thoughtfully.

"You have the opportunity of making such a marriage?"

Helen Adrian laughed a little scornfully.

"Any time the last two years. He's a big business man up in the north. He heard me sing and went in off the deep end. Any amount of money, and I've only got to say yes. Well, ever since I was ill I've been thinking about it. Chances like that don't go begging—if you don't pick them up, somebody else will. So I made up my mind I would. And that's where the blackmail comes in."

Miss Silver's needles clicked, the grey stocking revolved. Helen Adrian leaned forward and opened her bag. She extracted from it a rather creased envelope which she passed across to Miss Silver, who put down her knitting and opened it. There was a half sheet of cheap white notepaper inside. On it was printed in rough capitals:

WHAT ABOUT BRIGHTON LAST MAY?
WOULDN'T MOUNT LIKE TO KNOW!

"That's the man I'm thinking of marrying—Fred Mount."

Miss Silver read aloud with a touch of primness in her voice, "What about Brighton last May?"

Helen Adrian's colour had risen a little. It did not amount to a blush, but the tint in her cheeks was certainly deeper. She said quickly,

"There wasn't anything in it at all. I was singing at a concert, and naturally my accompanist went down with me."

"A man?"

"Of course—Felix Brand. He's a marvellous accompanist, and such a good contrast—the dark tragic type. It all helps, you know—throws me up."

"Did you stay at the same hotel?"

"A friend asked me to stay. Look here, I'll tell you the whole thing. There wasn't anything in it, but it could be made to look funny. My friend asked us to stay, and when we got there one of her children was ill at school and she was just off. What were we to do?"

"What did you do?"

"We stayed for the week-end. What else was there to do? The place was packed. I couldn't put Felix out into the street."

"Is this young man, your accompanist, in love with you?"

"What do you think! He's crazy about me. That's what makes it awkward." She took another letter out of her bag and tossed it over. "Here's number two."

In the same scrawled capitals Miss Silver read:

F. BRAND MIGHT PROVE A FIREBRAND IF FRED KNEW ALL. IF YOU WANT THE WEDDING BELLS TO RING YOU HAD BETTER COME TO TERMS. WHAT ABOUT MAY LAST YEAR?

She said, "Dear me!"

Miss Adrian nodded.

"That was only the beginning. A day or two later I was rung up on the telephone. It was from a call-box—you can always tell—and someone said, 'You've had my two letters about F. Brand and F. Mount. If you want those wedding-bells to ring you'll have to shut my mouth. I want fifty pounds down, and you can buy your wedding-dress. One pound notes, please, and you'll put them in an envelope and address

69

them to Mr. Friend, 24 Blakeston Road, S.E. You'll be sorry if you don't.' I said, 'What's the good of talking to me like that? Once I was fool enough to pay you, what's going to stop you going right on?' He said, 'What indeed! Fred has got a lot of money, hasn't he? You're not going to tell me you won't be able to get some of it out of him once you're safely married!'"

Miss Silver coughed.

"And what did you say to that?"

"I lost my temper," said Miss Adrian frankly. "I said, 'Go to hell!' and hung up."

"And then?"

"There was an 'And then' all right. Here it is."

Another of those sheets of writing-paper came out of the bag. The capitals said:

NASTY TEMPER. IF YOU DO THAT AGAIN FRED
WILL KNOW ALL. WHAT ABOUT THE MIDDLE OF
LAST JUNE?

Helen Adrian stared defiantly across the table.

"That's as far as we've got."

"When did this come?"

"This morning. That's when I rang you up."

Miss Silver continued to knit.

"Miss Adrian, do you know who is blackmailing you?"

"How should I?"

"I cannot tell you that. The address would, of course, be an accommodation address. If you went to the police, they would advise you to send a letter as requested. They would then watch the place and endeavour to trap the blackmailer."

"I won't go to the police."

Miss Silver looked at her shrewdly.

"I think you may have some idea of the blackmailer's identity. Did you, for instance, recognize the voice which spoke to you on the telephone."

"No. He was making it all squeaky—like a Punch and Judy show."

"It was a man?"

"Oh, yes."

Helen Adrian said,

"Well, there was someone down at Brighton last year—we were in a concert party together a couple of years ago. He was doing a sketch with Althea Paine. He was rotten, but she'd got a crush on him. Women fell for him—he was that sort. Cyril Felton is the name. It was just the sort of thing he might do. Of course—" The words came out in a hesitating manner.

Miss Silver said,

"I think you have someone else in mind, Miss Adrian."

"Well, I don't know. . . . Yes, I suppose I'd better tell you. I won't say I haven't thought it might be Felix himself—Felix Brand, my accompanist. He's crazy about me, and jealous of Fred—that's my fiancé, Mr. Mount—and he might think it was a way of getting it all broken off."

"Would he ask you for money?"

"I don't know—that might be just a blind, and to get me deeper in. I shouldn't be surprised if he hadn't got a revengeful nature, and though there isn't anything in it of course, there's Fred. He's jealous, and all his people are Chapel—you know the sort of thing. The first time he heard me sing I was having a big hit with a number about a child saying its prayers and the father and mother making it up— the God bless Mummy and Daddy touch. 'God bless our Home' it was called, and that was the refrain—

'God bless Mummy and Daddy,
God bless our home.'

71

Real hot sob-stuff. Felix said it made him sick, but it went over big and Fred fairly lapped it up. I'll say this for him, he doesn't let the grass grow under his feet—the next thing I knew, he was asking me down to meet the family. There's an old maid sister that keeps house for him, and a lot of married brothers. Well, that meant business, so I had to sit up and take notice. They were all very friendly, and I sang for them at a Chapel sociable. 'God bless our Home' went down like hot cakes. Fred told me I was his idea of an angel, and that's the way he's thought about me ever since. All very well, you know, but it means you have to mind your p's and q's. If he'd even half an idea there's ever been anyone else—week-ends, you know, and that sort of thing—well, there wouldn't be any wedding-bells, that's all. There isn't anything modern about Fred. There are good women and bad women. If you're a good woman you get the wedding-bells, if you're a bad woman you don't. Nice, simple, easy way of looking at things, isn't it?"

After a thoughtful silence Miss Silver said,

"I cannot take up your case, Miss Adrian, but I will give you some advice. You ought to take these letters to the police. But if you will not do so you would, I think, be well advised to tell your fiancé that an attempt is being made to blackmail you. You would, no doubt, be able to put the whole thing in such a way as to convince him that you are being subjected to an unscrupulous persecution. You should not, I think, find it difficult to convince him of your complete innocence."

If Miss Silver's tone was unusually dry, Miss Adrian did not notice it. She said with all the emphasis at her command,

"You don't know Fred."

72

CHAPTER 10

Helen Adrian arrived at Cove House on the following day. In some extraordinary way her presence immediately pervaded it. A scent of violets came and went, clashing a little with the naphthalene which was Mrs. Brand's specific against moth. It even came over into Marian's side of the house, which was mercifully free from moth-ball, Martin Brand having disliked the smell, maintaining that there had been no moths in his mother's time, and that she used nothing but lavender to ward them off. To which Eliza Cotton had been wont to respond that some people *drawed* them.

The violet scent was only one manifestation of Miss Adrian's presence. The shutters were open and the curtains drawn back in the drawing-room. The sound of the piano could be heard continually, and the notes of a high and lovely voice went floating up, and up, and up, and then down, and down, and down, as she practiced scales, and runs, and trills, never really letting her voice out, but keeping to the enchanting half-voice which tests the breath-control and imposes no strain on the throat. Felix, plunged head over ears in his dream, was like someone moving on another plane.

Eliza, ejecting a queen wasp from a honeypot, remarked with a rasp in her voice that, insects or men, it was all one when there was honey about, they were bound to trap themselves no matter what came of it.

"And no use your looking like that, Penny my dear. If he knew what was good for him he'd do different, but men don't and never will."

Penny said in a small dejected voice,

"I don't know what you mean."

She stood looking out of the old kitchen window, one hand absently stroking Mactavish, who was sunning himself on the window ledge. Through the half-open casement Miss Adrian could be heard trilling melodiously.

Eliza looked grimly at Penny's back. It would have given her a good deal of pleasure to have started a barrel-organ in opposition. She would also have liked to tell Felix what she thought of the silly way he was acting—black as a May thunderstorm and sour enough to curdle the milk one minute, and grinning like a Cheshire cat the next. "And what I've always said, and always will say, is, being in love is all very well in reason, but no need to make a show of yourself!" This last bit came out aloud to the accompaniment of a vigorous rattling of pots and pans.

Penny said in a still smaller voice,

"I suppose he's in love with her." Then, after a pause, "I said that to him one day, I said it right out—'I suppose you *are* in love with her.' And what do you think he said?"

Eliza snorted.

"Something soft!"

Penny didn't turn around. She went on stroking Mactavish.

"He looked at me. You know the way he can look—black, like you said just now—and he said, 'Sometimes I think I hate her!' and he went out of the room and banged the door."

Eliza said harshly,

"She's the tormenting sort. Maybe she'll do it once too often. Hatred's like muck—it breeds things."

Penny nodded.

"He didn't mean it—not really—at least—" Her voice trailed away.

"Better say it."

"It's wicked to hate. I suppose I'm wicked. I do very nearly

74

hate her—when she—makes Felix—look like that." Then, with sudden energy, "And when that scent of hers comes crawling up into my attic, I'd rather it was moth-ball, and that *shows!*"

Mactavish, who had been on the edge of purring, uttered a sharp protest. The stroking fingers had become quite hard. They had pressed upon a tender spot, they had actually hurt. It was not his habit to suffer in silence. Since the fingers were Penny's, he refrained from biting them. Instead he rose to his majestic height, dazzled her for a moment with an orange glare, and leaped out of the window.

Penny said, "Oh!" and Eliza scolded.

"Now look what you've done—put him right out of temper!"

The sound of Miss Adrian's voice came in at the open window, floating down from its high trill. Penny jerked round, stamped her foot hard on the stone floor, and ran out of the room.

In the study the telephone bell was ringing. Marian Brand, who had been going through the writing-table drawers, pushed a pile of papers out of the way and pulled the standing instrument towards her. A man said "Hullo!" and all in a minute time and distance had slipped aside and a hand was holding hers in the dark under the rubble of a wrecked train.

She said, "Marian Brand speaking," and was pleased because her voice was full and steady. Something in her shook. She had thought that he was still in America. Perhaps he was . . . . That was nonsense. He might have been in the room. These thoughts were all there together at the same time.

And he was speaking again.

"How are you? Did you know my voice? I should have known yours anywhere."

Ina opened the door. When she saw that Marian was at

the telephone she went away again. She had the air of an intruding ghost, unwanted and forlorn. Marian had not even seen her. She was saying, "I thought you were in America."

"I was—I'm not any longer. One flies. Did you get my letters?"

"Yes. They were very interesting."

"How did you know we were here?"

"Your Mrs. Deane. I missed you by a couple of days. May I come over and see you?"

"Where are you?"

"Practically next door, in the hotel at Farne. When may I come and see you?"

"Would you like to come to lunch?"

"Do you mean today? . . . . . I'd love to."

"We're about a mile along the coast road. You can't really miss us. The house is white, and there are twin front doors painted blue."

She hung up and went to interview Eliza.

"I do hope you can manage. It's rather short notice."

Eliza looked gloomy.

"It'll have to be something out of a tin, which is what I never thought I'd come to, but there's not many can say they've not had their spirits broke by the war—when I think how I wouldn't have margarine inside my kitchen, let alone having to manage with drips and drabs of fat, and go on your knees to the butcher for the bones to boil it off!"

"But you're such a lovely cook. That's where real cleverness comes in—everything tastes as if you had pounds of whatever you wanted."

If there had been one shade of insincerity in her tone, or even in her thought, Eliza would have been on to it like Mactavish with a mouse. There being nothing but sheer conviction, she allowed herself to accept the tribute.

When they had considered that a coffee-cream could not

76

be ready in time, and that there was not lard enough to make a tart, Eliza came down firmly upon Queen pudding, there being two eggs left over and the grocery order due again tomorrow.

Then as Marian turned to go, Eliza stayed her.

"There is something I think I'd better say, Miss Marian—"

Marian's heart sank. After only two days she could feel that it was going to be a wrench to part with Eliza, and it sounded dreadfully as if Eliza was going to give notice. And then remorse smote her. If she felt like this all in a flash, no wonder Aunt Florence and Aunt Cassy were sitting on the other side of the wall being jealous and angry because of having Eliza reft from them. There had been a couple of dreadful communal meals at which this had been made quite clear. She braced herself for the blow.

Eliza stood up tall and stiff, with the bone of her nose showing yellow under the skin and her eyes the colour of the sharp steel knife which she had just taken out of the table drawer. She said,

"It's always best to get things settled, and I'd like to be sure where I stand, so perhaps you'll let me know if you would be thinking of making a change."

This didn't sound like giving notice, but you couldn't take anything for granted.

"I don't want to change anything at all, Eliza."

"Then I'm sure I shall be very pleased to stay. I always did say this was the better range of the two, and Mactavish has settled down."

"I'm very glad, Eliza. The only thing is, I feel bad about Mrs. Brand and Miss Remington—"

Eliza did not exactly sniff. The muscles of her nose twitched. She said firmly,

"Mrs. Bell is doing for them, and her sister Mrs. Woolley

will come up mornings and cook for them. I've put her in the way of the range, and they can hot up what she leaves for the evening. It's all fixed, and nothing for you to worry about. And if you and Mrs. Felton'll do your own rooms—"

"And the study," said Marian quickly—"I'd like to do the study."

"We'll get along fine. And if I may say so, I'll be glad for Penny to have a little more company, and Felix too."

CHAPTER 11

On the other side of the wall Miss Remington lifted her head with a jerk.

"I'm sure it's a blessing this room doesn't face the same way as the drawing-room."

The ladies were in their own sitting-room. It looked towards the road and had a view of wind-driven shrubs on this side and rising ground beyond. There was a good deal of furniture and a great many knick-knacks. Every inch of the wall space was taken up. A number of small tables cluttered the floor. The blue plush curtains were heavy. The Brussels carpet had worn remarkably well, its harsh blues and browns being practically intact.

Mrs. Brand said, "We don't get the sun, or the view of the sea."

Cassy tossed her head.

"You don't care for too much sun, and I'm sure the sea makes quite enough noise on this side. So does Helen Adrian. I shall speak to Felix. They really ought to keep the window shut when they're practising. I don't see why we should have to close ours." She went quickly to the casement as she spoke and jerked it to with a bang.

Florence Brand was darning a stocking. She looked up. She allowed her eyes to rest upon her sister for a moment, and then went on darning, taking a thread and leaving a thread in a slow, deliberate manner.

"People pay to hear her," she said.

Miss Cassy turned round.

"I don't know why you have her here."

"I don't have her here. And Felix won't much longer."

Cassy stared.

"How do you know? She'd marry him for two-pence."

Florence Brand shook her head.

"Oh, no—not now—not without Martin's money."

"Well, she'd be a good riddance," said Cassy Remington.

As she spoke, the door, which had been slightly ajar, was pushed a little wider. Mrs. Bell's lugubrious face with the fair streaky hair coming down in loops looked round it.

"Emma's doing fish for you, Mrs. Brand. She's brought it with her, but there wasn't any haddock, so it's cod, and a few herrings for breakfast."

She went back through and told her sister Mrs. Woolley that Miss Remington had turned up her nose, but what was the good, someone had got to eat cod, and they were carrying on like nobody's business about that Miss Adrian.

In the drawing-room Felix lifted his hands from the keyboard and said,

"Not much wrong with the voice. Let's run through that again. And try letting it out a little."

The sun streamed in through the three windows. The two double casements stood wide, but the window in the middle, which was really a door, was closed. All the curtains were of pale brocade with the colour bleached out of it. The room

79

corresponded to Martin Brand's study on the other side of the wall, and it looked and felt as if it had never been lived in. An ivory wall-paper with a satin stripe was here and there interrupted by watercolours with wide white mounts and narrow gold frames. The furniture was, as Penny had described it, gilt and spindly. Most of it was shrouded in dust-sheets, but the covers had been carelessly pulled off two of the larger chairs and tossed in a heap upon an Empire couch.

In the midst of all this stiffness and pallor Helen Adrian looked as warmly alive as sunshine. Her hair was very nearly as golden. Her skin glowed with health, and her eyes were just that one shade deeper than sky-blue which makes all the difference. She shook her head and said,

"No, that's enough."

Felix jerked back the heavy lock of dark hair which was always falling into his eyes.

"Just let your voice out. I believe it's better than ever."

She was leaning over the piano towards him.

"No—I don't want to."

He said accusingly, "You're scared," and she nodded.

"I'm afraid of singing out. I don't feel—"

"You don't need to feel. Sing! It's all there—just let it go."

He struck the opening chords, but she remained leaning there, tracing an imaginary pattern on the dark wood and looking down at her own finger with its polished rosy nail.

"Felix—"

He banged out a bar and stopped.

"What is it?"

"It's no good. I can't go on to a concert platform and sing in a whisper, and I'm not going to let my voice out and crack it."

"What are you driving at?"

"Oh, well—"

"You've got an engagement in Brighton in a fortnight's

time. How are you going to keep it if you won't try your voice?"

"Well, that's just it—I don't think I'm going to keep it."

"And all the rest of your engagements?"

"I don't think—"

"You don't think? You've *got* to think!"

"I'm not going to crack my voice."

"There's nothing the matter with your voice."

She straightened up with a little laugh.

"Well, it *is* my voice, darling—I'm glad you admit that— and if I don't want to sing, you can't make me."

He swung round on the piano-stool.

"Do you mean anything by that?" Then, with the blood rushing into his face, "What do you mean?"

She was watching him. Now she smiled.

"I just don't want to sing, darling."

He got up and came towards her quite slowly and deliberately.

"Do you mean now—or—"

"I mean now."

"All right, then we try again tomorrow—is that it?"

"No, I don't think so. Felix, do be reasonable."

The blood had drained back. The lock of hair had fallen forward again. It emphasised his pallor.

"What do you mean by being reasonable?"

She laughed lightly.

"It's not anything you'd understand very well, is it, darling?"

He said heavily,

"No, I'm not reasonable about you—you needn't expect it. But you're going to tell me what you mean."

"Am I?"

He said with sudden violence,

"Some day you're going to get yourself murdered!"

81

Quite involuntarily she flinched. It was only Felix in a temper, but just for the moment something in her wavered and was afraid.

She stepped back, and the movement brought the door into her line of vision. The ivory panels, the china handle and door-plates with their pattern of small pink roses, stood very slightly at an angle. The door was not quite shut. She went over to it, opened it, and looked out. A yard away Mrs. Bell was on her hands and knees in the passage, polishing the floor-boards.

Helen Adrian shut the door in a controlled manner and went back. Felix was still in a temper, but he didn't frighten her now. She stuck her chin in the air and said,

"Next time you feel like murdering anyone, darling, I don't think I should tell the daily first." Then, with a laugh, "Oh, come off it, Felix! Let's go down and see if it's warm enough to bathe."

CHAPTER 12

Richard Cunningham walked out along the cliff road. He knew that nothing in the world would have prevented him from coming down to Farne and going to see Marian Brand. If he had been twenty, he couldn't have been more set on doing a foolish romantic thing. If he had been twenty, he wouldn't have thought about it being foolish or romantic, he would have just done it. Since he was thirty-five, he was fully aware of the folly and on the edge of being able to laugh at the romance. No, that wasn't true. He would have liked to be able to laugh at it, to keep a back way out in case the whole airy structure crashed and let him down flat after the manner of so many castles in Spain. But he couldn't manage it. If the castle came down, it came down, but nobody or nothing was going to stop him walking into it with his eyes open.

He told himself, as he had done at intervals during the past month, that he was allowing an obstinate whim to drive him. To which there always came the spontaneous reply that it might not be a whim at all but an instinct. He had seen Marian Brand once as he passed the window of her compartment before the train was wrecked, and once for a moment before he fainted when they had just been dug out of the débris. There had been dust in her hair, and blood on her face. He had talked with her on and off for something like two hours with a smashed railway carriage tilted over them in the ditch which had saved their lives. He had sent her flowers, and a copy of *The Whispering Tree*. He had written to her three times. During the rush of his business in the States he had found it a refreshment to write those letters. They did not touch on intimacies, but they were intimate because they had been written without taking thought as to what was said or how it would be received. The whole world might have read them, but they could only have been written to one person.

There was the background. And now he was going to lunch with her. Either the thing was an instinct, or it was a folly. He would know at once. It was a lovely May morning with a blue sky and just enough light cloud moving to keep the sea in change instead of that eternal blue glitter which tires the eye.

He came to the white house standing behind its wind-driven shrubs, walked up to the twin blue doors, and knocked on the right-hand one. It was opened. He stood looking at Marian Brand, and she at him.

At once everything was quite easy. He might have been walking up to that front door every day of his life. There wasn't any castle in the air. There was a welcoming house, and the woman he wanted. It was as simple, as inexplicable, and as comfortable as daily bread. He held her hand and laughed, and said,

"Take a good look at me! I'm clean, which is more than I was when you saw me before."

She said, "I knew exactly what you would look like."

"How?"

"I don't know—I did."

And then she was taking him through to the study, and they were talking about the house, about his journey, and each of them had so much to say that they were taking turns, catching each other up and laughing about it, interrupting and being interrupted, like friends who have known each other for a long time and don't have to bother about being polite. It wasn't in the least the way that Marian had thought it would be. She had been so pleased and proud about his coming, and then quite terrified. If she could have run away and kept a single shred of self-respect she would have done it. She had wondered what they would talk about, and been quite sure that, whatever it was, he would find it dull. And then it didn't matter. They were easy and comfortable together. She could be just herself. It didn't matter a bit.

When he asked about Ina she could say just what was on her mind.

"I'm worried about her. I told you about Cyril. He's gone off in a temper."

"Because you wouldn't give him half your kingdom?"

"Something like that."

"You won't do it?"

"Oh, no—he'd only throw it away. But Ina's fretting."

"Is she fond of him?"

84

"She was."

He whistled.

"Like that, is it?"

"She's very unhappy. I'm afraid she won't be here for lunch—she's gone out—" She hesitated, and then went on. "She didn't tell me—just left a message to say she was going down into Farne to see about a library subscription and wouldn't be back. She didn't know you were coming."

"And you are thinking she may have gone to meet her husband?"

She looked startled.

"How did you know?"

Their eyes met, and he smiled. There was a moment when they looked at one another. Then he said,

"Wouldn't he come here?"

"Well, I think he would try and get round Ina first."

"Does it worry you?"

"I don't want him to make her unhappy."

"I expect he knows which side his bread is buttered."

"Oh, yes."

"Then he may behave reasonably now he's had time to think things out."

Cyril being reasonable sounded too good to be true. She found herself saying so with a rueful laugh. And quick on that she had a sense of immeasurable relief. She had never had anyone with whom she could talk things over—never in all her life before. Now there was Richard. The feeling didn't get into words, but it was there.

The bell rang for lunch.

When it was over they went down the garden steps to the cove and watched the tide go down, leaving first wet shingle, and then a stretch of sand with a double line of rocks running out into the shallow sea. Sometimes they talked, sometimes they were silent. It was a very happy, peaceful time.

Coming up the steps, they met Felix and Helen Adrian coming down. She wore grey slacks and a hyacinth-blue pullover, and her hair dazzled in the sun. She might have stepped off the cover of any Summer Number. The steps were narrow. Felix and Helen waited on the lowest of the garden terraces. As Richard Cunningham came into sight, she called out and ran to meet him.

"Richard—*darling*! Where did you spring from?"

He was pleasant without enthusiasm.

"My dear Helen—what a surprise!"

She linked her arm in his.

"Is that all you've got to say? Where on earth have you been?"

"In the States."

"You never wrote me a line! You're not going in, are you? Come along down to the beach! I've got a million things to say to you. This is Felix Brand, my accompanist. I'm staying with his people. And—I suppose you know Marian—"

Felix looked murder at him.

Richard said, "Marian and I are very old friends. You'll find it lovely on the beach. We've just been there. Now we're going in. If you're staying here, I expect I shall be seeing you."

He went into the house with Marian.

Helen Adrian looked after them for a moment before she turned to Felix with a laugh.

Eliza brought tea to the study and said no, Mrs. Felton hadn't come in, and she didn't know where Penny was either. She retreated in a vaguely offended manner which Marian guessed might be put down to Miss Adrian's account. It came over her that here was a beautiful woman with a beautiful voice, and nearly everyone in both houses disliked her cordially. Felix was in love with her, but she had a conviction that he didn't like her the better for that, or any more than the rest of them.

With this in her mind, she looked up from the tea she was pouring and said,

"Do you know Helen Adrian well?"

It was very pleasant in the study. A light air came through three open windows and brought the scent of flowers. A bumble bee zoomed in, and out again. It was all quite extraordinarily peaceful. He looked at Marian in the old blue and white cotton dress which she had worn for three summers, and which had never pretended to anything but utility, and thought what a restful woman she was to be with, and how she made any place she was in feel like home. Even if he hadn't fallen in love with her he would have liked her more than anyone he had ever met. It was just as if her thought about Felix had touched him, because he remembered that he had once been in love with Helen Adrian without liking her at all. Without thought or effort he found himself saying,

"I was once in love with her—for a week."

She said gravely, "Were you?" and gave him his tea.

"I heard her sing. Have you?"

"Just practising with Felix. It's a lovely voice."

"The correct expression is that she sings like an angel. People were saying so all round me the first time I heard her, but even that didn't stop me thinking it was true. And she looked like an angel too—white satin and lilies, and the light shining down on her hair. I went right in off the deep end."

"What happened?"

He laughed.

"I came to the surface again and discovered that we bored each other stiff."

Marian lifted her cup to her lips and drank. When she had put it down again she said,

87

"Do you often do that kind of thing?"

"What kind of thing?"

"Falling suddenly in love, and then out again."

Well, he had asked for it. He laughed again and said,

"No. And anyhow 'in love' is the wrong word. It was more like going under ether. I wouldn't be talking about it if it had been serious—would I?"

"I don't know." Her voice took a note of surprise. "I don't really know—you—at all."

"I wonder. I think I know you very well."

She began to smile, but couldn't trust her lips. She said in a quiet voice,

"There isn't much to know. You would soon come to the end of it. Then it would bore you."

"Would it? If you take most of the things that really matter, they may be profound, but they are fundamentally simple. You don't get tired of the sun, and the sky, and fresh air, and water, and bread. There is nothing complicated about them. They are always there. If they weren't, we should die. You don't get tired of what you need."

It came out slowly, a bit at a time, more as if he was thinking aloud than speaking.

Before she could say anything there was a step on the flagged path outside. Penny came up the two shallow steps and into the room. She looked as if she had been crying her eyes out. She had tried to wash away the marks with cold water, the bright brown curls on her forehead were damp. She hadn't bothered with powder or lipstick. She held Mactavish in her arms, and he wasn't liking it. She said in a small, flat voice,

"Eliza said you wanted me."

And then she saw Richard Cunningham, and wanted to run away. Only, of course, when you've been nicely brought up you can't, so she came and shook hands instead. Mactavish, whom no amount of bringing up had ever been able to deflect from doing exactly what he wanted to, gave Penny a fierce rabbit kick and jumped down. After which he arranged himself in Marian's lap, refused a saucer of milk, and remained for some time with his eyes mere orange slits and the extreme tip of his tail flicking to and fro.

Penny drank two cups of tea, said a very few things in that little exhausted voice, and presently slipped away again through the open door.

When she had gone Richard looked at Marian.

"What's the matter with that nice child?"

There was a spark of anger in her eyes.

"She loves Felix a great deal better than he deserves. Helen Adrian is tormenting them both."

"Does Helen want him?"

"I shouldn't think so. He doesn't even think so himself. She might have taken him if he had come for Uncle Martin's money, so I'm afraid that goes down to my account."

"He ought to thank Heaven fasting. He would probably get to the point of murdering her in less than six months. He doesn't look far off it now."

"That's what worries Penny."

"Is the child engaged to him?"

"No—just brought up with him. She's some kind of distant cousin. I don't see how anyone could love Mrs. Brand and Miss Remington, so it's all gone to Felix."

They went on talking.

CHAPTER 13

Miss Silver came up from the beach where she had left her niece Ethel Burkett sitting comfortably in the lee of a breakwater with little Josephine digging in the sand beside her. Farne has a very good beach though not a large one. Later on in the year there would not be room to move, but on this May morning Miss Silver considered it very pleasant—very pleasant indeed. She had enjoyed the delightful air and Josephine's infant prattle. She had recalled with pleasure Lord Tennyson's poem about the "fisherman's boy" who "shouts with his sister at play," and the "sailor lad" who "sings in his boat on the bay," together with the much less well-known lines about the eagle:

> "Ring'd with the azure world, he stands.
> The wrinkled sea beneath him crawls."

Not that Farne Bay could at the moment exhibit a fisherman's boy sporting with his sister, or even a sailor lad on its at present empty sea, and there was no tradition of its having ever attracted an eagle. But you do not, of course, expect poetry to be literal.

After a couple of hours of the beach and Lord Tennyson, Miss Silver considered that a little movement would be agreeable. Ethel and Josephine could remain on the beach whilst she herself did some shopping. She did not care for the book they had given her at the library yesterday, and she thought she would change it. She would prefer a novel in which the characters had at least heard of the ten commandments and did not begin drinking at ten in the morning after having kept it up for most of the night. Their behaviour under this alcoholic stimulus she considered to be totally lacking in interest.

She came up from the beach and made her way along the front until she came to Cross Street. Up here in the wind she was really very glad of her coat. It did not trouble her in the least that it was now ten years old, and that its black cloth surface had a dingy look in the bright spring sunshine. As the breeze caught it, a breadth of olive-green cashmere came into view beneath. She had found her ribbed woollen stockings a little heavy on the sunny beach, but it was not her practice to change them for lisle thread until May had not only come but gone, and she was really quite glad of them now. On the same principle, she was wearing a winter hat—not the felt which she had bought two years ago, but the one which had been her best until then. For seaside wear she had removed an elderly bunch composed of two pansies in a circle of mignonette, leaving it simply trimmed with loops of black and purple ribbon, rather limp after four years of faithful service. Instead of her usual chintz knitting-bag she carried, as more suitable to the seaside, a bag of black cloth stoutly lined with the shiny black Italian that she had used to make her windows light-proof during the war. The bag had neat cord handles unpicked from an elderly cushion and was both strong and capacious. It contained at the moment one made and one half-made stocking for Derek Burkett, a ball and three two-ounce skeins of grey wool, four steel needles, a purse, a handkerchief, a black and purple neck-scarf, some oddments, and her own and Ethel's library books.

She turned into Cross Street, and was sheltered from the wind. Really, if she had been going to stay on the Front, she would have had to put on her scarf, but now it would not be necessary, and in any case the library was quite close. She came up the steps, passed through the outer shop devoted to picture-postcards, photograph frames, cheap editions, shrimping-nets, and other miscellaneous articles, and made her way to the rather dark cavern behind it. There were a number of people changing books. She turned to a shelf near the counter and began to scan the volumes on it. Really, people thought of the oddest titles: *Four Cold Fishes in a Bath; Crimson Wormwood; The Corpse in the Refrigerator*—very distateful indeed.

She was dipping into *Medley for Maurice* and wondering if even the author knew what it was all about, when someone just behind her at the counter said, "Yes, a two-book subscription for three months—Mrs. Felton—Mrs. Cyril Felton. And the address is Cove House. It's on the Ledstow road." The name struck a chord. Helen Adrian had used it in speaking to her the very day she had received Ethel's letter begging her to come to Farne. Neither the Christian nor the surname were common ones. Linked, it seemed impossible to suppose that they had no connection with the young man whom Miss Adrian had named as a possible blackmailer.

With *Medley for Maurice* in her hand Miss Silver turned to take a look at Mrs. Cyril Felton. She saw a pretty girl with a loose coat over a blue linen dress and a bright handkerchief tied over curly dark hair. She would have been prettier if she had had more colour, and if she had not had such a worried, nervous look. She took her receipt from the girl at the counter, put it away in a very new handbag, and drifted over to the far end of the room.

Replacing *Medlley for Maurice* upon its shelf, Miss Silver moved in the same direction. The books here were of the kind not in extensive demand. People do not come down to a seaside to read statistics on emigration, or works on what to do with the dispossessed populations of Europe. Culling a volume at random from the shelves, Miss Silver found herself with *Some Considerations on the Sociological Aspects of Inflation*.

Glancing at Mrs. Felton, she observed her to be making no pretence of being interested in her surroundings. Her eyes were upon the archway leading to the library. When the bell upon the outer door tinkled she changed colour and looked eager. Upon the entrance in rapid succession of a mother with a small child, a stout elderly person with a shopping-basket, and a provocative young woman with so little on that she might have been expected to die of exposure if it had not been for the oil with which she had smeared her skin, the nervous look returned to Mrs. Felton's face. It would have been obvious to anyone much less acute than Miss Silver that she had a rendezvous, and that the person whom she was expecting to meet was a man. If it should happen to be Cyril Felton, Miss Silver felt that it would interest her to see him. She therefore moved to an even darker corner and became to all appearances completely immersed in *Sociological Aspects*.

She had hardly effected this manoeuvre, when Ina Felton caught her breath, ran forward, and then, checking herself, came back again, to snatch a book from the shelves, open it at random, and stand there trying not to look as if she were expecting anyone.

An attractive young man with fairish hair and a roving blue eye came through the arch from the outer shop and looked about him. The eye lit upon the dark-haired girl in the corner. As he strolled over to her, she stopped pretending to read, crammed the book back anyhow, and gazed at him with brimming eyes and changing colour.

"Oh, Cyril!"

So it was the husband. Miss Silver was deeply interested. A goodlooking young man of the type which women often found attractive. Not very steady, she feared. It did not show

93

much yet, but to her experience the signs were unmistakable—weak, pleasure-loving, and selfish. Yes, she thought he might quite easily have turned to blackmail.

He put a hand on the girl's shoulder and said,

"Hullo, Ina!"

There had been a quarrel, and he was anxious to make it up. He was smiling at her in a manner that was meant to charm, and she was shrinking away from him. Her voice trembled as she said,

"I nearly didn't come."

He laughed in a pleasant manner.

"But you did come—so why worry? Look here, how's the barometer? Marian still angry?"

"She isn't pleased."

"Then you'll have to soothe her down. I'm sorry I lost my temper and all that, but you must allow it's pretty maddening to have her holding the purse-strings. If you had had half as you ought to have done, we'd have been all right."

He was speaking quite low, but Miss Silver had excellent hearing. In her elderly dowdy clothes, her attention apparently riveted upon the duller of the dull books, she was just one of those negligible spinsters who haunt the libraries and find a vicarious life upon their shelves. You may be Miss Blank, subsisting in a bed-sitting-room without very much to live for or many people to care whether you live or not, but for a pound or two a year you can battle for lost causes, sail beyond Ultima Thule, ascend into the stratosphere, love and be courted, adorn a glittering throng with your glamorous presence, tumble over a corpse on the mat, probe the mystery of the Poisoned Penwiper, and never have a dull moment. These reflections had occurred to Miss Silver from time to time, but she had no leisure for them at the moment. She merely felt secure in her protective colouring and continued to listen to the conversation of Mr. and Mrs. Cyril Felton.

94

At the sound of Helen Adrian's name her interest was doubled. It was Cyril who introduced it.

"Helen Adrian is here, isn't she?"

Ina said, "How did you know?" and he laughed.

"Because I've made it my business to know. I want to see her."

She was looking at him doubtfully.

"Oh, Cyril—why?"

"Well, it's just a professional matter, and there's no need for you to ask a lot of questions about it. And I'm not making a pass at her, so you needn't be jealous. She's out for the big money. Means to land it whilst the going's good, and I don't mind giving her a helping hand—for a consideration."

Ina said, "Oh! But she's having an affair with Felix! I don't mean anything wrong, of course, but you know she's staying in the other half of our house with the Brands, and Felix is frightfully in love with her."

"That won't get him anywhere, poor devil. Now if your Uncle Martin had left the money to him instead of to Marian, there might have been something doing. Look here—I want to come back to my darling wife and my dear sister-in-law."

He had a hand on her shoulder and a smile whose charm made the words just a family joke.

"You've got to soothe Marian down."

"Have I?"

"Ina!" He sounded really hurt. "Look here, darling, don't be silly! I couldn't be happy away from you if I tried—you know that."

"You haven't been very much with me in the last eight years, Cyril."

"My sweet! *Ina*—you mustn't say things like that! You know I'd have given anything in the world to have you with me."

"Would you?"

"Of course I would! And now, when we can be together, you're not going to let a silly quarrel keep us apart. Look here, you tell Marian I'm simply frightfully sorry and ashamed about losing my temper. Just ask her to forget about it. Make it right for me to come up this evening. To tell you the honest truth, I haven't got the price of a bed. If you've got a pound on you you'd better hand it over. It'll look a bit odd if you have to pay for lunch. Make it two if you've got it."

"I haven't."

"All right, I'll have to make do with one. Let's have it!"

Ina was pale and grave. He hadn't ever seen her quite like this before. She would come round all right when he made love to her. He took the pound note which she got out of her purse, noted that there was only a little loose silver left, and said lightly,

"Cheer up, darling—there's a good time coming. I've booked a table for lunch at the hotel. The food isn't bad there, I'm told."

CHAPTER 14

Miss Silver changed the library books. She was fond of a good historical novel, and found one by an author whom she admired. Her niece being one of those who prefer to read about people whose circumstances as nearly as possible resemble their own, she asked the girl at the counter to recommend a novel of strong domestic interest, and was provided with what proved to be a pleasantly written tale of family life. There was a father who was a solicitor, a mother

96

of almost exactly Ethel's age, and four children, made up of three boys and a girl. Hastily looking at the end to make sure that no harrowing incident cut short any of the infant lives, and finding the entire family very happily grouped round a Christmas tree on the last page, she bestowed one of her kindest smiles on the helpful assistant and said it would do very nicely indeed, thank you.

Coming out into the sunshine, she decided to walk the rest of the way down Cross Street, and then after turning to the left take a parallel road back to the Front. She had not yet located a fancy-work-shop, and would be pleased to do so. It was very agreeable to be able to saunter along in a leisurely manner and look in at the shop windows.

It was just before she came to the corner leading back to the Front that she came face to face with Helen Adrian. The recognition was mutual and immediate. Neither could, indeed, have been easily mistaken for anyone else. Miss Adrian appeared to be in very good spirits. She was accompanied by a dark moody-looking young man whom she introduced briefly as "Felix Brand—my accompanist." After which she told him to go away and buy cigarettes, because Miss Silver was an old friend and she wanted to talk to her—"And we'll be right over there in that shelter out of the wind."

When he had gone away in gloomy silence she slipped a hand inside Miss Silver's arm and took her across to the shelter. The sun was delightfully warm, and it really was pleasant to get out of the wind. Since it was now almost one o'clock, the Front was practically deserted. They had one side of the shelter entirely to themselves.

By the time they were settled Miss Adrian had explained that she was staying at Cove House. With a very little encouragement she was induced to explain a good deal more than that. Miss Silver was given a full account of the Brand family, the two households, and the iniquities of the will under which Martin Brand's large fortune had passed to a hitherto unknown niece.

"And the extraordinary thing is this Marian Brand who comes in for all the money—well, it's her sister Ina who turns out to be married to Cyril Felton. You remember I told you about him."

Miss Silver coughed in an enquiring manner.

"Did you know of the connection?"

"Well, I did and I didn't. Cyril didn't exactly advertize that he was married. As a matter of fact, I was one of the few people who knew. He told me her name had been Brand, but I didn't really connect her with Felix, you know. Actually, Cyril didn't himself. There had been a family quarrel, and they didn't know each other. It's funny the way things turn out, isn't it? If Felix had got the money instead of this girl Marian, I'd probably have been marrying him, but Fred Mount will be a lot easier to live with, so I expect it's all for the best. And Felix has some pretty poisonous relations. That's another thing to Fred's credit—he hasn't got any parents, and I always did say I wouldn't marry anyone but an orphan."

Her gaze was one of angelic candour, a fact of which she was perfectly well aware. She would have been very much surprised if she had known that Miss Silver was thinking what an extremely ill-bred young woman she was. She continued to gaze and to prattle.

"You remember I showed you those letters and told you I thought it might be Cyril who was trying it on. I actually did think so all the time. Blackmail isn't exactly the sort of thing Felix would go in for, and it was bound to be one or other of them. At least that's what I thought, because of what the letter said about last June. You remember, it said, 'What about last June?' So it was more or less bound to be either Felix or Cyril, because they were the only two who knew."

98

Miss Silver coughed.

"Was there anything to know?"

"Well, there was in a way," said Miss Adrian in a nonchalant manner. "I expect I'd better tell you about it, or you'll be thinking it was worse than it was. Actually, you know, it wasn't anyone's fault. I told Felix he'd done it on purpose, but I don't think he did—he's not that sort. You see, there's a cave just round the point from the cove. All that bit of beach belongs to the Brands, and there's this cave. It's not very big, but a year or two ago Felix found a sort of crack through to a second cave. He widened it enough to get through, and it's his own special place—not many people know about it. I was staying at Cove House in June last year, and we slipped out after everyone was in bed and went down on the beach. It was a lovely night, and we talked about bathing, but in the end we didn't. We went into the cave instead, and—you know how it is—we rather lost count of the time. And there it was, we got cut off by the tide and had to stay there all night."

Miss Silver said, "Dear me!"

"Oh, well, there wasn't anything in it. And no one knew up at the house. We got home to breakfast, and they just thought we'd been out for an early bathe. That cook they've had for donkey's years, I thought she had a nasty suspicious eye, but she didn't say anything, and nobody could ever have done more than guess if I hadn't been fool enough to let on to Cyril."

It was by now quite apparent to Miss Silver that Cyril Felton's relations with Miss Adrian were certainly not those of a mere casual acquaintance encountered some time ago in a concert-party. There was no expression to her voice as she said,

"And what made you do that?"

"Too many cocktails," said Miss Adrian frankly. "It seemed

a good idea at the time, if you know what I mean. We both laughed about it a lot—Mrs. Brand and Miss Remington being so out of the way proper, and not having any idea that we had been out all night. And then I more or less forgot the whole thing, but it looks as if Cyril didn't. And you know, if he went and told Fred, it wouldn't be anything to laugh about. Fred hasn't got that sort of sense of humour.''

Miss Silver made up her mind. Miss Adrian had approached her as a client, and though she had not taken the case she felt a certain obligation to be frank. She said with some gravity,

''You intend to marry Mr. Mount?''

The blue eyes widened.

''I can't afford to miss the chance.''

Miss Silver coughed.

''When you came to see me, I advised you to take those letters to the police. When you said you could not do that, I recommended you to tell Mr. Mount about them yourself.''

Miss Adrian shook her golden head.

''You don't know Fred.''

Miss Silver continued as if she had not spoken.

''You now say you are sure that Mr. Cyril Felton is the person who has been attempting to blackmail you. I am inclined to agree with you. Are you aware that he is in Farne?''

Miss Adrian exclaimed in a manner which Miss Silver considered profane. Rightly conjecturing that this indicated surprise, she continued.

''I heard Mrs. Felton give her name in the library just now, and subsequently witnessed a meeting between her and her husband. From their conversation I received the impression that there had been some kind of quarrel which Mr. Felton was anxious to make up, since he was so short of money that

100

it was a matter of urgency that he should be received at Cove House."

Helen Adrian nodded.

"Yes—that's Cyril. And, from what I've heard about Ina and seen for myself, she's the kind of girl to let him walk all over her like a door-mat."

Miss Silver gave her slight prim cough.

"Even a door-mat may become worn out in time."

"Meaning?"

"That it is possible that Mr. Felton may be disappointed."

Helen Adrian appeared to be considering the implications of this. The angelic look was replaced by a shrewd one as she said,

"If he's as hard up as all that, I could have a stab at buying him off. Look here, it's an idea! I don't think Ina could hold out against him—once a door-mat, always a door-mat. But Marian Brand is a different proposition. According to Cyril, she's been supporting his wife for years and taking him in whenever he was on the rocks, which is about the only time he went near them. But I don't think he cuts any ice with her really. Ina is fond of him, and Marian is fond of Ina. If Ina cooled off, I don't think Cyril would get yes for an answer, so if Ina is really peeved with him, this is the time for me to drive my bargain. I tell you what I'll do—I'll tell Cyril I know he wrote those letters. He can take ten pounds to hold his tongue, or I'll go to the police. That's just what I'm going to *say* to him, you know—I won't really. If he's as hard up as you say, he'll take the ten pounds. Of course he'll mean to come back for more, but he won't get the chance. I'll tell Fred he can see about a licence, and once we're married, well, it's done. And I shall tell Cyril that if he makes a nuisance of himself, all he'll get is Fred will just about make him wish he'd never been born. And the worse he behaves, the less

101

Fred will believe anything he says about me. How's that?"

Miss Silver's neat features expressed none of the distaste which she felt. If there was a slight dryness in her tone, her companion did not notice it. She said,

"It would appear to be quite a prudent course of action, Miss Adrian."

CHAPTER 15

When Richard Cunningham had gone away down the road to Farne, the part of Marian's mind which had been troubled about Ina began to take charge. It was nearly seven o'clock. She had not realized that it was so late until Richard looked at his watch. He had exclaimed, and she had known very well that he would have liked to stay on, but she had not asked him. There had been a sudden withdrawal, a cold breath of fear not definitely attributable to anything special. It was just as if they had been sitting out in a sunny place and all at once the sun was gone and it was cold. She walked with him to the gate, and he said,

"When shall I see you again?"

"I don't know. Would you like to come over tomorrow?"

"You know I would. What time?"

She said, "Lunch, if you like," and watched him walk down the road before she turned back to the house and to the realization that she was definitely worried about Ina.

But she was only half way up the stairs when she heard a step going to and fro above. She came out on the landing, to see that the door of one of the two empty bedrooms was open and Ina standing there waiting. She looked pale and tired. As Marian came up to her, she said in a plaintive voice, "What ages you've been."

"But I didn't know you were in. I've been worried."

"You didn't sound worried. I've been in my room, and I could hear you and that man talking. You just went on, and on, and on—I thought he was never going to go. I suppose it was Richard Cunningham?"

"Yes."

Ina caught her breath.

"I heard you on the telephone." She flung her arms suddenly round Marian's neck. "Oh, darling, I'm a pig! Did you have a nice time? I do really hope you did. I saw him when he was going away, and I thought he looked terribly nice. Is he going to come again? Shall I see him? I wanted to come down, but I was afraid I was going to cry."

Marian said, "Why should you cry?" But of course she knew.

Ina let go of her with a sob.

"I'm so unhappy!"

"You've been meeting Cyril?"

"Yes. He rung up when you were in the kitchen with Eliza. I went to meet him in Farne."

"Why didn't you tell me?"

Ina dabbed at her eyes.

"It really was partly because I didn't want to spoil your day. I opened the study door when you were talking to Richard Cunningham, so I knew he was coming over—at least I didn't think it could be anyone else."

Marian said, "I wanted you to meet him."

"I met Cyril."

"And what did Cyril want?" Marian's tone was dry.

There was a pause before Ina said,

"He hasn't any money. He wants to come here."

Marian thought, "Well, we've come down to brass tacks.

Money—that's all that ever does bring him back, but she's never faced it before. Poor Ina!"

She saw the colour run up to the roots of Ina's hair.

"Marian—"

"When does he want to come?"

"Now—tonight—for supper. I told him to wait till then. He hasn't got any money at all. He was expecting some, but it didn't turn up. He—he—said to tell you he was sorry—about the things he said. He didn't mean them. Everybody says things they don't mean when they're angry—I do myself."

It was a lame and faltering performance. There was no conviction in Ina Felton's voice. She looked anywhere except at her sister. Marian couldn't bear it. She never had been able to see Ina hurt. She said as lightly as she could,

"That's all right. Of course he can come, and we'll talk things over. But he must try and get a job."

Ina nodded.

"He says he will." She turned abruptly to the window.

It wasn't until then that Marian noticed that the room had been got ready for a visitor. There was soap on the washstand, and two clean towels on the old-fashioned towel-horse. The carafe had been filled, and the bed made.

Standing at the window with her back to her, Ina said,

"I've put him in here."

Cyril strolled in a quarter of an hour later with a deprecatory "My dear—" for his sister-in-law and a sunny smile for his wife. For eight years Marian had managed to keep her eyes shut to the fact that these manifestations really meant nothing at all. Cyril might not be a very good actor on the stage, but in private life he could play any part with ease and charm, and so convincingly as to be quite carried away by it himself. At the moment he was, in all sincerity, the careless, impulsive fellow whose tongue has run away with him, but whose heart

104

is so very much in the right place. He made no attempt to conceal the fact that it overflowed with brotherly affection for Marian and devotion to his wife. He was wounded but uncomplaining over the spare bedroom, and exerted himself to be the best of good company at supper.

Penny, invited to come over and have coffee, was given what might be called a preview by Eliza Cotton, who had stepped in for the purpose, supper being cold and all put out on the table.

"Tongue like a leaky tap—drip, drip, drip, and nothing that's any more good than what you'd let run down the sink. Darling this, and darling that!"

"He *didn't*!"

Eliza snorted.

"Not to me, he didn't." Then, after an ominous pause. "Not *yet*. But I don't doubt he'll come to it. Darling, or sweet or both—they just run off his tongue. It's 'Marian darling,' and 'Ina my sweet,' and arms round their shoulders, and bouncing up to open doors enough to turn you giddy. Tried it on Mactavish—called him 'Puss' which he hates like any poison—and who wouldn't—and snapped his fingers at him to come."

"What did Mactavish do?"

"Didn't let on he so much as knew he was there—waved his tail and went out of the window. And if he'd touched him he'd have scratched."

Penny's eyes were round and serious.

"Poor Ina! Eliza, are you sure? Perhaps he just doesn't know about cats."

Eliza looked down her nose.

"Never was surer about anything in my life. There was one like him down at Bury Dene where I used to stay with my aunt. Jim Hoskins his name was—curly hair and blue eyes, and all the girls running after him. Joked with all of them, kissed a good few more than ever told, and married the one that had the most in her stocking foot, poor girl. She never was sorry for it but once, and that was all her days. Next thing anyone knew, the money was gone and so was he, and she was taking in washing to provide for his twins."

Penny giggled.

"Well, Ina hasn't got twins."

"Not yet," said Eliza, and departed in the odour of disapproval.

Penny went over. She wondered afterwards whether Cyril would have charmed her if Eliza hadn't got in first with her Awful Warning. Perhaps he would, and perhaps he wouldn't—she didn't know. She saw that neither Ina nor Marian was being charmed. Marian was quiet and thoughtful, and Ina had smudges under her eyes. Nobody talked very much except Cyril, and the more he talked and the more charming he was, the less Penny liked him. Felix might have the worst manners in the world, but he didn't smarm. He didn't say darling unless he meant it, and if it didn't happen very often, that was because he was so desperately unhappy, poor lamb. Baa, baa, black sheep, have you any wool? Felix was being shorn to the quick, and when there wasn't any more to be got Helen Adrian would just toss it all away and go and look for somebody else. Like an odd sympathetic echo set off by the nursery tag, there slipped into Penny's mind the words of a proverb she had heard Eliza use. Something about going out for wool and coming home shorn. She was to remember that afterwards.

CHAPTER 16

Miss Silver was at breakfast next day with her niece Ethel and little Josephine, when the telephone bell rang. Mrs. Burkett had been reading selected passages out of a letter just received from her husband, and Josephine was taking advantage of the fact to fish all the bits of crust out of her bread and milk and drop them one by one upon the carpet. Miss Silver's attention being divided between the latest news from Europe and the less stirring events retailed by John Burkett, the manoeuvre had been very successful. It was not, in fact, until Miss Silver had lifted the receiver and said "Hullo!" that she heard Ethel exclaim in a dismayed voice from behind her, "Oh, Josephine! How naughty!" Glancing over her shoulder, she was aware of Josephine being an angel child, all smiles, curls, and innocence.

And then Miss Adrian's dulcet voice was thrilling along the wire.

"Is that Miss Silver?"

"Miss Silver speaking."

"This is Helen Adrian. Wasn't it clever of me to remember the name of the house your niece had taken! That's how I got your number. I rang up the Supervisor, and she gave it to me at once. And I expect you're wondering why I wanted it, but as a matter of fact—well—you remember what I came to see you about?"

"Certainly."

"I thought it might be a good plan if you were to meet the crowd up here. Cyril rolled up last night, too sunny for words. We haven't got down to anything yet. There's no hurry, you see. He's quite comfortable, and he can just go on spreading a little happiness and being mother's bright-eyed boy until he thinks he's got me nicely softened and ready to part." She broke into a trill of laughter. "I hope he isn't listening in! The two sides of this house are on the same line, so he'd only have to lift the receiver on the other side of the wall, but I think I should hear the click. Well, what I was going to say was, Miss Remington's got some awful sort of panic affair on this afternoon—she's the aunt I told you about. We all met in the garden after supper last night, and Cyril buttered her up like mad. He's the answer to the old maid's prayer all right—and doesn't he know it!"

Miss Silver coughed. Really, Miss Adrian's tone! And the expressions she used—quite unbelievably ill-bred! It was a significant cough. It would have checked a person at all sensitive to the finer shades. Musically, Miss Adrian might have a sensitive ear, but in no other respect. She continued as if there had been no cough.

"What I was trying to explain was, we shall all be making one happy party down on the beach for tea. And when I said you were an old friend of mine and staying at Farne, Miss Remington said wouldn't I like to ask you to join us. So I thought what a good opportunity it would be for you to see Cyril and Felix and the whole set-out. And actually, of course, it's supposed to be a very pretty cove, and the view is rather special. And if you're interested in authors and that sort of thing, Richard Cunningham will be there. You know, he wrote *The Whispering Tree*. He was in that railway accident I told you about with Marian Brand, but as a matter of fact he used to be rather a special friend of mine."

Miss Silver coughed with considerable firmness.

"If this is a professional invitation, Miss Adrian, I must remind you that I declined to handle your case."

"Yes, I know you did. And that's quite all right, because I am quite sure I can handle it myself. But I thought perhaps you would come out and have tea just in a friendly sort of way. I thought perhaps you might be interested, and then just in case anything went wrong—not, of course, that anything is likely to, but if it did, and I wanted some advice, well, you'd have met everyone, wouldn't you? And if it came to that, of course I'd be quite willing to pay a fee."

Just what was in her mind when she said that? There was something about the words, the tone, the manner, that stirred Miss Silver's professional instinct. Perhaps stirred is too strong a word. The instinct was a very sensitive one. It received and responsed to the faintest possible touch.

Helen Adrian was quite unaware of having touched anything at all. She said,

"You'll come, won't you?"

There was that almost imperceptible stimulus, there was Miss Silver's quite insatiable interest in other people's lives, and there was something else. It was this with which she chose to cloak her acceptance.

"Thank you, I shall be very pleased to come. I shall be interested to meet Mr. Cunningham. A cousin of his is a valued friend. Will you thank Miss Remington for her invitation?"

Helen Adrian said,

"That's all right. They tell me there's a bus from the hotel at a quarter past four, and you can't miss the house. Come along and give us all the once over."

The distaste with which Miss Silver heard this final remark very nearly made her retract her acceptance, but, before she had time to do more than experience a strong desire to say that after all she did not think that she could leave her niece, Miss Adrian had rung off.

She turned round, to see little Josephine with the marks

of tears on her face partaking of half a dozen small pieces of crust especially cut for the purpose, since the pieces so naughtily rejected could hardly be gathered up from the floor and put back in her bowl of bread and milk. Encountering Miss Silver's eye, she waved her spoon and remarked in a virtuous tone,

"Josephine *good* girl now."

CHAPTER 17

Just what had put the idea of a communal picnic into Miss Remington's head it was impossible to say. She had liked men's society, and always felt herself to have been unfairly deprived of it. This, and the fact that the next-door party appeared to have been augmented by two attractive men, may have been a contributory cause. There may have been other reasons—a desire to annoy Marian and Ina, who would doubtless prefer to keep their own party intact—Felix, whose manner had been quite insufferably rude for days—and her sister Florence, who detested picnics but would certainly not stay at home and allow Cassy to play hostess and run the show. Be this as it may, the idea having been once entertained, it became an overriding necessity that it should be put into action. As Eliza Cotton had it, "When Miss Cassy takes a thing into her head, she'll go through with it whether or no."

Cakes were baked, sandwiches were cut, everyone in both houses was pressed into service, and Florence Brand's afternoon rest was interfered with. Not that she herself took any part in the preparations—on that point she could be, and was, inflexible. But how enjoy the meditative calm so propitious to digestion—the feet on a raised stool, a cushion behind the head, a light wrap over the knees, and a book whose pages were never turned laid open there—when Cassy was liable at any moment to come running in for this, that or the other, and go running out again, very likely omitting to close the door? Mrs. Brand's slow, mounting resentment not only banished sleep, but induced a heavy frown and an unbecoming purple flush.

The dislike which she usually felt for the other inmates of the house assumed menacing proportions. Felix had been behaving abominably. She had never been fond of him, and she now found him quite unendurable. Helen Adrian was a light woman—in her own mind she used a blunter term than this. Marian Brand and her sister had practically stolen Martin's money. When she considered all she had done for that man, giving up her independence to come and look after him, it just didn't bear thinking about. She practically never stopped thinking about it. Penny was a little fool. No doubt she had thought that Felix would be a good catch, and now she couldn't have him she had no more pride than to let everyone see how disappointed she was. Eliza Cotton—there was ingratitude and treachery if you like. A low, impertinent creature, ready to go wherever there was money to get, and probably counting on making a good thing out of the weekly books. Marian Brand wouldn't know whether she was being cheated or not. As for Cassy, she was simply getting up this picnic in order to push herself forward. That was Cassy from the nursery—playing up, and showing off, and pulling things round to suit herself. Her anger mounted, and her heavy blood.

It was a warm afternoon, but there was quite a pleasant breeze off the sea. Miss Silver had found it hot in the bus. She wore her olive-green cashmere and her black cloth coat, which she would not have cared to remove in a public conveyance. She was, therefore, very much pleased to find that it was pleasantly fresh in the cove. There was, of course, no shade, a circumstance which made her compare the seaside unfavourably with places such as glades, where a picnic meal could be partaken of under the boughs of some stately oak or spreading chestnut—these being the adjectives which presented themselves to her mind in this connection. She had, however, provided herself with a neat striped umbrella belonging to her niece Ethel, which could be used as a sunshade.

It was not really a comfortable meal. Of the two elder ladies, Mrs. Brand was in a state of smouldering anger which she made no attempt to conceal, and Miss Remington was as sharp, restless and disturbing as a wasp. No sooner did any two people fall into a conversation than she broke in upon it, dancing hither and thither, pressing food on people who did not want it, snatching at the half-emptied cup in order to brim it with bitter tea, and generally making everyone as uncomfortable as possible.

Helen Adrian, who had begun a low-toned interchange with Cyril Felton, was driven into relinquishing him, but no sooner had she started all over again with Richard Cunningham than Miss Cassy broke off her own conversation with Cyril to say with an edge to her voice,

"Dear me, Helen, I had no idea that Mr. Cunningham was *your* friend. We all thought it was Marian he had come to see." She turned to Miss Silver. "So romantic, you know—they were buried under a train together for hours."

Marian found herself able to smile.

"You wouldn't have thought it so romantic if you had been there," she said. "Poor Richard had two ribs broken, and I thought I was never going to get the dust out of my hair. I came home looking as if I had robbed a scarecrow. You never saw such a mess."

Across the currents of enmity of which Miss Silver was intelligently aware she saw Richard Cunningham's eyes rest for a moment upon Marian Brand, and she thought that Miss Cassy had spoken a true word in bitter jest. It was a very fleeting look, and perhaps no one else saw it at all. She went on taking everything in whilst she made a little difficult conversation to Mrs. Brand, who could hardly be induced to say more than yes or no, and pronounced even those monosyllables in an inimical manner.

Ina Felton and Penny Halliday were both unhappy. She saw Penny look once at Felix Brand's dark, tormented face with the unguarded look of a mother watching her sick child. It had nothing to hide and everything to give. It suffered because he was suffering. Helen Adrian never looked at him at all. She laughed and jested with Cyril Felton. She slipped her hand inside Richard Cunningham's arm and dropped her voice to reach his ear alone.

Ina kept her eyes on the fine shingle of the cove. There were small shells mixed with it, most of them broken to pieces by the grinding of the stones. You have to be tough, or you get ground to bits. The shell hasn't really got much chance.

The meal came to an end, a good deal to everyone's relief. Whilst Miss Cassy was making the three men gather up the fragments and re-pack the picnic-basket Miss Silver approached Helen Adrian.

"There was a view you were going to show me. Round the next point, was it not? It will be pleasant to walk for a little. I find sitting on the beach rather cramping."

Helen Adrian nodded.

"It's the clothes—you want to be in a bathing-dress. But I suppose you wouldn't agree with that."

They had been moving as they spoke, and were now

well away from the picnic group. Miss Silver coughed.

"Why did you ask me here, Miss Adrian?"

"Oh, I don't know—"

"I think you do."

"Oh, very well then—I wanted you to see them all."

"Why?"

There was a hesitation, a sense of something withheld and then quite suddenly released.

"I wanted to know if it was all right to do what I said. About Cyril—and all the rest of it. I got a feeling—I expect it was stupid—"

"What kind of feeling?"

"Oh, I don't know—"

Miss Silver looked at her very directly.

"I think you were afraid."

"Why should I be?"

"I think you were. And I think you have reason. I think you are playing a very dangerous game. You are stirring up feelings which you may not be able to control."

Helen Adrian laughed.

"I'm sorry—I really can't help it. Cyril!"

Miss Silver shook her head.

"Not Mr. Felton—Mr. Felix Brand."

Helen laughed again, this time with contempt.

"Oh, Felix? He'd lick my shoes if I wanted him to!"

Miss Silver said very seriously indeed,

"You asked me to come here this afternoon because you wanted me to see these people. Shall I tell you what I saw? Hatred—jealousy—spite—wounded affection—resentment —deep unhappiness. These things are not to be played with. They are dangerous. You have come to me for advice, and I am speaking plainly. You are meddling with dangerous matters. Leave them alone. Leave these people alone. Leave their house and return to London. Go back to your fiancé. Tell him the truth and marry him. If you wish me to do so, I will see Mr. Felton on your behalf. I think I can undertake that he will not annoy you further. He is not a strong or a determined character, and a threat to refer the matter to the police would, I feel quite sure, dispose of him."

That sullen look which Miss Silver had seen before disfigured the curve of Helen Adrian's mouth. She said in an obstinate voice,

"I won't have the police brought into it."

"There will be no need to bring them into it. The threat will be enough."

The fair head was vigorously shaken.

"No—I'd rather take Cyril on myself." Then, with a half laugh, "I'm not afraid of him!" She turned round and began to lead the way back to the cove. "I'm not really afraid of anyone—I just got the jitters. I'm all right again now. I'll fix up with Cyril, and then perhaps I'll take your advice and send a wire to Fred to meet me in town. It's no good hanging on to things when they're over, is it?"

When Miss Silver presently took her departure the party had thinned out and scattered. Mrs. Brand had gone into the house. Felix had disappeared, and so had Helen Adrian and Cyril Felton. Penny had wandered down to the edge of the sea. The tide was now far out. She stood quite motionless, bare-foot on the shining sand, her head a little bent. Beyond her the shallow water caught and reflected the sun. The sky overhead had a faint haze across its blue. The breeze had dropped. Ina had remained where she was, sifting the fine shingle through her fingers and never looking up.

Miss Cassy was doing most of the talking. She did not very often have an audience like Richard Cunningham. She asked innumerable questions, often interrupting an answer in order to put another question, and always spitefully aware that he would rather have been talking to Marian Brand. It gave her

115

quite a lot of pleasure to prod him with her questions and make it impossible for him to get away. Marian, of course, was no match for her—a poor-spirited creature who didn't even get angry. She shot her a contemptuous glance, and saw her sitting there with a look of half-smiling abstraction. No one would take her for an heiress in that old serge skirt and home-made jumper. Some people might say that the colour suited her, but the blue had run—or faded. It wouldn't matter what she wore, she would never hold a candle to Helen Adrian. An odious girl, but you had to admit that she had looks and style. *And* a gift for walking off with the nearest young man. Where was she now? And where was Cyril Felton? And Felix? She went on rattling off questions at Richard Cunningham.

But when Miss Silver got up to go, he got up too. They walked up the terraced garden together and talked about Charles Moray, who was some sort of a cousin and a good deal of a friend.

With her slight prim cough Miss Silver admitted to a strong affection for Charles and Margaret.

"I have heard them speak of you, Mr. Cunningham."

"They have very often spoken of you. I don't know whether it is a forbidden subject, but I should like to express my admiration for your work."

Miss Silver's eyes dwelt upon him thoughtfully as she said,

"It is not generally known. It has always been possible to prevent my name appearing in the press. I should appreciate your discretion."

He laughed.

"No advertisement? How very remarkable!"

She smiled.

"I have often found it very useful not to be remarked."

"I know. I promise you I will be discreet. And you mustn't blame Charles and Margaret, because it was Frank Abbott who had already aroused my interest."

Miss Silver coughed.

"Inspector Abbott should have been more discreet."

She encountered a smiling gaze.

"Won't you drop the 'Inspector'? I really do know Frank very well. Cousins of his are cousins of mine, and the reason he was indiscreet was that one of these cousins was in a position which was, to put it mildly, delicate. I consulted Frank, and he suggested you. When I stressed the difficulties of the situation, he talked—in fact I may say he let himself go. I have known Frank a long time, and I thought I knew him pretty well, but I had no idea that he had it in him to be a humble disciple."

Miss Silver smiled indulgently.

"He sometimes talks a great deal of nonsense."

Richard Cunningham laughed.

"He doesn't usually run to humility. Frank has quite a fair opinion of himself. Well, as a matter of fact, the case I was concerned about cleared up without there being any need to trouble you. But I remained interested, and I am so very glad to have the opportunity of meeting you."

"Thank you, Mr. Cunningham."

CHAPTER 18

It was while the bus was conveying Miss Silver quickly and easily down the hill to Farne that two young people were making their way in the opposite direction. They had walked out from Farne and taken the footpath which leads across a field to the common land along the cliffs. The path goes no farther because the ground has never been enclosed, being too rough and uneven and continually cut up and worn away into small rifts and combes. There is some growth of rough grass, gorse, and bramble, and though the beach below is private and considered to be inaccessible, it is not really very difficult to climb down and steal a bathe.

Ted Hollins and Gloria Payne were about to scramble down what Ted indicated as "the place Joe and I got over," when they heard the sound of voices coming up from the beach. Ted stopped, listened, and went on again, moving gingerly and putting out a hand behind him to check Gloria. But when he came to a place where he could see over, there she was, right up against him, her shoulder bunching into his, craning her neck to see what he was looking at. And neither of them could see a thing.

The rift they were in had taken them half way down the cliff, the rest of the way was easy enough. They could see the long inviting stretch of sand left bare by the tide, a ridge or two of piled-up shingle, and then the bulge of the cliff was in the way. They couldn't see the two people who were standing right down under them where the beach ran in to meet this little combe. There was a man, because it was a man's voice which they had heard to start with—a man's voice, but not his words, only the angry echo as if they were something he was chucking about and getting chucked back at him again. But what the woman said was as plain as plain—"All right—go on and do it! You've said you're going to often enough. Go on and murder me if you feel like it!"

Gloria pursed up her mouth and said, "Ooh!" Her lips were so close to Ted's ear that her breath tickled him. He put up a hand to rub the tickle away just as if she had been a fly, and they both heard the man say, "I will when I'm ready—you needn't worry about that," and they heard him

118

go striding away over the shingle with the stones grinding and creaking under his feet.

Since the woman showed no signs of following him, Ted and Gloria made their way back to the top of the cliff, where they talked about how long it would be before there would be a chance of getting a couple of rooms let alone a house, and whether if the worst came to the worst, they couldn't just make do at Dad and Mum's. Since Gloria shared a room with a sister and there seemed to be nowhere else for Edith to sleep, it wasn't a very helpful prospect. And Ted's landlady wouldn't take in a wife, not if it was ever so. "Next thing you know, there's nappies on the line," was the way she put it. And when Ted up and said, "What's wrong with that?" Mrs. Crole, she looked at him like any thunderstorm and said, "You wait and see!"

"Reely anyone 'ud think a baby wasn't human, wouldn't you?" They had said this to one another quite a number of times, the accepted response being a gloomy "Seems like it."

"And all they go on saying to us is we're young." Ted pitched a pebble over the cliff. "Anyone 'ud think that meant you hadn't got your feelings, and no right to have them!"

Gloria said, "That's right."

They went on talking about themselves.

CHAPTER 19

Ina Felton was very unhappy. Once your eyes are open you can't help seeing things, and once you have seen them you can't go back to the time when you didn't know they were there. She locked her door, and thought about Cyril in the spare room. And wondered whether he would come and turn her handle and try to get her to let him in.

She stood a long time at her window looking out over the sea, but he didn't come. It was a relief, but it was the kind of relief which comes when you have made up your mind not to go on hoping any more. The night was lovely—no moon, but light coming from the sky, and the air a dark transparency. She could see the blossom against the garden wall glimmering like a ghost, its rosy colour gone. She could see the slow resistless movement of the tide. It was coming in. Where there had been smooth shining sand, the water deepened. As she stood there she could see how it kept rising, rising, without hurry and without rest. The point of rock which had been clear a little while ago was gone now, the water covered it without a ripple. You couldn't stop things like the tide, and thought, and what was happening in your life.

She stood there for a long time before she undressed. There was a clock on the floor below—a big old clock with a slow, soft tick, and a slow, heavy stroke for the hours. It stood in the hall, and if she was awake in the night she liked to feel it was there, and that if she listened it would tell her the time. She was awake a good deal in the night, and it was company.

She was turning back her bed when she heard it strike—just the one heavy stroke which meant that another day had begun. She stood there listening, because she had lost count of the time and she was not sure if there would be another stroke.

She was just going to move, when she heard a faint sound on the landing. It stopped her before she had really moved at all, because she knew what it was. The board outside the spare room creaked when you stepped on it. She had heard it every time she came and went, with soap, with towels, with bed-linen, getting the room ready for Cyril. All the other boards were steady. It was just this one that made the sound. She stood quite rigid with her eyes on the handle of her door and waited to see if it would move. The bedside lamp was on. All at once it went tingling through her that it might show a line of light under the door.

Before she knew what she was going to do her hand went out and turned the switch. Then she went over to the door and stood there, a finger on the handle to feel if it would move.

She couldn't hear anything. The board did not creak again. She had no feeling that anyone was coming nearer. She thought that if Cyril was crossing the landing bare-foot to her door, she would have some feeling. Her heart beat to suffocation, and it came to her that she did not know what the feeling would be. Everything in her couldn't have changed so much that she would find herself shrinking. Or could it? She didn't know.

There was another sound. It was nowhere near the door. Perhaps from the stairs. Perhaps even farther away—from the hall. She turned the key in the lock. Then she let her whole hand close on the door knob and turned it too. The door swung in.

The landing was dark and empty. A very faint light came

up from the hall. It was so faint that it was really only a thinning of the darkness, but she could see the line of the balustrade which guarded the stairs, heavy and black against the greyness below.

She came out of her room past the short passage which led to the other house. The door at the end of it was bolted top and bottom. There was one of these doors on every floor, and they were all the same, bolted on this side, with a key to turn on the other.

She came to the top of the stairs, but before she could come round the newel-post she heard the sound again, and this time she knew what it was. Someone was drawing back the bolts on the door in the hall.

She stood quite still where she was and listened. There was the same short length of passage that there was upstairs, and the door at the end of it with a bolt at the top and a bolt at the bottom. Since she had heard the sound twice, it would not come again, because both the bolts must have been withdrawn. The only other sound that could be looked for would be the turning of the key on the farther side. But it might have been turned already, before she came out of her room. If it had been, she would not have heard it. She listened to see if she would hear it now.

And then it came—just a faint click, and before she had time to think whether she had heard it or not she knew that the door was opening, and that someone was coming through. There were two people in the passage now, and one of them had come through from the other house. Two people—and one of them was Cyril, who had gone downstairs in the middle of the night and drawn back the bolts.

Her knees shook. She was holding to the newel. She let herself down until she was crouching behind the balustrade. It screened her, but she could see over it. She had let herself down because she couldn't stand any longer. Not to screen herself, or to see more. But in the result she found herself protected from being seen, and in a better position to see. If there had been a light in the passage now, she would have been able to see the whole length of it.

And then there was a light—the sharp white beam from a small pocket torch. It struck the surface of the door between the houses—old dark paint, rather scratched and chipped. It danced across, and there was no gap at the edge—the door was shut. It slipped like a dazzle on water across a woman's dark skirt, a woman's white hand with shining blood-red nails, and came to rest in a trembling circle on the floor.

As soon as Ina saw the hand she knew that it was Helen Adrian who had come through the door in the wall. Anger, humiliation, and pain suddenly rushed in upon her. It was one o'clock in the morning, and Cyril had slipped down to let Helen Adrian in. They were there in the passage now. She could hear them whispering there. It was the faintest of faint sounds, like a stirring of leaves in the wind. The round eye of the torch stared on the floor, and its reflection shook, and moved, and shifted there. There was a row of pegs with coats hanging from them—old raincoats, hers and Marian's, umbrellas, and a scarf or two. The torch swung up. Cyril had it in his left hand. She saw his right hand come through the beam and unhook one of the coats. Then it came down again. A scarf of Marian's came down with it. It was a new one she had bought. A square. Very gay and pretty—shades of blue and yellow. It fell right through the beam of the torch, and Ina was vexed, because it was new, and because Marian liked it, and it was one of the very few things she had got for herself. Right in the middle of all that was happening she could feel vexed about Marian's scarf.

And then she was more than vexed, she was angry. There was a rustling. Helen Adrian was putting on Marian's coat.

It was just an old raincoat, but she hadn't any business to come in here in the middle of the night and take it.

The beam of the torch swung out and back across the blue and yellow of the scarf lying there on the floor. She saw Helen Adrian's arm in the shabby sleeve of the raincoat come down into the light, she saw the hand with the crimson nails. The torch swung round towards the hall. The two people in the passage came that way. Helen Adrian was tying the scarf over her hair. She didn't quite laugh, but her whisper had a laughing sound. It carried up the well of the stair. Ina heard her say,

"Safe enough now."

And Cyril said,

"You can't be too careful."

It was all just on the edge of sound. It was so nearly over the edge that she might not have heard it at all. Through all the days that followed she was to ask herself what she had really heard. But it always came back to that "Safe enough now," and, "You can't be too careful."

They crossed the hall to the study door, and went in and shut it after them.

CHAPTER 20

The hotel in Farne was really very up to date. Not only was the food exceptional and the service prompt, but there was a telephone in every bedroom. Richard Cunningham had one beside him as he lay watching a light haze draw up off the sea and melt into a cloudless sky. He could rise early when he chose, but he had not chosen today. It was too pleasant to be at nobody's beck and call, with another perfect day in prospect. All this, and Marian too. They had travelled a long way yesterday. They would travel farther today, and tomorrow—

The telephone bell rang. He put out his hand, took up the receiver, and Marian was speaking.

"Richard—is it you?"

At once there was a shadow. Her voice was steady only because she would not let it shake. That came to him. Control. What had happened that Marian must control her voice when she spoke to him? This in a flash while he said,

"What is it?"

"Something has happened."

"What?"

"Something dreadful. There's been an accident."

"To whom?"

"To Helen Adrian. Richard, she's dead."

"How?"

"We don't know. The two women who help next door, Mrs. Bell and Mrs. Woolley, they get here at eight. The aunts have tea in their rooms—Helen too. She wasn't there. They thought—she and Felix—had gone down—to bathe. Mrs. Woolley went a little way, to see if they were coming. She couldn't see them. She went down farther. She saw Helen Adrian lying on the beach where the last lot of steps go down. You remember how steep they are. Mrs. Woolley thought she had fallen and hurt herself. She went down to see. And Helen was dead."

He had a picture in his mind of the last steep drop to the beach. The path took a turn. There was no rail—or was there? For the moment he wasn't sure. Then the blurred picture cleared. The garden was terraced to the beach. The last steep steps went down from the lowest terrace to the shingle of the cove. A railing guarded them. But there was no railing

125

to the terrace itself. It followed the sloping line of the cliff, and on the narrowest side it fell steeply.

Into the picture in his mind there came, small and clear, Helen Adrian lying under the drop, her hair bright against the stones. He said,

"Horrible!"

He heard her take her breath.

"Yes. I rang to tell you not to come out. It won't be—very pleasant. There will be the police—" She wouldn't let her voice shake, but she couldn't make it go on.

He knew just why she had stopped like that. He said,

"Marian, let me come. It's horrible for you and Ina. There might be something I could do. I'd like to be there."

She got her voice going again. It was steady but faint. It said,

"You'd better not. You don't want to get mixed up in it. There'll be—reporters. You see, it wasn't—an accident. They think someone—killed her."

He said her name quickly, insistently. And then,

"But of course I'll come! What did you think—didn't you know? Look here, I'll be out as soon as I can make it."

"You mustn't—"

He said, "Don't talk nonsense!" and hung up.

When he got out to Cove House Mrs. Woolley was still alternating between being overcome by her feelings and the urge to enlarge upon the most exciting experience that was ever likely to come her way. She had already told the whole thing a good many times—to her sister Gladys Bell between hysterical sobs; to an augmented audience of Penny, chalk-white and rigid; to Mrs. Brand and Miss Cassy; to Eliza Cotton; to Miss Marian Brand and Mrs. Felton; and finally to the police, who rather belatedly instructed her not to gossip. The narrative had by now become set. She used the same words, and stopped to cry in the same places. She went through it all again for Richard Cunningham, from the moment when, receiving no answer to her knock, she had opened Miss Adrian's door and looked in to find the room empty, to the moment the recollection of which really did make her heart thump and her head swim when she had looked from the narrow end of the last terrace to the beach and seen a body lying there on the stones below. "And I don't know how I got down those steps—I don't reely. Seems to me one minute I was up there looking down at her, and the next there I was, taking her poor hand. And of course I knew she was dead, because it was as cold as ice, let alone her head being all smashed in, poor thing."

There was a police sergeant from Farne in charge, but within the next half hour superior authority had begun to function. Inspector Crisp arrived from Ledlington and at once proceeded to make himself felt. The whole ghastly business which waits on murder was set in motion. Mrs. Woolley went through her story again, photographs were taken, and one by one every member of the two households were interviewed. Every member except one. Felix Brand was not in his room. Had not been in his room when Mrs. Bell went up and knocked on the door, which was just before her sister ran in panting and crying from the beach. He was not in the house, or in the garden, or in the cove. Nobody, in fact, had seen him since half past ten the evening before.

CHAPTER 21

When Richard arrived at Cove House Eliza met him at the front door and took him through to the kitchen. She had her own views as to what his place in the family was going to be, and she considered that he did ought to know what was going on. Miss Marian's raincoat found down by the body, and Miss Marian's scarf with a great bloodstain on it hanging up in the passage which led through to next door. And Sergeant Jackson taking charge of it, and in there in the study this minute asking all manner of questions which no one could answer. She did think Mr. Cunningham ought to know. And when she had told him all about it, so did he.

Then, right on the top of that, there was Mrs. Woolley at the back door. He never really knew what excuse she made, or whether she troubled to make one, because the minute she saw him she burst out crying all over again and began to tell him about finding the body.

The ground floor door between the two houses stood open as he walked through the hall from the kitchen. Sergeant Jackson went down the passage which led to it and passed out of sight on the other side. His solid blue back brought home the realities of the situation with something like a physical shock. Marian's house wasn't her own any longer. It was merged with a house where someone had been murdered. All its doors and all its rooms were open to the police. And if anyone in either house had any secret thing to hide, it would be open too.

Marian came out of the study. As soon as she saw Richard

she put a finger to her lips and went back. He followed her and shut the door, but she stepped away from his out-stretched hand.

"Richard, you mustn't get mixed up in this."

She was dreadfully pale. There was the control of which he had been aware when she rang him up. He said,

"My dear, I am mixed up in it—at least as much as you are. It's been a great shock, but it's not as if you were involved in any way."

She looked at him. He was aware that she had an impulse to speak, and that she checked it. She stood in the place to which she had fallen back after shutting the door. She did not move from it. But the distance between them had widened, her thought had withdrawn.

He went on to say quietly,

"After all, you hardly knew her. I gather that the Inspector from Ledlington has just arrived. He sounds very vigorous and efficient. If Mrs. Woolley hadn't been over here visiting Eliza, I feel sure that I wouldn't have had the chance of seeing her. One of the constabulary has now recalled her to the fold, and she will have to tell her story all over again. She's enjoying it, you know. Nice amiable creature, and quite properly shocked and horrified, but just at the moment she's got the centre of the stage and she can't help enjoying it."

Her mind shuddered, but she held her body still. He was as much aware of that as if it was his own thought that was shaken. He said,

"Felix Brand is missing?"

"Yes."

"That means the police will suspect him."

She said, "Yes," again. And then, "I haven't seen Penny. Eliza says she's like a bit of stone. She loves him dreadfully."

He nodded.

"How is Ina?"

129

She took a long breath.

"It's been a most frightful shock."

"Where is she?"

"In her room. She won't come down."

"The police will want to see her."

"The sergeant asked us all whether we had heard anything in the night. They think she would have—cried out. Nobody seems to have heard any cry. He said the Inspector from Ledlington would want to see us when he came, and not to go out. But Cyril says he has to go up to town."

"He'd better not."

"He says he has an audition."

"He'll have to tell that to the police."

As he spoke, Cyril Felton walked in. Like everyone else in the two houses, he looked the worse for wear. He had shaved carelessly and cut himself. Richard thought there was a moment in which he was undecided as to how he should play the part which had been thrust upon him without rehearsal. He came down on the side of being shocked but brave—the man of the world who knows that life and his own affairs must go on. He came forward with his hand out.

Richard felt that a really good producer would have cut the handshake down to a nod, but the "Hullo, Cunningham— shocking business this," achieved quite the right casual note.

Richard said, "Yes."

Cyril continued.

"Naturally they think it's Felix. Frightfully silly of him to do a bolt like this. Of course the chap was insane with jealousy."

"Cyril!" Marian's voice cut in with a note of anger in it.

He stared at her.

"What's the matter?"

"You've no right to say it was Felix!"

"All right, all right—I'm not saying it, but the police will.

130

As as matter of fact I don't see why it couldn't have been an accident."

Marian grew perceptibly paler.

"You would if you had listened to Mrs. Woolley."

He gave a vague half shrug.

"Oh, well, I should have thought pitching down over that drop on to the shingle would account for anything. But the police will have it their own way. It's no concern of mine. I just felt sorry for the chap, that's all. Look here, what's the matter with Ina? I've got to get up to this audition today, and there she is, locked in her room. I can't get up to town without some cash—I'm cleaned right out. And there she is, locked in her room and won't let me in."

"The police won't let you go."

He raised his eyebrows.

"Darling, they haven't the slightest right to stop me. It's all quite simple. I believe the Inspector from Ledlington has arrived. I just go through and tell him what I know, which is just about nothing at all, and I catch the next bus to the station. If he insists, I can come back tonight, but I must get up for that audition. So if you can make it a fiver—"

Marian looked as if she was going to say something, and changed her mind. She went out of the room, leaving the door open behind her. They heard her run up the stairs.

Cyril stuck his hands in his pockets, whistled a few bars from "Only Fancy Me," and drifted over to the glass door leading to the garden. Standing there, he remarked conversationally,

"Nasty business all this. But I must say I think Ina might pull herself together. Shutting herself up like this. I mean, it's the sort of thing that puts ideas into people's heads—the police, you know. I mean, it's not as if she even liked the girl. Other girls didn't. And no need to go locking herself in her room and behaving as if she'd lost her dearest friend.

Not reasonable, I mean—is it? Look here, if you get a chance you might put that to Marian. She'll listen to you, and there's an odd chance Ina will listen to her. You put in a word and see what you can do about it. I mean, there's no sense in putting ideas into people's heads, is there?"

Richard observed him with interest. A young man with one idea, and that one Cyril Felton. Most people were selfish, but there was quite often a blend of other interests. In this case the mind appeared to have but a single thought.

They heard the running feet on the stairs again. Marian came back into the room with a little packet of folded notes in her hand. She gave them to Cyril and stepped back to avoid his casual embrace. She had a little more colour. It looked as if her patience with Cyril had worn very thin indeed. He kissed his hand to her, said, "Wish me luck with the police!" and wandered out of the room as if he had all the time in the world and nothing special to do with it.

When he had gone Marian made an exasperated movement.

"What am I to do? He'll come back without a penny, and we shan't even know whether there was an audition or not. This is the first time it's been mentioned. If he really had one, why didn't he say so before? I think he just wants to get away from all the unpleasantness."

"I shouldn't wonder." Richard's tone was dry.

She turned round to him with both her hands out.

"And you come into it when you needn't—when there isn't the slightest obligation. We shan't ever forget that."

He took the hands, held them strongly for a moment, and let them go again. It would be easy to go too far and spoil everything. What she needed just now was friendship and stability—the feeling that there was someone who wouldn't fail her. At least that stiff control had broken. He said lightly, but with an underlying seriousness,

132

"Well, here I am, and here I'm going to stay. You'll have to make use of me."

The look she turned on him was full of trouble.

"Richard—you shouldn't! There are things—you don't know."

"Suppose you tell me what they are."

"I don't think I can."

He put a hand on her shoulder.

"You can tell me anything. Don't you know that? I believe you do." He withdrew his hand, but went on speaking in the same low, intimate tone. "There isn't anything you can't tell me, and very little that needs putting into words. Where most people have walls between them, you and I have windows. I knew that when I walked down the corridor of that train. I only saw your face for a moment, and I don't think you saw me at all—you didn't look as if you did. But just in that moment I knew more about you than I do about people I've known all my life. It's something like being on the same wave-length, and there's just nothing you can do about it, my dear. So now are you going to tell me what's bothering you and let me do what I can to help you?"

She went on looking at him. The trouble darkened her eyes. He saw how beautiful they were like that, wide and deep, but they tore his heart. He said,

"If it's anything that touches you, it touches me. If it touches Ina too, I'll go as far as you will. And now will you tell me what's on your mind?"

At the almost imperceptible movement which meant, "Yes," he said,

"Very well then. Now come and sit down. And just remember nothing is ever quite so bad as you think it is."

They sat down on Martin Brand's comfortable, shabby old couch with its wide seat and deep padded back. Marian leaned against the cushions and thought how wonderful it was to have someone who wanted to help, and how easy to let him do it.

"What is it? If it's the raincoat, you don't suppose Mrs. Woolley held her tongue about it, do you?"

"Oh!" It was just an involuntary catch of the breath. Her hands took hold of one another, but she was able to manage her voice.

"What did she say?"

"That your raincoat was found hanging over the back of the seat on the terrace from which Helen Adrian fell. You didn't put it there, I take it."

She shook her head. Her eyes were clear on his face.

"Or Ina?"

There was a pause before she said, "No."

"Was it left down on the beach after the picnic? You were sitting on something of the sort, weren't you?"

She thought, "He notices everything." Then, aloud, "No, it wasn't left out. You brought it in yourself."

He said, "So I did!" and for an odd intimate moment they smiled at one another. Then he laughed. "I brought it in, and I hung it up in that bit of passage where the door goes through to the other house. That's where you keep it, isn't it?"

"Yes."

"Anyone could take it from there."

She said, "The door was locked."

"You mean, Helen Adrian couldn't have taken it?"

She said again,

"The door was bolted. There are bolts on our side. We keep them shut."

"You mean, someone from this side must have taken your coat?"

"The police will say so."

He said, "I should think they would be too busy suspecting Felix Brand."

134

She shook her head.

"The sergeant asked me about the coat—he wanted to know how it got there. He asked us all, and we all said we didn't know."

Richard said in a reasonable tone,

"Well, I should say offhand that if anyone is lying it would be Cyril."

She said, "Why should he take my coat?"

"I don't know. I don't know why anyone should, but somebody did. It may have been just accidental, or there may have been a motive behind it."

"What do you mean, Richard?"

"I mean, someone may have taken your coat because they wanted one and yours was handy. Or they may have taken it because it was yours, to turn suspicion towards you—away from someone else."

"That's—horrible."

"Yes."

"Richard, there's something more."

"I knew that. What is it?"

She said, speaking slowly with pauses between every few words,

"I have—a blue and yellow scarf—a square to tie over the head. There's so much wind here—it blows my hair. I got it in Farne—the day after we came down—it's rather pretty and bright. It was hanging in the passage—with my coat. The sergeant wanted to see—where I kept the coat—so I showed him. The scarf was there—hanging on the peg—so he took it down and looked at it. He asked—if it was mine. I said it was. Then he held it out—for me to see." A long shudder went over her. She said, "It was—stained—"

"Blood?"

"Yes."

He sat quite still for a moment, frowning and intent, his

mind working, emotion shut off. Then he said,

"Your scarf—stained and put back. That's proof that some-one wants to bring you into it."

Her lips just moved. He barely caught the words they formed.

"Unless—they didn't know—"

"You mean, the person who was wearing the scarf might have put it back without knowing it was stained. What sort of stain was it—slight?"

"No—dreadful."

"Then whoever handled it must have known."

"I don't see how they could help it."

He got up and walked to the glass door. It stood open. A bee blundered by, heavy with pollen, a scent of flowers was distilled upon the sunny air—the sort of day one calls heav-enly. And things moving in some perverted mind—sick, evil things reaching out to injure and befoul. He had a moment of awareness that set every nerve tingling. He turned and came back.

"Marian—"

She looked up, startled.

"What is it?"

"There's something deliberate about this. I can see no mo-tive for bringing that stained scarf back into this house except the damnable one of trying to involve you in the murder. But look here, my dear, that lifts your worst fear. You needn't tell me what it is, for I know. You've been afraid about Ina. But you needn't be. The worst of this kind of shock is that it puts your thinking out of action and hands you over to your emo-tions. Now just pull yourself together and think! Yesterday afternoon Cyril was having the kind of casual flirtation with that young woman which I suppose he, and she, would have with every second person they met. That is so, isn't it?"

"I suppose so."

"Do you really think it upset Ina so much that she contrived to lure Helen Adrian down to the beach in the middle of the night and murder her there?"

Marian's colour came back in a rush. She said,

"No—no—of course I don't."

He went on ruthlessly.

"And if you did manage to believe that, could you believe that she would wear your raincoat and your scarf, leave one on the scene of the crime, and bring back the other all messed up with Helen Adrian's blood and hang it in the hall for the police to find? Now, Marian, get your brain to work! It was done to incriminate you. Would Ina do that?"

She put up her hand to her head.

"No—no—of course not. Richard—*please*."

"I'm putting it bluntly, but that's what you've been letting yourself be afraid of. Isn't it? Once it's put into words, you can see that it's all nonsense. Get it into words to Ina. Go up now and ask her if she took your raincoat or your scarf. The Inspector may ask for you at any moment, and we've got to know where you stand."

He saw relief flash over her face. She ran upstairs. After a moment's hesitation he followed, to find her at Ina's door, her head bent, one hand on the jamb. She called softly,

"Ina—it's Marian. Let me in."

There was no answer.

"Ina, we shall have to see the Inspector. I must see you first. If you don't let me in, I shall have to climb from the bathroom, and if you shut the window I shall break the glass."

This was a Marian whom he hadn't seen. Something inflexible in her bearing, in her voice, but all very quiet.

Before he had time to wonder what would happen there was the sound of the key turning in the lock and the door opened. Ina stood there with the back of her hand to her eyes as if she was shielding them. When Marian put an arm around her the hand came down and caught at her. She looked dazed, and she was wearing the dress she had worn the night before. He wondered whether she had undressed or slept.

She said, "Where's Cyril?" and Richard answered her.

"He said he had an audition. He is seeing the Inspector about going up to town."

"Will they let him go?"

"I don't see why not."

She showed no surprise at his presence, no embarrassment. Her voice was gentle and a little dull. He thought, "She's had a bad shock." He began to wonder about Cyril Felton.

CHAPTER 22

It was no more than five mintues later that a constable came through to say that the Inspector would be glad if they would step along to the drawing-room next door and answer a few questions.

The two girls were in Ina's bedroom with the door shut, but Richard went to it and knocked. They came out at once. A resourceful woman can do a good deal in five minutes. He had heard water splashing in the basin, and guessed at a vigorous sponging of Ina's drawn face and tired eyes. She certainly looked a good deal more alive. Powder had been applied, and a very little rouge—not enough to stand out from the pallor beneath, but enough to mitigate it. The dark curls had been combed and the crumpled dress replaced by a skirt and jumper.

They went down the stairs, along the passage where the

raincoat and scarf had hung, and through to the drawing-room of the next house.

The dust-sheets had been removed from the furniture, and the scene had a kind of caricature resemblance to one of the more ghastly forms of tea-party. Mrs. Brand and Miss Remington sat side by side on a gilded sofa between the windows. Cyril, in his town suit, was standing beside the piano looking like any guest who wishes he had not come and is counting the moments till he can get away. Penny, in a dark skirt and the old white sweater, sat stiffly on a small gilt chair, her hands in her lap, her eyes never lifting from them. There was even a tea-table, a gimcrack inlaid affair, but instead of a tea-tray it was laid out with writing materials, and behind it, to dispense not hospitality but justice, sat Inspector Crisp, stocky, wiry, efficient, and very much concerned with getting to the top of his own particular tree. To do this it was necessary that he should get to the bottom of this and every other case which came his way. From the set of his head with its harsh dark hair, his bristling eyebrows, and quick frown, to the way in which he handled the papers before him and kept his feet firmly planted upon a rather anaemic rose wreath in the Brussels carpet, everything about him declared that he was a man who would stand no nonsense. The young constable who sat on the piano-stool with pencil and notebook ready kept a wary eye cocked in his direction, and was obviously ready to spring to it at the mere flick of an eyelash.

Marian and Ina sat down together on a second small sofa. Richard pulled up a chair beside them.

Eliza Cotton stalked in with an air of extreme disapproval and went to stand behind Penny with a hand on the back of her chair.

The door to the garden was open and a soft air came in, but the room had a chill.

139

Inspector Crisp looked them all up and down and rapped upon the table.

"Everyone here who slept in either of the two houses last night?" he said in a barking voice.

Richard was just thinking that he reminded him of a terrier—the whole air of him, and the eyebrows bristling out over the small bright eyes when they were suddenly turned on himself.

"Who are you, sir? Were you here last night? I haven't got you down. Who are you?"

"Richard Cunningham. I am a friend of Miss Brand and Mrs. Felton. I didn't sleep in the house, but I was here all day."

"When did you leave?"

"About half past ten."

Crisp stared at him for a moment, said, "Very well, you may stay," and rapped again. "I would like everyone to give me their attention. I have here a list of the bedrooms in both houses which look out towards the sea. I am going to check up on them."

He picked up a sheet of paper and read from it.

"In this house:—

Attic bedroom, occupied by Miss Halliday—box-room next door.

Next floor:—

Two bedrooms—Miss Remington and Miss Adrian."

Cassy Remington made a fidgeting movement.

"Of course, Inspector, it's really my niece Penny's room—Miss Halliday. Only she isn't actually my niece but rather a distant cousin, though she has always called us Aunt."

She wore her lilac cardigan and a long chain of gold links and amethysts. Her fingers played with it continually. Her blue eyes dwelt on the Inspector and sustained his frown.

"That is beside the point. You are not suggesting that Miss Halliday did not occupy the attic room last night?"

140

"Oh, no, Inspector."

"Or that Miss Adrian was not occupying the bedroom next to yours?"

She darted a little edged glance at him.

"Not really next, because the bathroom is in between. It used to be a dressing-room, you know, but Mr. Brand's father had baths put in on both sides of the house."

Mrs. Brand's colour had been deepening alarmingly. She said, "Really, Cassy!" in an exasperated voice.

Crisp said sharply,

"Miss Remington, I must ask you not to speak unless you have something relevant to say. You and Miss Adrian were occupying the two bedrooms above us now, and they both look out towards the sea. Mrs. Brand and Mr. Felix Brand have the rooms which look towards the road?"

Miss Cassy fiddled with her chain.

"Oh, yes, Inspector. My sister finds this side of the house too bright, but I like all the sun I can get."

Crisp opened his mouth, closed it again with something uncommonly like a snap, and returned to the paper he was holding.

"In the next house, which is on exactly the same plan, Miss Eliza Cotton has the attic bedroom, Miss Brand and Mrs. Felton the two rooms looking towards the sea on the bedroom floor. One of the rooms looking towards the road was empty, and Mr. Felton was in the other. That is correct?"

Cassy Remington twisted the links of her chain.

"Oh, quite," she said brightly. "Except that you've forgotten the bathroom. But it's just the same as the one on this side. It was the dressing-room of the best bedroom, you see, so it is between Miss Brand's room and her sister's."

Crisp said, "Yes, yes, we've had all that! Now, if you please, I want to know whether anyone heard Miss Adrian cry, or call out. I want to know whether anyone heard any unusual sound of any kind. I want to know whether anyone heard her come downstairs or leave the house. This glass door into the garden was found open this morning by Mrs. Bell. It may have been opened by Miss Adrian, or by Mr. Felix Brand, who is missing. I want to know whether anyone heard it opened. You, Miss Remington—your room is immediately over it. Did you hear the door being opened?"

She put her head on one side and gave him a bright, birdlike attention. Anyone who knew her well would have known that she was enjoying herself. Eliza Cotton eyed her with disapproval. People hadn't any business to enjoy themselves when there had just been a murder in the house.

"The door? This door? Oh, no. But then if I was asleep I don't think I should. All our doors and windows open very quietly—none of them creak."

"Did you hear any cry?"

"Well, there you put me in a difficulty, Inspector. I must absolutely refuse to swear to it."

Everybody was now looking at her. Eliza's impression that she was enjoying herself deepened, so did Eliza's disapproval.

Crisp said with restraint,

"You are not being asked to swear to anything. I am asking you whether you heard a cry."

Miss Cassy said in a bright voice,

"I couldn't possibly say whether it was a seagull."

"In the middle of the night?"

"Now, Inspector, you mustn't try and catch me. I didn't say it was in the middle of the night. I woke up, I heard this cry, and I went to sleep again. I had no opportunity of consulting my watch, which was on the dressing-table."

"I suppose you know whether it was dark?"

"Oh, quite dark. Quite, quite dark."

"Then it wasn't a seagull."

"But it might have been a bat," said Cassy Remington.

"A bat!" The Inspector's restraint was wearing thin. The word came out with a snap.

"Oh, yes, Inspector. You may not be aware of the fact that bats have quite a sharp cry. It is so high in the scale that most people are unable to hear it. I happen to be one of the exceptions."

Crisp tapped with his pencil in an exasperated manner.

"You woke in the dark at some time which you cannot fix, and you heard something which may or may not have been a human cry."

Miss Cassy jingled her chain.

"Of course it may have been a cat. They come here after Mactavish."

Crisp pounced on the name.

"Mactavish?"

"Our cat, Inspector—a very fine half-Persian."

It is probable that Mactavish heard his name. He obliged with a dramatic entry, walking in through the open door, his tail held high and all his orange fur fluffed out. Seeing his whole family assembled, and not caring for the manner of it, he surveyed the strange man at the table with hauteur, opened his mouth in a soundless mew of protest, and went disdainfully back down the two shallow steps into the sunny garden.

The Inspector rapped.

"You heard something in the nature of a cry. Did you hear any sound of movement in the house? Did you hear Miss Adrian leave her room? I don't mean when you were all going to bed, but later when the house had settled down."

She shook her head regretfully.

"Oh, no, I don't think so—only this cat, or bat, or whatever it was."

He swung round on Penny, who had not moved at all.

"You, Miss Halliday—did you hear anything outside or in?"

She said, "No."

Her face was bloodless under its tan. He could only just hear the word. Well, thank God everyone wasn't a gas-bag. He swung back again.

"Mrs. Brand, your room looks the other way, but you could have heard sounds in the house. Did you hear anything at all?"

She sat there stout and shapeless in the black dress with the brown and red pattern which looked like smears of mud and red ink. Her large smooth face, usually of an even pallor, was considerably flushed. Her prominent brown eyes were fixed in an angry stare. She had a linen handkerchief in her hand, and every now and then she fanned herself with it. She said in her heavy voice,

"No, I didn't hear anything."

"Mr. Felix Brand's room is next to yours. Did you hear him leave it?"

"No. I am a sound sleeper."

He made an abrupt movement.

"Well, that's everyone on this side of the house—Miss Adrian being dead and Mr. Felix Brand missing. I'll now take the next-door people. Miss Brand—did you hear anything?"

Marian returned his look with a steady one.

"I don't know, Inspector. I woke up suddenly in the night, but I don't know what it was that waked me. I couldn't say that it was a cry, but I woke with the feeling that something had startled me. I sat up in bed and listened, but I didn't hear anything more, so I went to sleep again."

"Can you fix the time at all?"

"I didn't look at my watch. It was high tide."

He came back quickly.

"Sure about that?"

144

"I could hear the water. You don't hear it when the tide is out."

He looked round the circle.

"Anyone know when the tide would be high?"

Richard Cunningham said,

"It was pretty far out at seven o'clock yesterday evening."

"Low tide seven-twenty," said Eliza Cotton.

Crisp nodded.

"That's near enough. We can check up on it. Then it would be high tide round about one a.m. Low again about half past six, and coming up now. If you heard the sea when you woke up, Miss Brand—well, I suppose it might be high enough for you to hear any time between twelve and two, or say a bit more margin than that."

The constable on the piano-stool wrote in his notebook, using a clear, neat script.

Crisp passed on to Ina.

"Mrs. Felton, your room is next to your sister's—looks the same way. Did you wake in the night at all?"

Marian put her hand over her sister's and found it cold. She felt it give a little nervous jerk as Ina said in a breathless voice,

"No—I didn't wake."

It went through Marian's mind that if you haven't slept you cannot wake. She did not think that Ina had slept at all. She had not taken off the clothes which she had been wearing the night before. She had not slept.

"You didn't wake up, and you didn't hear anything?"

The hand that Marian was covering twitched again. Ina said,

"No."

His keen bright eyes remained fixed on her.

"Was Miss Adrian a friend of yours?"

She shook her head, then, as if realizing that something more was needed, came to hesitating speech.

145

"I didn't know her—at all—only these two or three days."

"Any quarrel with her?"

She was startled into awareness.

"Oh, no. I don't think I spoke to her more than twice, and then only a few words."

He said sharply,

"I ask because you look as if this has been a considerable shock."

Ina felt the hand on hers press down with a strong, comforting warmth. Marian said quietly,

"It has been a very great shock. My sister isn't strong."

He gave a sort of nod and swung round to Eliza.

"Now, Miss Cotton—you're in the third room facing that way, the attic, aren't you? Did you hear anything?"

Standing there with her hand on the back of Penny's chair, Eliza sniffed.

"I did not."

"Sure about that?"

There was a second and more portentous sniff. When Penny or Mactavish heard that sound they knew enough to make themselves scarce. Inspector Crisp did not.

Eliza's temper had been working up for some time. She now let it go with what was no longer a sniff but a snort.

"There are those that'll lie as soon as look at you, and there are those that won't whether they've taken a Bible oath or not. Thank God I've got my sleep, and when I go to my bed I'm not listening for any bats, or cats, or such—or expecting that people'll be murdered and police officers come asking a lot of questions nobody can answer."

Crisp was irresistibly reminded of his Aunt Aggie, a lady whose temper intermittently afflicted her family. She would come on a visit and stay until some dynamic quarrel hurled her on to the next suffering relative.

146

He said hastily, "That's all I want to hear, Miss Cotton," and came round with relief to Cyril.

"Well, Mr. Felton, you're on the wrong side of the house, unless—you weren't sharing your wife's room last night?"

Nothing could have been pleasanter than Cyril's,

"Oh, no. She hasn't been very well."

"Did you hear anything?"

"I'm afraid not. I am a pretty sound sleeper."

Crisp looked from one to the other, frowning.

"When Sergeant Jackson got here this morning it was stated that the whole party, including Mr. Cunningham who didn't sleep in the house, another visitor who left early, Miss Adrian, and Mr. Felix Brand, were all together for several hours at a picnic in the cove. Mr. Cunningham is stated to have left at half past ten." He turned to Richard. "That correct?"

"Yes."

"The parties on the two sides of the house had supper and spent the evening on their own premises, but both parties say they had separated for the night by a little after half past ten. That is correct? I just want to confirm it."

There was a general murmur of assent. Miss Cassy said brightly,

"A quarter past ten is my hour, Inspector—winter or summer."

He rapped on the table.

"I will ask you again. Did anyone hear Miss Adrian leave the house? Or Mr. Felix Brand?"

A deep persistent silence followed each of these questions. He made an impatient movement.

"Mrs. Brand, you told Sergeant Jackson that none of your son's clothes were missing except the pair of flannel slacks and the pullover which he was wearing last night?"

Florence Brand said, "That is all."

"Except his bathing-suit," said Cassy Remington. She

147

turned helpfully to the Inspector. "Plain black stockinette. So neat and workmanlike, I always think. And he is such a good swimmer."

He gave her his most repressive stare.

"I was speaking to your sister. Mrs. Brand, I want to know how your son would dress if he were going out for an early morning dip."

Florence Brand said,

"Like that. He would put on a pair of trousers and a sweater over his bathing-suit unless it was really hot." She paused, fanned herself with the linen handkerchief, and said in her slow, deep voice, "I had better put you right about our relationship. Felix is not my son."

"Not? Do you mean that he was adopted?"

"No. I married his father." She fanned, and added, "When he was two years old."

It was a public repudiation. Since Felix was probably a murderer, she would have none of him. There was not anyone present who was not aware of the implication. Even Crisp was taken aback. Eliza gave another of those formidable snorts. And for the first time Penny moved. Her little stiff body remained rigid, but she turned her head. Her clear brown eyes rested for a moment upon Florence Brand. They said, "Judas." Her clear young voice said,

"You are in a great hurry, Aunt Florence."

Cassy Remington came into the silence that followed. Her chain jingled. She said in what Eliza called her vinegar voice,

"Always a most uncongenial child. Such a shocking temper."

Penny looked away. It was perhaps the more damning gesture of the two. She went back into her stillness.

The sound of heavy feet came in through the garden door. A constable came up the two steps and stood there looking across at the Inspector.

148

"Excuse me, sir—"

"Well, what is it?"

"We've found the clothes."

"Where?"

"Shoved in under the bank above high water mark."

Crisp had a frowning stare. He barked out,

"All right, what are you waiting for? Bring them in!" The frown was turned on Florence Brand. "Son or stepson, madam, I suppose you can identify his clothes?"

She sat affronted. Cassy Remington played with her chain, primmed up her lips, patted the regular waves of her hair.

Coming out of the bright sunshine, the constable found the room embarrassingly full of people. It was really quite light, but it didn't seem so, coming in like that. He had to thread his way amongst the chairs, the tables, the people. He felt as crowded and uncomfortable as if he was wearing a suit that was too tight for him, but he got up to the table without mishap and dumped the clothes he was carrying in front of Inspector Crisp.

Felix Brand's old grey flannel slacks. The Inspector picked them up and held them dangling. He addressed Florence Brand.

"Are these your son's?"

She stared back at him with her prominent brown eyes.

"If they belong to Felix they will have his initials inside the waistband. I have already told you that he is not my son."

"F.M.B.—is that right?"

"Felix Martin Brand—yes, that is right."

He let the slacks fall in a heap and picked up the sweater. As he shook it out, there was a sound in the room, a movement, a drawing in of breath. The front of the sweater was stained and spotted, and the right sleeve soaked with blood from elbow to wrist.

CHAPTER 23

When Miss Silver got back from the beach that morning she found Richard Cunningham waiting for her. She had intended to write some letters, but a single glance informed her that they would not be written. She took him into a bright bare room which contained a sofa, two chairs, and a carpet—very little else. She indicated the largest chair, removed her coat before taking the sofa corner, and extracted Derek's current stocking from the bag which she had taken to the beach.

Richard watched her without impatience. No hurry and no fuss. He could imagine that she had been brought up on such maxims as, "Self-control is the essence of good breeding," and "A gentle-woman is never in a hurry." He found her reposeful, and very steadying to the nerves.

When she had taken up her knitting she gave him her peculiarly sweet smile and said,

"What can I do for you, Mr. Cunningham?"

He was leaning forward in the rather unyielding chair. He made no pretence to anything except gravity as he said,

"I hope you can help me."

Her eyes dwelt thoughtfully upon his face.

"Something has happened?"

"Yes. Miss Adrian has been murdered."

After the briefest possible pause she said,

"Yes?"

"You are not surprised?"

She coughed.

"The abnormal is always surprising, and murder is always abnormal."

"But you are not surprised?"

She was knitting evenly and fast. Her regard dwelt on him as she said,

"It is the abnormal itself which is surprising, not its results."

"And you were aware that the conditions at Cove House were abnormal?"

"I think you were aware of it yourself, Mr. Cunningham."

"Not to that extent. I wonder whether you would tell me just what you were aware of."

Miss Silver quoted from the Book of Common Prayer.

" 'Envy, hatred, and malice, and all uncharitableness,' Mr. Cunningham. Where these are present, murder can never be surprising. May I ask who is suspected of having caused Miss Adrian's death?"

He said, "Felix Brand. But I don't know—I am very uneasy. That is why I am here. May I give you the facts very shortly?"

She inclined her head.

"Pray do so."

"Miss Adrian's body was found at half past seven this morning by Mrs. Woolley, the daily cook who works for Mrs. Brand. Finding that neither Felix nor Helen Adrian were in their rooms, she imagined that they had gone for a swim, and went down the garden to see if they were in sight. She had made some tea, and was afraid that it would spoil. She found Helen Adrian lying dead under the steep drop where the steps go down from the last terrace to the beach. She may have fallen over, but it was not the fall that killed her. There were horrible injuries to the head. It had been literally battered in—probably with one of the larger stones. The place is above high water mark, and there are plenty of them lying about. No weapon has been found, but if a stone was used it could have been very easily disposed of. The tide was high between twelve and two last night, and that seems to be the most likely time for the murder to have been committed. Miss Remington says she heard a cry, but she cannot fix the time, except that it was dark, and she tangles the whole thing up by suggesting that what she heard was a seagull, a bat, or a cat—I think she put them forward in that order. Now Marian did not hear anything, but she woke very much startled just about high tide. She heard the water very plainly, and you don't hear it unless the tide is high. I haven't the slightest doubt that it was a cry that waked her, but she didn't actually hear anything, so it's no good as evidence. Everybody else says they didn't hear anything at all. Helen Adrian went out, and Felix Brand went out, but nobody heard them. Helen was found dead at half past seven this morning, and Felix hasn't been found at all."

The busy needles checked for a moment. Miss Silver said, "Dear me!"

"He apparently went out in a swim-suit, slacks, and a sweater—he often went out to bathe like that. Well, the sweater and the slacks have been found pushed in under the bank above high water mark. The sweater is quite horribly stained—the lower part of the right sleeve practically soaked with blood. If he didn't kill Helen Adrian he must have handled the body. Whichever way it was, it looks as if he had stripped and just swum out to sea. He couldn't have got anywhere in a swim-suit, and if he'd meant to try and make a get-away he'd have come back to the house for clothes and money. Whether he killed her or not, he was crazy enough about her to drown himself when she was dead."

Miss Silver coughed.

"You say 'whether he killed her or not.' There is some doubt in your mind?"

He nodded.

"It looks like the plainest of plain cases, but—well, there are one or two things that stick in my throat."

Her needles clicked.

"I shall be interested to hear what they are."

"If I was sure that Felix Brand was the murderer I shouldn't be here. You saw him for yourself. He had the sort of crazy passion for Helen Adrian which could quite easily end up in a case of murder-cum-suicide. That is just what this looks like. But there are one or two things that don't fit in. Marian had an old raincoat down on the beach yesterday. The shingle was damp where the tide had left it. There were a lot of these rugs and old coats—"

"Yes, I was provided with one myself."

He nodded.

"They were taken in afterwards. I carried Marian's. It is kept hanging on one of the pegs in the passage which leads to the door between the two houses. I hung it there. There was a scarf on the peg already—a blue and yellow square which she wears over her hair when it is windy. I took it down in order to hang up the coat, and then put it back again."

"Yes, Mr. Cunningham?"

He went on in the same quiet, even tone.

"The door between the houses is locked on the far side, bolted on the nearer side. It is the same on all three floors. Marian did not go out again, but in the morning when Helen Adrian's body was discovered this raincoat was down on the terrace from which Helen was pushed or fell. There is a seat there, and it was lying on the seat. But the scarf—"

"The scarf, Mr. Cunningham?"

"The blue and yellow square, which I had put back on the same peg, was still there, but it was badly crumpled and stained with blood."

Miss Silver coughed.

"And what deduction do you draw from that?"

He made an abrupt movement.

"It looks like an attempt to involve Marian. Her raincoat down on the terrace. It has her name inside the neckband. Her scarf, which everyone knows, messed up and put back on the peg. What else can it be? But it doesn't tie up with Felix Brand. I can imagine him murdering Helen and swimming out to sea to drown himself afterwards. But I don't see him taking Marian's raincoat down to the terrace for one clue, and messing up her scarf and putting it back for another. Murder and suicide are compatible with a state of reckless passion, but not with this cold-blooded attempt to throw suspicion on somebody else. That's the psychological difficulty. But there's a physical one too. Those doors between the houses are kept locked on one side, bolted on the other. The outside doors and windows on the ground floor were all shut when we came in soon after seven. I am sure that the scarf and raincoat were still there when I went through the hall just before half past ten, because Marian was talking about the doors between the houses and I glanced along the passage. There was a good overhead light, and I am sure I should have noticed if her coat and scarf had not been there. Well then, how could Felix Brand have taken them? How could anyone in the other house have taken them? Or put the scarf back after it was stained?"

Miss Silver coughed.

"Very clear, very lucid," she said. "May I ask whom you suspect?"

He said drily, "Not Marian or her sister."

She coughed again.

"I will neither endorse nor question that."

"Miss Silver!"

She had a faint reproving smile.

"Pray let us avoid coming to conclusions which may be

premature. You have stated the facts. They may be explained in more than one way. For the moment what I want to ask you is this. Just why are you here?"

His manner had become a shade more formal.

"I want to protect Miss Brand."

She was knitting steadily.

"You want to protect her, and you come to me. In what way do you imagine that I can help you?"

He sat up straight, one hand on the arm of his chair.

"I will tell you. I am—very uneasy. I think there is an attempt to involve Marian Brand. I think there may be a money motive behind it. She has recently come in for a considerable sum of money."

"Oh, yes, there has been a good deal of local talk about that. The late Mr. Brand was very well known and respected, I understand. When he left his entire fortune to a niece whom nobody had ever seen, there was bound to be a good deal of comment. Mrs. Lester's maid is a cousin of the Mrs. Bell who works at Cove House, so she was full of it. Her story is, I suppose, correct. Miss Brand was her uncle's sole heiress?"

"Yes. He left her everything. Ina Felton has no share. He distrusted her husband, and he had confidence in Marian. It is not true to say he had never seen her. He did see her once, in circumstances which enabled him to form his own opinion of her character, and he had for some years been receiving reports about her and her sister. He felt that he could trust her, and he did not feel that he could trust Cyril Felton. But if anything were to happen to Marian, half of what he left would go to her sister, and the other half would revert to Felix Brand, his mother, and his aunt."

Miss Silver stopped knitting for a moment. She said, "I see—" in a very thoughtful voice, and then, "Pray go on."

He said,

"I am in a difficulty. Martin Brand didn't trust Cyril Felton.

Marian doesn't trust him at all, and nor do I. I don't want those two girls to be there alone with him. I can't produce any proof, but I am thoroughly uneasy over the whole business. I want to be on the spot, I want to be in the house. I don't want those two girls to be alone, or with Cyril. But I am not in a position to put myself forward. I am quite sure that you know how I am placed. I hope to marry Marian Brand, but we have actually met only three times. It is just one of those things—they can't be explained, and one doesn't want them to be gossiped over. If I were to go and stay there alone, it would certainly set up a lot of talk. I don't want to rush anything. We are not engaged—I have no status. Cyril has gone away—he says to an audition. He'll be back for the week-end, if not before. He hasn't a penny except what he gets out of Marian—" He broke off and looked at her entreatingly. "Miss Silver—will you come and stay at Cove House?"

She said, "Dear me!" Derek's stocking revolved. Her expression was mild and thoughtful.

He felt emboldened to proceed.

"It would, of course, be a professional engagement."

She gave her slight cough.

"As a chaperone, Mr. Cunningham?"

He felt an unwonted embarrassment.

"I've been stupid. I've muddled everything up—put the cart before the horse. The fact is, I am very anxious about Marian, and a good deal concerned about the best way of dealing with the situation."

She smiled indulgently.

"Pray do not think that you have offended me. I understand that your position is a difficult one."

"But I want you to understand something more than that. I want you to understand that I think those two girls are in need of protection. If anything were to happen to Marian,

Ina would be at the mercy of a very unreliable husband. If I must put it quite plainly, I don't trust Cyril Felton, and I want your professional help to see that he doesn't get away with anything."

Miss Siver's smile had faded. She knitted in silence for a time. Then she said,

"If I were to come into this case in my professional capacity I could give no guarantee as to what the result might be. Miss Adrian has been murdered. I cannot undertake to prove that any given person is innocent—or guilty."

"No, no—of course not."

"That must be quite clearly understood. I would like you to consider this in all its aspects. Suppose Mr. Felton to be implicated in this murder—I do not say that he is implicated, but I want you to consider the possibility. Miss Brand and Mrs. Felton will not think that you are doing them a service by exposing him."

Richard Cunningham looked at her very straight and said,

"If he had anything to do with Helen Adrian's death, then he is the person who is trying to implicate Marian. And if he has murdered Helen and is planning to get rid of Marian, how long do you suppose it would be before something happened to Ina? I'm not taking any chances, and—Marian asks you to come."

She took her time before she said, "My niece has a friend coming to stay for a few days. I could leave her. But there is something more to be said. I think I must tell you something which I will ask you to keep to yourself. I shall feel obliged to communicate with the Chief Constable on the subject, but it should not, I think, go any farther except at his discretion."

"You mean I am not to tell Marian?"

She said, "I do not know. I will ask you to be very discreet."

He began to wonder what was coming. And then, prefaced by that slight cough, it came.

"Miss Adrian was being blackmailed. She came to see me in town and asked me to take up the case. I did not see my way to doing so, but I gave her certain advice. She did not take it. I had no idea that she was coming down to Cove House. I came to Farne myself to be with my niece, whose little girl has been ordered sea air after an illness. Yesterday morning, when I was changing some books in the local library, I heard Miss Adrian's name. It was spoken by one of the people whom she had mentioned to me as a possible blackmailer."

"Who was it?"

"It was Mr. Felton."

Richard Cunningham exclaimed.

"Who was he talking to?"

"To his wife. He said, 'Helen Adrian's here, isn't she?' And when Mrs. Felton asked how he knew, he said that he had made it his business to know, and that he had to see her on a professional matter. After which he talked about being very hard up, reflecting angrily on the fact that Miss Marian Brand held the purse-strings, and ending by borrowing all the money Mrs. Felton had with her. He said it would look so bad if he couldn't pay for the lunch they were having together. There had evidently been some quarrel which he was anxious to make up, for he told Mrs. Felton she must make it all right for him to come and stay at Cove House, saying that he hadn't the price of a bed."

Richard Cunningham said,

"Blackmail. That's pretty nasty. You say Helen suspected him?"

Miss Silver inclined her head.

"After I came out of the library I met her quite by accident. She was with Mr. Felix Brand, but she sent him away, and we sat in one of the shelters on the Front and talked. She was extremely frank. She told me that the person who was blackmailing her must be either Mr. Felix Brand or Mr. Felton, since no one else had any knowledge of the incidents upon which the blackmail was based. I told her Mr. Felton was in Farne, and she was very much surprised. Before we parted she told me she really was quite sure that it was Mr. Felton who was blackmailing her. She said it would not be in Mr. Brand's line. She said she had quite made up her mind what she would do. She was going to see Mr. Felton, tell him she knew that the letters she had received were from him, and that she would give him ten pounds down. If he held out for more, she said she would threaten him with the police."

"Did she meet him?"

"That is what we do not know. They certainly met and talked at the picnic, but she had not had any private meeting with him then. You may have noticed that I had a short stroll with her. It was at her instance that I was asked to Cove House, and I wanted to know why she had suggested the invitation. She said she wanted me to see the people there. I told her some of the things I saw, and I gave her some advice. I told her that the whole situation was dangerous, and I advised her to leave and return to town. I offered to see Mr. Felton on her behalf, telling her that I was quite sure he would not be difficult to dispose of. She replied that she would rather take him on herself, adding that she was not afraid of him or of anyone. It was obvious from this that there had been no private meeting between them, but that she meant to effect one. I think that is all I can tell you, Mr. Cunningham."

He said, "She could have met him that night."

The busy needles clicked.

"I think she intended to do so."

There was a pause. Then he said,

"Why should he kill her? If he was blackmailing her he

159

was hoping to get money out of her. I shouldn't have thought—"

"She may have threatened to expose him. She did, in fact, intend to use that threat. All this I shall feel it my duty to communicate to the Chief Constable. Do you still wish me to come to Cove House?"

He met her eyes full and said,

"Yes, I do, Miss Silver."

CHAPTER 24

Before going up to Cove House Miss Silver had some preparations to make. Richard Cunningham left her to them and went back to be firm with Marian Brand.

"She will be here by four o'clock, and whether you like it or not, my dear, I've brought a suitcase, and I'm staying too. I can sleep on the study sofa."

Marian looked at him. She had much ado not to show all the relief she felt. She said gravely,

"There are two spare rooms. I will put you in the one Cyril had."

"Isn't he coming back?"

"Not today, or tomorrow. I don't feel that we can look any farther ahead than that."

When Ethel Burkett came up from the beach Miss Silver was packing a well worn suit-case. She exclaimed, and received an affectionate smile.

"So fortunate that your friend Miss Blundell should be arriving this evening. Really quite providential. It would have distressed me to feel that I was leaving you alone."

"But, Auntie—"

"A professional call. And you will enjoy a tête-à-tête with your friend. I shall not be at any distance, and shall hope to return before Miss Blundell leaves."

Her packing completed and lunch disposed of, she rang up the exchange and gave the Chief Constable of Ledshire's private number. When his familiar voice came on the line she allowed no restless hurry to intrude upon the occasion.

"My dear Randal—"

"Miss Silver! Now where have you dropped from? You don't sound like London."

"No—I'm at Farne with my niece Ethel and her little girl. Such delightful weather. But tell me of yourselves. Rietta is well?"

"Blooming. And the boy is immense. We have begun to call him George."

"And your dear mother? . . . . . . And Isabel—and Margaret?"

He had with these two sisters once shared a schoolroom over which Miss Silver presided. Her voice could still evoke its memories. The delicate spoiled little boy whom she had taken over had outgrown these drawbacks. She would never have admitted to having any favourite among her pupils, but she had remained on terms of close affection with the March family, and during the last few years had been more than once brought into what she herself would have described as professional association with Randal. His feelings for her were those of affection, gratitude, and the deepest respect, with an occasional tinge of impatience. She had a way of cropping up in the middle of a case and disrupting it. The fact that she was so often right did not really make things any better.

As he answered her warm enquiries he could not help wondering whether her call was a purely friendly one. He would like to see her, Rietta would like to see her, and they would both like to exhibit George in the breath-taking performance of pushing himself up on to his feet, staggering three steps, and sitting down bump with a fat face wreathed in smiles. So far the natural man. But the Chief Constable could not help remembering that a rather well-known young woman had just been murdered no more than a mile from Farne. Crisp was investigating the affair. There should, of course, be no connection with Miss Silver, but if there were, he felt sorry for Crisp, who had encountered her before. A most excellent, zealous, and efficient officer—his mouth would always twist a little over the commendation.

Miss Silver's discreet cough came to his ear. The social preliminaries were over.

"I should be glad of an opportunity of talking to you, Randal."

He thought, "Now we're getting down to brass tacks," and said aloud,

"About anything special?"

"About Miss Adrian."

"Don't tell me you are mixed up with that affair!"

"To some extent, Randal. She approached me professionally just before I came down here at the beginning of the week. I did not see my way to undertaking the case. I met her yesterday morning in Farne. We had some further conversation. I was subsequently invited to a picnic that afternoon. I went. I was there for some hours. I met a number of people in whom you will now be interested, and I had another conversation with Miss Adrian in the course of which I advised her to leave at once and go back to town. I have today accepted an invitation to stay at Cove House with Miss Marian Brand."

The reaction of the natural man to this was, "The devil you have!" The Chief Constable suppressed it. After no more than a moment's pause he said,

"I think I had better see you before you go."

162

Miss Silver coughed.

"Thank you, Randal. I think it would be as well. I shall be catching a bus at the station just before four."

He could picture her, neat, shabby, indefatigable, suit-case in one hand, handbag in the other, the flowery chintz affair with her knitting hanging from a wrist. She was probably going to be a nuisance. Crisp was certainly going to be very much annoyed. But when all was said and done, she was the one and only Miss Silver. He said in an affectionate voice,

"You can give the bus a miss. I'll drive you out when we've had our talk. I'm telling Crisp to meet me there. I want to see the lay-out."

An hour later she had told him what she had already told Richard Cunningham, with some additions.

"I do not know if you are aware that Miss Adrian was engaged to be married."

They were in Muriel Lester's bare, bright sitting-room, Miss Silver in the sofa corner, March in the least uncomfortable of the chairs. A narrow strip of orange linen framed the wide window without offering any suggestion that it formed part of a curtain or could contribute to screening the room at night. There was nothing on the walls except distemper, but the narrow mantelshelf supported a writhing torso. There was no clothing, there were no arms or legs, there was no head. Miss Silver regarded it with philosophic detachment, but little Josephine still said "Poor!" whenever it attracted her attention.

March shifted his chair so as not to have to look at it.

"Engaged to be married, was she?"

She was knitting briskly.

"To a Mr. Fred Mount, a well-to-do business man a good deal older than herself. He and his family hold strict views about morality. It was on this account that Miss Adrian would neither go to the police nor take my advice and tell her fiancé the whole story."

163

He looked at her quizzically and said,

"And what was the whole story?"

"I do not know. She did not admit that there had been any-thing between her and Felix Brand, but his feeling was very obvious, and I have no doubt that she had encouraged it. Just at the end she said to me, 'It's no good hanging on to things when they're over, is it?' That was when I took that walk with her during the picnic. She had asked me for my impressions, and I gave them to her for what they were worth."

"And what were they?"

She repeated the words which she had quoted to Richard Cunningham.

" 'Envy, hatred, and malice, and all uncharitableness.' "

"On the part of Felix Brand?"

"I would not say that. He was in a state of jealous passion and despair. She was tormenting him by paying as much at-tention as possible to the other two men. But he was not the only unhappy person there. Mrs. Felton was obviously in a state of deep depression. She was unhappy about her hus-band, about their relationship, about the financial demands he was making on her sister. She hardly spoke or raised her eyes. Penny Halliday was equally unhappy. She has been brought up with Felix Brand, and she loves him with all her heart. She is a young girl, very single-minded and devoted. She has had to stand by and see another woman playing havoc with his health, his career, his whole character."

"It was like that?"

"I think so. He has shown promise as a composer, but he has left everything go for Miss Adrian. Then there is Mr. Felton, an insincere young man a good deal concerned with the impres-sion he wishes to produce. He does not support his wife, and objects to supporting himself if anyone else can be induced to do so. I think there is very little doubt that it was he who was blackmailing Miss Adrian. And there are the two older ladies,

Mrs. Brand and her sister Miss Remington. They are full of resentment at the disposition of Mr. Martin Brand's fortune. Apart from this, Mrs. Brand appears indifferent to the members of her family, whilst Miss Remington's behaviour suggests that she feels an active dislike for them."

He raised his eyebrows.

"My dear Miss Silver!"

" 'Envy, hatred, and malice, and all uncharitableness,' Randal."

There was a pause, during which it was obvious that he was considering what she had said. For her part she continued to knit. After a minute or two he said,

"Helen Adrian was being blackmailed. I think you said there were letters and a telephone call. Did she identify either the writing or the voice on the telephone?"

"The letters were printed, the telephone voice disguised. Her reason for suspecting Cyril Felton was to be found in the subject matter of these communications. Two episodes were referred to, the first at Brighton in May a year ago, the second in June. Miss Adrian told me that Felix Brand and Cyril Felton were the only ones who knew of these episodes, and she did not think that blackmailing was in Felix's line."

"The episodes were damaging?"

Miss Silver coughed.

"In the first she arrived with Mr. Brand, who was her accompanist, to find that the friend with whom they were to stay had been called away but had left her flat at their disposal. They stayed there for the week-end. There was a professional engagement involved."

"Well, there need have been no harm in that."

"She declared that there was not, or in the June episode, when she and Felix Brand were cut off by the tide and were obliged to stay there all night. They had gone out to swim by moonlight, and when they came back to the house in the

165

morning it was merely supposed that they had been out for an early dip. But she told Cyril Felton—"

March raised his eyebrows.

"She seems to have been on pretty intimate terms with him."

"I think so, Randal."

He said, "Well, none of this seems to give grounds for any very serious blackmail."

"I agree. But you have to remember that Mr. Mount is rich, strict, middle-aged, and jealous. Miss Adrian was nervous about her health. She had a delicate throat, a very serious thing for a singer. She made no secret of the fact that she wished to be married to a man who could provide for her. In the ordinary way she would, I think, have snapped her fingers at Cyril Felton, but she was nervous of a possible threat to her marriage. She told me Cyril would take ten pounds to hold his tongue. What she meant to do was to leave Cove House this morning, meet her fiancé in town, and tell him that she was willing to marry him without delay. Once they were married, I think she felt quite confident that she could dispose of any further attempt at blackmail."

"She was going to leave Cove House this morning?"

"Yes, I think so."

"And she intended to have an interview with Felton before she left?"

"Yes, Randal."

He said in a thoughtful voice,

"I wonder if she did have that interview."

CHAPTER 25

For the second day running Miss Silver arrived at Cove House in time for tea. She was glad to avail herself of the lift which Randal March had offered, but, like Mrs. John Gilpin, she arranged for the conveyance to stop somewhat short of its destination—not, as in the case of the eighteenth-century lady, because she would not have the neighbours think her proud, but because she considered it unnecessary to advertize the fact that she had driven out from Farne with the Chief Constable. She therefore allowed him to precede her, and then walked leisurely in between the rough pillars at the gate and deposited her suit-case on the mat before using the heavy old knocker on the right-hand front door.

Once arrived, she proceeded to settle down and become part of the household. From the study windows the Chief Constable was observed to emerge from the glass door of the drawing-room in the other house and, accompanied by Inspector Crisp, to proceed across the lawn to the steps descending to the cove. Sometime after his return he rang the front door bell on this side and asked to see Miss Brand and Mrs. Felton.

Miss Silver, offering to leave the room, was invited to remain. He asked them no more than a few questions, relating chiefly to such small points as the time of their return from the shore and the locking up of the house. Marian replied that they had come in between seven and a quarter past, and as it was turning chilly, she had herself shut the doors and windows.

"When you say shut, Miss Brand, do you mean that they were locked? I see you have the same glass door into the garden that they have in the next house."

She said, "Yes—it was locked. I'll show you."

She jumped up, went to the open door, and drew it to. As the handle turned it drove an iron bolt into a prepared socket, an old-fashioned arrangement which took him back to the house which his mother had had in his schoolroom days.

He said, "I see. And the front door?"

"Eliza will know about that. It was locked when I let Mr. Cunningham out at half past ten."

"And you locked it after him?"

"Oh, yes."

Eliza, sent for, asserted that the front door had been locked from the time the party went down to the beach. She didn't hold with leaving it open, and always turned the key if she was alone in the house.

"And the door to the kitchen—it's at the side, isn't it?"

"It was locked."

The next question was addressed to everyone there.

"Then there was no door or window open on the ground floor after you came up from the beach?"

Marian said, "No—it was getting cold."

To which Eliza added that she had shut the upstairs windows a good half hour before.

"And the doors between the two houses?"

Marian answered this.

"They are kept bolted. Until today they hadn't been opened since we came. Eliza will tell you the same."

Eliza told him.

Ina Felton was leaning back in one of the big comfortable chairs. She looked small and frail. Her dark hair appeared to melt into the brown leather upholstery. Her face was white against it. She had not spoken at all, but when March asked

168

her if she agreed with the others she found an exhausted voice and said, "Yes." Just the one word, but it sounded as if it was too much trouble to say. He thought the girl was ill, and reflected that Miss Silver would look after her.

A few questions about Marian Brand's raincoat and scarf elicited no more than he already knew. The coat had been down on the beach, but the scarf left hanging on its peg by the door through to the other house. The bolted door. Richard Cunningham had brought the coat in and hung it up on the same peg as the scarf at a quarter past seven. In the morning the coat was on the seat near the place from which Helen Adrian had fallen. The scarf was still on the peg, but most horribly stained with blood. And all the house was shut. Not a door had been opened when Mrs. Woolley ran up screaming from the bottom terrace to say that Miss Adrian was dead.

When this point had been established the Chief Constable got up and went away.

Miss Silver was no stranger to an atmosphere of unhappiness and suspense. It had often been her professional duty to move amongst those who had sustained some shock of terror or of grief. She had sat at many a table where members of the same household looked at one another in fear and looked away again in haste lest they should see what they could not afterwards forget. She had a fund of quiet small talk which served to mitigate these occasions. She knew how to impart a soothing sense of the commonplace. Her presence made a small oasis of cheerfulness and afforded relief from strain.

Before the evening was over she had come to comfortable terms with Eliza over the desirability of inducing Penny and Ina to have a good drink of hot milk and get off to bed.

"Which if you'll take on Mrs. Felton, I'll go in next door and see to Penny. They haven't eaten enough to keep a mouse alive since it happened, and we don't want illness in the house on top of everything else. I can stand over Penny till

169

I get it done, because I've had her from a child, but I think you'd be best for Mrs. Felton. She just keeps on saying, 'No,' or 'Let me alone,' to Miss Marian and me, but you've a kind of a firm way with you, and I think if you was just to walk right in and not take no for an answer—"

Ina drank the milk because she didn't like to be rude, and because it was less trouble than going on saying no. She dropped asleep after it, and could not remember that she had dreamed, only there was a crushing sense of fear that went with her into her sleep.

Rightly concluding that Miss Brand and Mr. Cunningham did not really require the society of a third person, Miss Silver proceeded to pay a call of condolence next door. This visit may be considered as an instance of the power of character to triumph over environment.

It was easy to see that her presence was not desired. Mrs. Brand sat blankly immobile with a newspaper on her lap. She did not read it, she did not turn a page. She just sat there and made no attempt to talk. Miss Remington, on the other hand, was voluble. It was indeed difficult to imagine any circumstance which would reduce her to silence. She rehearsed the events of the day, repeating what Mrs. Woolley had said, what she had felt like when she heard her say it, what they had all felt, said, done, from Inspector Crisp to "poor little Penny who is quite crushed. No stamina, no courage, no will-power. Now I am sure you have noticed that about the young people of the day. I don't know whether it was the war, or what, but I am sure you must have noticed it. They simply cannot confront an emergency."

Miss Silver said mildly that she had not noticed it. She had produced Derek's stocking and was knitting comfortably.

Cassy Remington gave a shrill protesting cry.

"No stamina at all! The least strain and they give way! Look at Ina Felton! She has collapsed in the most ridiculous manner.

She hardly knew Miss Adrian—unless, of course, there was something going on that we don't know about. But I suppose the police will make full enquiries. I wouldn't like to accuse her of anything—you must understand that. Then there's Penny. No one can pretend that she had any affection for Helen Adrian. In fact quite the reverse—we all know that. But she is just giving way. I'm sure if I have told her once that it is her duty to rouse herself, I have told her fifty times. But no, she just gives way—goes off to her room and shuts herself up there."

Miss Silver coughed.

"It is sometimes better to leave people alone after a shock."

Miss Cassy jingled her chain in a contemptuous manner.

"All these young people are the same. Look at Felix! He loses his head over this girl and rushes off to drown himself. Most selfish, most inconsiderate! My sister and I have this dreadful tragedy happening in our house, and we do not collapse—we behave with dignity, we carry on. Nobody pampers us."

Miss Silver continued to knit. She murmured that it was all very sad, very distressing.

Cassy Remington sent her a darting glance.

"Half an hour ago I met Eliza Cotton going up to Penny's room with a cup of hot milk. Pampering I call it! And how she has the face to come over here leaving us the way she did—"

Miss Silver murmured in a non-committal manner which did not soothe. There was a toss of the head with its well-arranged waves.

"Not that our house is our own in any way at present." She repeated the last words with malice. "Not in *any* way. I'm sure the police walk in and out as if the whole place belonged to them. That horrid Inspector Crisp was here again just as we were sitting down to tea. And brought the Chief Constable! And there they were, out and down to the cove, and up on every floor, looking at the doors going through to

171

the other side of the house, and Crisp going round to open them, though what it's got to do with them how many locks and bolts and bars there are, I'm sure I can't see. I may be stupid—I suppose I am—''—the head was tossed again—''but I can't see what a purely domestic arrangement like that has got to do with the police. I'm sure it's bad enough having one's own niece bolting doors against us as if we were a lunatic asylum or a menagerie of wild beasts!''

Mrs. Brand came out of her silence with a "Really, Cassy!" Her voice was heavy with resentment. She said,

"Marian Brand is my niece by marriage only. She is your second cousin twice removed. The houses were originally two. They have now been divided again.''

Cassy Remington's colour rose to an angry flush.

"Oh, if you like it, Florence, there's no more to be said. I'm sure I have no desire to claim relationship with Marian and Ina—or perhaps you think I should speak of them as Miss Brand and Mrs. Felton.''

Florence Brand made no reply. Her large pale face showed nothing. Presently, however, she intervened with a remark about Miss Silver's knitting and Cassy Remington's complaints were interrupted.

Miss Silver stayed for an hour, and had managed to draw Mrs. Brand into a slight show of interest over a pattern for long-sleeved vests and the address of a shop where the wool suitable for making them could be bought. It transpired that Florence had always worn wool next to the skin, and had now arrived at measurements which made it practically impossible for her to procure the necessary underwear. She got as far as saying that she might have some wool upstairs in the box-room, and Miss Silver offered to help her look for it in the morning.

CHAPTER 26

Penny lay in bed in the attic room. She had drunk the milk which Eliza brought her, just as she had taken the soup and the lightly boiled egg which had been presented to her for her supper. If she refused, and for as long as she went on refusing, Eliza would stay. She loved Eliza, but she wanted to be alone, so she drank the milk and the soup and ate the egg, and Eliza patted her and called her "my lamb," and presently she went away.

She went through into the next house by the door on its attic floor, and when Penny heard her shoot the bolts behind her she got out of bed and locked her own door. Nothing was less likely than that either of the aunts would come up. The stair was ladder-steep for one thing, and they wouldn't be interested for another. The thought of Aunt Florence sitting immobile at the foot of her bed and looking at her with bulging eyes, or of Aunt Cassy fidgeting and jingling and saying things about Felix, was just pure nightmare. The sort in which you want to scream and run, and there isn't anywhere to run to.

She locked her door and lay down again. The bed was close up to the window and she could look out over the sea. She lay there watching it. She couldn't see the other side of the cove. She couldn't see the place where the steps came down and Helen Adrian had fallen and died. Her view began where the fine shingle changed to sand. The tide was out. Dry sand, wet sand, and shoaling water. Rock, and pool, and orange seaweed. The sky losing its blue, paling before it darkened.

Time went by. No one came near her. The tide turned. There were sounds in the house below—Cassy Remington's voice, Florence Brand's heavy step, the sound of water running in the bathroom, the sound of doors opening and shutting, and, at last, silence settling in the house.

Penny waited for a long time. Then she got up and dressed herself—stockings and shoes, her old thick skirt, Felix's old shrunk sweater, an old tweed coat. She was cold with the bitter chill of grief. The shoes were sand-shoes, they would make no noise.

She went down the attic stair to the landing, and from there to the hall without making any sound at all. She moved in the silence without jarring it. No one could possibly have heard her pass from the hall to the drawing-room. The chairs were all still there in the dark, turned from their usual places to face the table behind which Inspector Crisp had sat and questioned them. Penny could see the room as if it was full of light. She could see them all sitting there. She could hear Florence Brand saying, "Felix is not my son." She could see the constable from Farne coming up the steps from the garden with a bundle of clothes—grey slacks, and a sweater stained with Helen Adrian's blood. The picture was there in every detail, bright and clear. The room was dark about her, and her eyes told her that it was dark, but the picture of the lighted room was clear in her mind. She could cross to the glass door and open it without so much as brushing against one of the chairs which looked towards the Inspector's empty seat.

When she opened the door and came down the two steps to the paved path at the back of the house she had a sense of escape. It was dark outside, but not with the enclosed darkness of the house, and it was cool, but not with the heavy chill of the room she had left. There was no breeze, only a faint movement of the air setting in from the sea with the flowing tide.

She went across the lawn and sat on the stone steps which went down to the next terrace. The tide was coming up fast. She sat there listening to the movement of the water. All day she had been calling Felix. That was why she had wanted to be alone. Everything in her called to him. Now perhaps he would come.

There was a story which she had heard Eliza tell when she was a child. She hadn't been meant to hear it. Eliza wouldn't have told it if she had known that Penny was outside the kitchen window, pressed up against the wall listening. It was an old story from Eliza's mother's side of the family, and it was about a woman who had called a dead man up out of the sea. There was a lot about charms and a full moon and the turn of the tide that went by her, but some of it she never forgot. She was remembering it now. A fine summer afternoon and the sun hot on the wall. Eliza's voice coming out through the open kitchen window as she talked to her friend. "Sarah Bethel was the woman's name." Penny always remembered that part, because of Bethel being in the Bible. And that bit at the end, "So she waited on the turn of the tide like the wise woman told her—'He went with the tide and he'll come with the tide, if so be he comes at all, and no good counting on it.' But he did. So my mother told me, and it was her mother told her, and she knew the woman well. The tide was far out and the moon rising, and with the turn of the tide he came. First she knew of it something splashed in the shallow water, and then she saw him black against the moon. It was one of those big full moons, as yellow as an orange. She saw the shape of him against it, and the splashing came on up to the edge of the water and stopped there. Sarah Bethel said she didn't know whether she was dead or alive with the fear that came on her. She stood where she was, and the splashing stopped, and there was a darkness between her and the moon. She couldn't see nor she couldn't hear.

175

And when she could move again she come away, running and falling and catching her breath, and beating on the first door she came to be taken in." That was the story—a full moon, and the turn of the tide, and a dead man coming up from the sea. And Sarah Bethel who called him and turned coward when he came.

Penny had always thought very little of Sarah Bethel. She didn't think about her now. She thought about Felix. If he would come to her by any means, in any way, from any depth, how wide her arms would be to welcome him! She let her love flow out. It felt as strong and resistless as the tide that was coming in from the deep places of the sea, only it was warm and comforting, and the sea was cold. If Felix came to her out of the salt cold of the sea, she felt as if her love was strong enough to warm him and bring him back to life again. It was so strong, and warm, and living that it took away the pain which had been part of her all through that dreadful day. Whether he was dead or alive, nothing could stop her loving him.

The sea moved below her. It was over the shingle now. She thought about Sarah Bethel and the footsteps that had come from the sea.

But when the footsteps came they did not come from that side at all. They came from the other side of the house, they came from the road. If she had not been strained to the limit of what is possible and a little beyond it, she would hardly have heard them. They were faint, and far, and stumbling, but she felt the beat of them as if they were falling on her heart. She ran across the lawn and round the house and out on to the road, and heard the footsteps halting and coming on again, halting and coming on. The road was brimmed with shadow. Someone came out of the dark with a flagging step. Penny ran to him and caught him in her arms, and said his name as if she couldn't be tired of saying it.

"Felix—Felix—Felix—"

He was cold to her touch. He leaned on her and shuddered, and said in a lifeless whisper,

"I've—come—back—"

She held him with all her strength and with all her love. The only words that she could get were, first his name, and then,

"You're cold—you're cold—you're cold—"

He said, "Yes." And then, "Let's come in."

She took him round the house and through the dark drawing-room and hall to the kitchen. There was an old shapeless wicker chair which Mactavish liked to sit in because it sagged in the middle. As soon as Penny put on the light Felix let himself down into it and sat there, leaning forward over his knees and staring down upon the floor.

Whilst she was stirring up the fire, putting in sticks and coal, and a drip out of the paraffin bottle to make a blaze, he neither moved nor spoke. She put water to heat, made a steaming cup of cocoa, and beat an egg into it, but he didn't seem to know what was going on. He was wearing somebody else's clothes—a pair of corduroy trousers that were too short and an old pullover which strained across his chest.

She came to him with the cup of cocoa in her hand and kneeled down in front of him, setting it on the floor.

"Nice hot drink, darling."

When she had said it half a dozen times he said, "What's the use?" and began to shudder, so that his whole lean body was shaken.

Penny got up. She wasn't going to have her cocoa spilled. She got another cup and poured off about a quarter of what was in the first one. Then she knelt down again and held the second cup to his lips.

"Drink it up, darling. It will do you good."

His teeth chattered on the rim, but she got the quarter

cupful down, and the rest was easier. When both the cups were empty she said in an accusing voice,

"When did you have anything to eat?"

"I don't know—this morning—"

She was still kneeling there in front of him. She said, "Silly!" And he made an abrupt movement.

"Don't!"

"Felix—"

He caught at her then, holding her roughly, desperately, his face against her shoulder, his sobs shaking them both. After a little she began to murmur the foolish loving things you say to a hurt child.

"Darling, don't cry. It's Penny—tell Penny. I won't let anyone hurt you—I won't let them. Tell me—darling—only tell me. I know you didn't—"

That was the most dreadful moment of all, because he lifted his head and said in a convulsed voice,

"Didn't I?"

Penny felt as if her heart would stop, but it didn't. She held him tight and said,

"Of course you didn't! Why did you go away? I thought you were dead."

He said in a confused way,

"I don't know—I wanted—to be—"

She thought he was going to say "dead," but it didn't come. He hid his face against her again. The sobbing had ceased, but sometimes she could hardly hear the words. It was more as if she felt them, as she felt the labouring breath and every now and then the deep shudder that shook him in her arms.

"I didn't sleep—I couldn't. It was all over. She was going away—she was going to marry Mount—it was finished. As soon as it began to be light I went down to the cove. I was going to swim right out. I think I meant to come back—I don't know. But when I saw her—lying there—"

She had to hold him whilst the agonized shudder passed. "You found her dead?"

He said in an exhausted voice,

"I think so—" Then, with an effort at control, "When I'm telling you like this, I know that I couldn't sleep, and that I went down to bathe, and found her. But when I start from the other end and look back, sometimes—I can only see myself kneeling there, touching her—and the blood—" His voice left off.

She held him until the rigid muscles relaxed.

"You didn't hurt her. Darling, you wouldn't hurt anyone."

He said, "Don't! I've got a foul temper—but I didn't touch her—I know that—really. As long as I'm sane I know it—only every now and then I feel as if I was going over the edge—and then I'm not sure."

"That's the shock, darling. It was a most dreadful shock. I'm going to get you something to eat."

"I couldn't!"

"There's some good stew. It won't take a moment to heat, and you can go on telling me what happened."

He did not realize how much of his burden she had lifted, but he was able to find the relief of words.

"I only thought about getting away. I wanted to get out of it all. I meant to swim right out and go on swimming till I went down. I stuffed my clothes in under the bank and waded in, and then—I just went on—swimming—"

When she had put the saucepan on the fire she came back to him.

"I thought you were drowned."

He said, "Better if I had been. They'll think—I did it." Then, with a sudden jerk of the head, "Who did?"

"They don't know."

"They'll think it was me."

"They'll find out. Go on telling me. You swam—and then—"

179

"There was a chap in a yacht—just himself and a boy. I was about finished. They got me in. A nice chap. He lent me some things—money to get home with. He landed me along the coast. I thought I would wait till it was dark before I came back. I walked from Ledstow."

"And nothing to eat all day?"

She jumped up and went to stir the saucepan. Mrs. Woolley made a marvellous stew. It was beginning to give off a savoury smell. All at once Felix was aware of tearing hunger.

CHAPTER 27

At a little after nine next morning Inspector Crisp was on the line to the Chief Constable.

"Felix Brand has come back, sir. Turned up last night and rang us up this morning."

"Has he made any statement?"

"A lot of cock-and-bull stuff about finding her dead and swimming off into the blue. I should say it was a pretty clear case."

March said, "I don't know. Where are you speaking from?"

"Cove House."

"Well, just hold everything. I think I'll come along."

Crisp had a black frown as he hung up the receiver. Nature had made it easy for his bristling eyebrows to meet. They met now, making a lowering bar above alert and angry eyes. He was a zealous and efficient officer, but afflicted with an acute sense of class-consciousness. The Chief Constable came from the class of which he nourished an ineradicable suspicion. He had been to what the Inspector called a posh school.

People who went to posh schools hung together and made a common front against those who had been educated by the state or, as in his own case, at an endowed Grammar School. Ledbury Grammar School was an old and famous foundation. He was prepared to maintain its excellence at any time and to all comers. It even boasted an old school tie. But he nevertheless resented the fact that there were people who had been to Eton, Harrow, Winchester, and the rest. He considered that they possessed an unfair advantage, and that if he didn't stick up for himself it would be used to down him. The Chief Constable would try and get this young fellow off if he could. If he had come of an honest working-class family, there wouldn't have been so much of that "Hold everything till I come." In which he wronged Randal March, who was of a just and cautious temperament and constantly endeavoured to do his duty without fear or favour. On his side, he esteemed his Inspector's zeal and ability, but thought him inclined to be biased and more than a little apt to jump to conclusions. The Superintendent at Ledlington, usually a restraining influence, was at the moment laid up with a chill.

Arrived at Cove House, March interviewed the Inspector, the drawing-room being placed at their disposal by Miss Remington, who had so much to say that it was some time before they could get down to business.

"I really must apologize for the room. The fact is we don't use it—only Felix for his music—and the Inspector yesterday when he interviewed us all, and then it was just left. I'm sure if we had known you were coming—"

"It doesn't matter at all."

"And we are short-handed—only dailies—so inconvenient. And Felix coming back in the middle of the night—most inconsiderate. If Penny hadn't happened to be up, we should all have been disturbed, and I daresay I shouldn't have got off again—I am an excessively light sleeper."

"Do you know what time it was when he came home, Miss Remington?"

She tossed her head. The household might be upset, but those careful waves of hers were just as they had come from the hairdresser's hand. He found himself entertaining a faint speculation as to whether Miss Cassy wore a wig. Surely any hair that grew on the human head would become disturbed by all this fidgeting and tossing. Even her voice jerked as she said,

"We didn't even know he was back till this morning. Creeping into the house like that! I don't really know when I had such a shock."

"But I thought you said you didn't hear him."

"Not last night. But I did this morning, and I could hardly believe my ears. And of course we thought he was drowned—what else was there to think? And indeed it might have been better!" There was another toss, and a very sharp one. "Well, I suppose I mustn't say that, but he's been nothing but a trouble always. He is not really my nephew, you know. Alfred Brand was a widower when my sister married him, and of course we have always done what we could, but he has a very difficult nature."

March got rid of her in the end. His comment when the door had been closed behind her was not what she might have expected. She had a pleasant picture of herself as a pretty, attractive woman being efficient, being helpful, being frank. Oh, yes, above all things frank. One should always be frank with the police.

What March was actually saying at the moment was,

"One of the rats to leave a sinking ship."

Crisp said, "That's right. And the other one's just as bad—the stepmother. Tumbling over each other, they were, to say he wasn't any relation of theirs. But it shows what they think. There's no doubt he did it."

182

March had seated himself. He looked like any country gentleman just come in from a morning walk with his dogs—rough tweeds, an open-air tan, thick hair burnt brown, eyes which looked blue against the ruddy brown of his face. He said,

"He's made a statement? Let's see it."

It was in Felix Brand's own hand, and it set down what he had said to Penny, and in very much the same words. He had gone out to bathe. He found Helen Adrian lying dead. He had handled the body to see if there was any spark of life. And then he had stripped and swum out to sea, not meaning to come back.

When March had finished reading Crisp said,

"The bit about the yacht is all right. I've been on the phone to the owner. Stockbroker of the name of Gaskell taking a long weekend from town—father a retired doctor living at Belmouth. He keeps the yacht there. He picked Brand up like he says, a couple of miles out and just about finished."

March gave him a long steady look.

"You know, the rest of it might have happened just like he said it did. If he came on her in the state she was, the shock might have been quite enough to send him off his balance. He says he meant to swim out and not come back. He's a highly strung chap—it might take him that way."

The Inspector bristled visibly. His expression became that of a terrier who sees a chance that his lawful rat may escape him.

"And who killed her, sir?"

March's look did not change.

"I don't feel satisfied that it was Felix Brand. I'd like to see him. But I'd like to see the girl first—Penny Halliday. She let him in, you say?"

He remembered seeing Penny the day before, shocked, frozen, monosyllabic. When she came in now he would hardly have recognized her. She had come alive again. He asked her to sit down, and she did so, her colour stirring under the smooth brown skin, her eyes on his face, bright and brown as peat-water.

"Miss Halliday, will you tell me just what happened last night."

"Felix came back."

"Were you expecting him?"

The eyes clouded.

"I thought he was dead."

"You let him in, didn't you? How did you know he was there?"

"I couldn't sleep—I was outside—I heard him coming up the road."

"What sort of state was he in?"

"He was—done. He had walked from Ledstow—he hadn't had anything to eat all day."

"Did he tell you what had happened?"

She looked at him steadily.

"Yes."

"Will you tell me what he said."

She repeated it, hardly varying a word from the written statement in his hand.

"You have seen what he wrote down for Inspector Crisp?"

"No. He hadn't written anything before the Inspector came."

Crisp said, "That's right, sir."

March went on.

"You were brought up with Felix Brand?"

"Yes."

"And you are very fond of him?"

Her colour ebbed rather than rose. When she said, "Yes," it was as if she was making a response in church.

"Do you think you would know whether he was speaking the truth?"

"Felix doesn't tell lies."

"Would you know if he did?"

"He doesn't—ever. He's telling the truth."

"He was very much exhausted when you brought him in?"
She took a long breath and said, "Dreadfully."

"When he talked to you about Miss Adrian, did he break down?"

Her eyes were bright with tears and anger.

"Of course he did! He cared for her—he found her like that. Wouldn't anyone break down?"

He said, "Yes, I think so. I just wanted to know. Was it while he was in this state that he told you about finding Miss Adrian's body?"

"Yes, it was."

"And you thought he was speaking the truth?"

Her colour came up brightly.

"I know he was. Mr. March, I do really know it. If you had heard him, you would know it too. Felix couldn't hurt anyone like that. And I'm not saying wouldn't, I'm saying couldn't. He *couldn't* hurt anyone like that. They'll tell you he has a temper, and it's true, but it's the quick, flaring-up kind. He frowns and looks as if he could murder you, but it doesn't mean a thing. Everybody could tell you that. But they don't. They tell you about his having a temper. But they don't tell you how he climbed the Bell cliff in a gale to save a puppy that had fallen over and got stuck on a ledge. Everyone who knew Felix—really *knew* him—would tell you just what I'm telling you. And I'll tell you something more. If Helen Adrian had got him so that he really didn't know what he was doing, he might have pushed her over the edge of that place where she fell. He didn't do it, and he wouldn't do it, but I can just imagine that he might have done it. There are things you

185

might just do if you were pushed farther than you can bear, but there are things that you know you *couldn't* do whatever happened or however hard you were pushed, and nothing in the world would have made Felix go down those steps and beat Helen Adrian's head in the way it was. If Felix had pushed her he'd have been sorry in a moment, and if the fall had killed her he wouldn't have wanted to live. He couldn't possibly have taken up a stone and beaten her with it."

March said, "Thank you, Miss Halliday. I just wanted to know how it struck you. You are a very good friend."

She said, "It's true, Mr. March—it's all quite true. I haven't made anything up."

He let her go after that.

CHAPTER 28

Crisp said, "I could have told you she'd back him up. She's fond of him—it sticks out all over her."

"Oh, quite. But she was speaking the truth, you know."

"Oh, I daresay he put up a tale to her. He would of course. And all that about pushing her over but not beating her head in—well, it doesn't mean a thing. When a man's crazy jealous and lets himself go he can't always stop himself. You get a case like that any day in the papers, and the chap says he doesn't know what happened. There's a bit of evidence came up last night from Farne. There was a girl and a young fellow up on the cliffs round about half past six the evening before the murder—Ted Hollins and Gloria Payne. Gloria Payne is a sister of Sergeant Jackson's wife. She told her sister what she and Ted had heard, and when Mrs. Jackson told her husband, he brought the two of them along to see me."

"Well?"

"They say they were up on the cliffs between Farne and the cove. Ted is a mechanic at Waley's garage in Farne. He's a very respectable boy, and he and Gloria have been going together since they were kids. They were half way down one of those combes that lead to the beach. They heard a man's voice coming from down below, very angry. There was a woman talking too. They didn't hear what was said, only the voices—the man angry and the woman talking back at him. But what she said at the end they both of them heard quite plain, and it was, 'All right—go on and do it! You've said you're going to often enough. Go on and murder me if you feel like it!' And the man said, 'I will when I'm ready—you needn't worry about that,' and went off in the direction of the cove."

"Did they see him?"

"No, they didn't—didn't see either of them. The cliff cuts under there. But it's all shingle, and they could hear him going off."

"You can't identify him with Felix Brand on that."

Crisp said stubbornly,

"It's a private beach. It belongs to Cove House. The whole lot of them were out in the cove having this picnic. Mrs. Brand and Miss Remington both say that Miss Silver and Miss Adrian took a stroll together, and shortly after they returned Miss Silver got up to go. She caught the bus that passes Cove House at six-thirty. Meanwhile, they say, Miss Adrian strolled off again—this time with Felix Brand. They went round the next point in the direction of Farne and were out of sight for the best part of twenty minutes. Then Brand came back alone and in a very bad temper, Miss Adrian following about a quarter of an hour later. Miss Remington says it was quite obvious that they had quarrelled."

"Very anxious to hang her nephew, isn't she?"

"Very anxious to explain that he isn't her nephew," said Crisp grimly. "Same with Mrs. Brand. He's only her stepson, and she's taking care to let everyone know it. The fact is he's one of those moody chaps—artistic temperament and all that, and they've got fed up with him. I grant you Miss Remington is spiteful—sticks out all over her. But she's telling the truth about Brand and Miss Adrian going off for this walk. She didn't know there had been anything overheard, and it all fits in. By what Gloria and Ted say they were out on the cliffs by a quarter to seven, and that was when they heard the voices from the beach. It all fits in. I'd say there was enough for an arrest."

March shook his head.

"You say it all fits in, but it doesn't. I don't think he did it. To start with, we know she was going to marry someone else. She told Miss Silver she had made up her mind to leave Cove House in the morning and tell her fiancé she was ready to marry him as soon as he liked. Presumably that is what she told Brand while they were out of sight of the others for those twenty minutes. I can well believe that he made a blazing row about it on the lines reported by Ted and Gloria, after which he flung off and came home alone. What I find difficult to believe is that, after all that, she slipped out of the house in the middle of the night and went down to that lonely terrace to meet him. Why on earth should she? She had had her scene with him and got it over. They were staying in the same house. If she had wanted to speak to him she could have done so. From supper-time till after they went to bed he was here in the drawing-room taking out his feelings on the grand piano. By all accounts nobody else uses this room. She had only to come to him here, and they could have a reconciliation, or another quarrel, or whatever they wanted. She wasn't romantic or passionate. She was a hard-headed

188

girl with a keen eye to the main chance. I simply don't see her going down to that terrace in the middle of the night to meet Felix Brand.''

"There's no saying what girls will do," said Crisp in a resentful tone. He was thinking of Ethel Sibley who had walked out on him and married an ironmonger. It was five years ago, but it still rankled. In moments of gloom he would tot up what he had spent taking her to the pictures. Only last week he had run into her in Ledbury High Street looking prettier than ever, with the twins in a double pram. That was the sort of thing that made you feel what a much better world it would be if there didn't have to be women in it messing things up.

March said, "Oh, well, that's how it looks to me. But putting all that on one side, there's this matter of Marian Brand's raincoat and scarf. I don't see my way to arresting Felix Brand until we've got it cleared up. Richard Cunningham is positive that he brought the coat up from the beach soon after seven and hung it on the same peg with the scarf. He is quite positive that the scarf was there. Everyone next door is quite positive that from that time onwards all the doors and windows in the house were shut, with the exception of bedroom windows opened when the occupants were ready for bed. With this exception everything was still shut when Mrs. Woolley gave the alarm next morning. How did Marian Brand's raincoat get down on to the terrace where it was found? How did her scarf become stained with blood? And after being stained, how did it get back upon the peg where Jackson found it within an hour of the alarm being given? Felix Brand couldn't have taken the raincoat or the scarf. He had no access to them. No one on this side of the house had access to them. In the confusion after the alarm had been given I suppose it is just possible that someone could have slipped in next door with the scarf and hung it up where it was found, but it certainly wasn't Felix Brand, who was miles away at the time on the yacht that had picked him up."

Crisp was an honest man. It was not in him to suppress evidence however little he liked it. He said in an unwilling voice, "That scarf couldn't have been put back after the alarm. It was put back with the blood on it wet enough to soak into the plaster round the peg. It's a dark corner, but if you shine a torch on it you'll see for yourself."

March said, "Well, there you are—we can't arrest Felix Brand. When is that fellow Felton coming back?"

"Felton? We've got his address. We can get him back."

"Yes, I think so. He was blackmailing Helen Adrian. She went to Miss Silver about it, as I told you. There's no absolute proof that the blackmailer was Felton, but she was convinced of it herself, and it seems likely enough. One of the last things she said to Miss Silver was that she meant to have it out with Cyril. She was going to offer him ten pounds down and tell him that once she was married he could do as he liked, but her husband would break his head if he bothered her. Miss Silver was trying to dissuade her from seeing Felton herself, but she had planned the interview and was determined to have it. Now when was it going to take place? Felton wasn't in the same house. He wasn't at her beck and call. She couldn't see him in the presence of his wife or sister-in-law. She couldn't ask him over here and have a private interview with the two old ladies watching and Felix Brand on the premises. She would really have a reason for leaving the house in the middle of the night to meet Cyril Felton, and no particular reason for being afraid of doing so. There were no passionate feelings involved—it was just a commercial transaction. It seems to me it would be quite in character for her to meet him like that."

Crisp made a sharp movement. He wanted to have his

190

say—he had been wanting to have it for some time. He came out with it now.

"You're saying he killed her. Where's his motive? More likely if it was the other way round. I've never heard of the blackmailer doing the killing."

"She told Miss Silver that if he gave any trouble, she was going to threaten him with the police. You've seen him—I haven't. Is he the kind that might panic and lose his head?"

"Goodlooking young fellow, and knows it. Never done a stroke of work he could help, I should say. Fancy manners. I can believe the blackmailing part of it all right. He's the sort that must have money, and don't care for the sweat of earning it."

March said,

"That's the sort that might panic and hit out. It wouldn't have been planned. Say she threatened him. He pushed her, she went over the drop. And then he went down and finished her off for fear of what she would say. It looks to me as if it had been like that."

"What about Miss Brand's raincoat and scarf?"

March was frowning.

"Easy, as far as having access to them goes. He had only to fetch them, leave the coat lying across the back of the seat, get the stain on the scarf, and bring it back to where he took it from."

Crisp looked up, brightly intent.

"And why would he want to do that?"

March said drily, "If Miss Brand were out of the way, his wife would come in for a very considerable sum of money which was left to her sister by the late Mr. Martin Brand."

"Mrs. Felton didn't get any of it?"

"No. I gather that Mr. Brand hadn't much opinion of Cyril. He left everything to his niece Marian."

Crisp jerked a nod.

191

"I remember hearing something about it—it made a lot of local talk. The next-door people didn't get anything either— it all went to the one niece. It's the sort of thing that makes bad feeling in a family. But if Miss Marian Brand was out of the way?"

"Then Mrs. Felton gets half, and the next-door people get half between them. Miss Silver is my informant. She always knows everything. And Marian Brand confirmed it to me yesterday, so it's all according to Cocker."

"Then all the relations on both sides of the house would have some sort of a motive for putting a murder on Miss Marian Brand."

March said very drily indeed,

"But only someone on her own side of the house could have taken her coat and her scarf to the scene of the crime and put the bloodstained scarf back again."

CHAPTER 29

Cyril Felton came back on Sunday morning. He had spent all the money with which Marian had provided him, and returned with a hangover to the only place where he could be sure of free quarters and free meals. If he expected a welcome he did not receive one. There seemed to be a consensus of opinion that his room would have been preferred to his company. And quite literally, since all four bedrooms were now occupied and Marian refused point-blank to allow Richard to turn out.

A curious little family scene followed. Miss Silver was about to walk down the hill into Farne in order to attend the morning service at St. Michael and All Angels, a new and very ugly red brick church with a new and very energetic Vicar whose sermons were the last word in frankness. They shocked everyone so much that people who hadn't been to church for years flocked there to hear them. She stood there practically unnoticed whilst Cyril went over to lean on the back of his wife's chair and say in what he intended to be a caressing tone,

"Oh, well, I can go in with Ina."

Ina Felton was already so pale that it would have been very difficult for her to turn any paler. What did happen was that the muscles under the bloodless skin became stiff and rigid, as if she braced herself to take a blow. Her eyes went to Marian, and Marian said,

"No, you can't do that. She isn't sleeping, and you would disturb her. There's a camp bed in the attic, and the little front room by the dining-room isn't being used. I'll have it put there for you."

It was Richard Cunningham who asked, "What about the audition? How did it go off?"

Cyril said in an injured voice that it was a washout.

"The whole thing's off. The backer backed out at the last moment. Of course I wasn't to know that."

Miss Silver found herself wondering whether there had ever been any prospect of an audition. She smoothed the black kid gloves which she wore on Sundays and proceeded on her way to church. On her return she was able to edify the party at lunch with quotations from the Vicar's sermon. It appeared that in the main it had met with her approval. She was not sure that it was altogether in good taste to refer to Miss Adrian's murder—"A shocking crime which has been perpetrated in our midst"—but she agreed very strongly with his subsequent remarks. He was an ugly, forceful young man, and he did not mince his words. "You have just heard the

193

fifth commandment read. I'm not going to tell you that it is wicked to commit murder. You all know it's wicked. You are all shocked when somebody else does it, but every single one of us every single day of our lives thinks, and says, and does the things which are the seed from which murder springs." Miss Silver had been much struck by the fact that he went on to quote the very words which she had used herself— "envy, hatred, and malice, and all uncharitableness."

When lunch was over Ina went up to her room. Miss Silver on her way to her own room saw her go in and heard the key turn in the lock.

When she came down again she found Cyril Felton alone in the study and very much at a loose end.

"Marian's gone off down to the beach with that fellow Cunningham. They're very thick, aren't they? As good as told me they didn't want me along. I shouldn't call it the thing myself, having a lot of strangers staying in a house when there's just been a murder there."

Miss Silver preferred a chair without arms. She settled herself and opened her knitting-bag. As she did so she considered Mr. Cyril Felton, who lounged upon the couch from which he had not troubled to rise when she entered. His skin was pasty, and he was heavy about the eyes. But quite a goodlooking young man, and not without ability. Possibly an only child—probably unwisely indulged. Certainly of very little use to himself or to anyone else in the world. A pity— a very great pity.

In this kind but firm attitude of mind she looked at him across Derek's stocking, now of considerable length, and said,

"Do you include me among the strangers, Mr. Felton?"

"Oh, well, you know what I mean. You needn't take it personally. But after all I'm Marian's brother-in-law and Ina's husband, and I should have thought—I mean, I just don't get the idea. You don't usually go and have a house-party when there's been a murder—I mean, do you?"

If Miss Silver considered this speech to be conclusive evidence of the faulty upbringing which she suspected she did not allow this to appear.

"Your sister-in-law and your wife are two young girls. I hope that my presence is some comfort and support to them. Mrs. Felton has had a great shock."

He stared and said,

"It's been a shock to us all. Why pick out Ina? It's not as if she and Helen were friends. They never set eyes on each other before this week, and no love lost when they did."

Miss Silver coughed.

"That is not a very prudent remark, Mr. Felton."

He made a pettish gesture.

"Oh, well, I didn't mean anything. Ina wouldn't murder a mouse—she'd be much too scared of hurting it. Nobody but a fool would imagine she'd do anything to Helen. She just didn't like her. Other girls didn't, you know. She got off with their men, and you couldn't expect them to like it. Jealous, you know, and wondering what she'd got that they hadn't. Not that I went in off the deep end about her myself. Not my type, if you know what I mean—and certainly not Ina's." He was getting out a cigarette and lighting it as he spoke, pitching the match in the direction of the fireplace without bothering where it fell. He inhaled a mouthful of smoke and let it out again slowly. "Now that chap Felix—he was in off the deep end all right. Funny thing his coming back like that. I mean it's practically committing suicide, isn't it? And if he was going to commit suicide, why didn't he just let himself drown instead of coming back here and waiting to be arrested—and then all that filthy business of being stood up in the dock, and all the stuff in the papers. Something odd about it, don't you think? I mean, why bother?

Much simpler and easier to drown, don't you think?"

Miss Silver was knitting briskly.

"People do not always do the simplest and easiest thing, Mr. Felton. Sometimes they do what they believe to be right. That surprises you?"

He hardly troubled to put a hand to hide a yawn.

"Oh, no—no—no. What I mean is, it's all very odd. I mean, why don't the police arrest him?"

"They may not believe that there is sufficient evidence."

He was leaning back in the sofa corner. With his eyes half shut, he drew in another mouthful of smoke.

"Oh, well, I just thought it was odd."

Miss Silver coughed.

"Mr. Felton, do you believe that Miss Adrian was murdered by Felix Brand?"

The eyes opened vaguely.

"Don't ask me. Anybody's guess is as good as mine."

The eyes closed again. The hand with the cigarette drooped towards the floor. Ash fell upon the carpet. The cigarette fell too. Miss Silver rose, picked it up, and dropped it on to the unlighted fire. She also picked up the match. Then she sat down again and went on knitting. Mr. Felton was asleep.

He was not, however, permitted to repose in peace. Sunday afternoon or no Sunday afternoon, Inspector Crisp was on the doorstep, the news of Mr. Felton's return having reached him at one o'clock. Cyril was obliged to wake up and answer a great many questions, which he did with the utmost vagueness and inattention. He yawned, he smoked, he fidgeted. He had constantly to be recalled to the point.

Crisp got nothing out of him.

"He's either much sharper than he looks, or he doesn't know a thing," he told the Chief Constable, who had arrived a little later.

March said thoughtfully,

196

"Well—he's an actor—"

"Not much of a one by all accounts."

"You never know—he may be better off the stage than he is on it. He didn't show any signs of nervousness?"

"Not a sign. Smoked and yawned most of the time. Didn't even seem interested."

March's look became alert.

"That's not natural."

"Well—"

"Overplaying the part. I'd say there's more in Cyril than meets the eye. Hang it all, man, he's blackmailing a woman, she's murdered within a stone's throw of him, and the police have got him on the mat—he ought to be nervous. And he simply can't help being interested. Indifference to the extent you describe just isn't possible. If it isn't genuine it's a smoke-screen. And if it is a smoke-screen, what is behind it? You didn't mention the blackmail?"

"No—I thought I'd hold that up. There's no evidence of course. She must have destroyed those two letters Miss Silver describes. She was going to get married, and she wouldn't want them about. No, I just took him through the picnic, the return to the house, the business about the doors and windows, and whether he had heard anything in the night."

"And what has he got to say to all that?"

"Nothing that amounts to anything. He saw Felix Brand go off with Miss Adrian at the picnic and noticed him coming back alone, but didn't see Miss Adrian come back. Says there were some raincoats and rugs about down on the beach, but doesn't know who they belonged to, and doesn't remember who brought any of them in. Says he only got up once during the night to go across to the bathroom and went straight off to sleep again. Says everything was quiet—no unusual sounds anywhere."

"What does he mean by unusual?"

"I asked him that. He said he could hear the sea."

"That means he was up somewhere between twelve and two. Do you know, I'm wondering about this visit to the bathroom. It's just the sort of story he might put up if he'd been out meeting Helen Adrian and was afraid he might have been heard. There's a creaking board just outside the room he was in then. He is new to the house, and might easily have stepped on it coming or going. If he did he'd be afraid and look round for a cover up. Which is just a lot of theory without a square inch of fact to balance on. We want to dig up some facts. What about this fellow Mount Helen Adrian was engaged to?"

Crisp nodded.

"He's been on the telephone. He was up in Scotland on business and didn't know a thing till he saw it in the papers this morning. Very upset and all that, but I gather he doesn't mean to come down. There was a lot about his business, and their not being officially engaged. If you ask me, I'd say he wanted to keep out of the limelight. You can't blame him of course—a business man doesn't want to get mixed up in a murder case. And there's no question of his being implicated. I asked Glasgow to check up on what he said about his movements, and it's all right. He registered at the Central Hotel on Thursday morning before breakfast, and he's been there ever since. Well, she was murdered between twelve and two on Thursday night, so it wasn't Mr. Mount that did it. Not that he was a very likely suspect, but just as well to get him out of the way."

March said, "Nice to get somebody out of the way. Well, we'd better get on with Cyril Felton. Let's have him in."

CHAPTER 30

The interview with Cyril Felton produced very little result. Regarded as a performance, Mr. Felton had profited by his rehearsal. It made the Inspector's description sound just a little crude. The lack of interest was less obvious. There was no more than a single yawn, carefully suppressed and apologized for with a "Sorry—I was up most of the night." Pressed as to how well he knew Helen Adrian, he assumed an agreeable frankness.

"Well, you know how it is—you knock up against people. We were in the same concert-party years ago, and we've come across each other at intervals on and off. Nothing much in it—always very good friends."

March said, "Were you lovers?"

"Oh, come, sir!"

"Were you?"

"No. I give you my word of honour we weren't."

March wondered how much it was worth.

"Any quarrel with her?"

"Not that I can remember. Nothing to quarrel about."

"Not a little matter of blackmail?"

Cyril looked horrified.

"Do you mind saying that again?"

"I said blackmail," said March, watching him.

He saw quite a good reproduction of the stock hero-falsely-accused situation. The slight start, the widened eyes, the squared shoulders, the look of noble scorn—they were all there. He had a feeling that Cyril ought to have been able to make a living on the stage. The tone in which he exclaimed "Blackmail!" was really pretty good.

"That is what I said."

"But I don't know what you mean. You can't suppose—"

"I am afraid I do. Miss Adrian received two letters and a telephone call referring to certain incidents and suggesting that she should pay fifty pounds to prevent her fiancé being informed about them. One of the letters began, 'F. Brand might prove a firebrand if Fred knew all.'"

Cyril raised his eyebrows.

"Poor girl—how very horrid for her."

"That was the first letter. Then there was a telephone conversation, asking to have fifty pounds in one-pound notes sent to Mr. Friend, 24 Blakeston Road, S.E., and adding, 'You'll be sorry if you don't.' Miss Adrian lost her temper and told you to go to hell. After which she received another letter, which said, 'Nasty temper. If you do that again, Fred will know all. What about the middle of last June?'"

He met the stare of affronted innocence.

"Look here, what *is* all this? Where are these letters? If you say I wrote them, I think I've got a right to have them shown to me, so that you can compare them with my writing."

That was the snag—they hadn't got the letters.

March said firmly, "Miss Adrian was convinced that the letters came from you. One of the incidents referred to was known only to yourself and Felix Brand."

"Oh, well, everyone knew he would do anything to stop her marrying Mount."

"So you knew that she was going to marry Mount?"

"Everyone knew she was thinking about it. Everyone knew that Brand was crazy with jealousy."

March said, "I think you know a good bit yourself, Mr. Felton. But perhaps you don't know that Helen Adrian informed Miss Silver that you were blackmailing her, that she had made up her mind to leave Cove House on Friday morning and return to town, and that she intended before she left to have an interview with you and offer you ten pounds down. If you boggled at taking it, she intended to threaten you with the police."

Cyril stared at him.

"This is terrible!"

"It may be—for you. This conversation took place with Miss Silver at the picnic on Thursday evening, just before half past six. Since everybody's movements have been checked, we know that Miss Adrian did not have that interview with you before half past ten, when the parties in both houses separated for the night. But Miss Adrian had expressed her intention of having that interview. That she had an appointment with someone on the lower terrace between twelve and two that night is certain. You cannot be surprised if we draw the natural inference that the appointment was with you."

He was dreadfully pale, his hands shook. All pretence at indifference was gone. He stammered out,

"No—no—you've got it all wrong. I wouldn't meet her in the night—why should I? If she wanted to talk to me she could have done it in the train—we were going to travel up together—I had my audition."

"You say you had arranged to travel up together in the morning?"

"Yes, we had. That is, she asked me at the picnic. She knew I had this audition, and she said she was off in the morning, and why not travel up together. She said she'd got something to talk to me about. But I give you my word I didn't know she'd got this blackmail idea in her head. Look here, Mr. March, anyone will tell you what sort of terms we were on at the picnic. She was as friendly as possible—anyone will tell you she was. As a matter of fact, she was too friendly for my wife. Ina didn't like it. She moped like any-thing—sat by herself and hardly spoke a word. Anyone will tell you that too. Now if she really thought I was blackmailing her, Helen wouldn't have been like that—I mean, would she? I mean, she couldn't really have thought I'd do that kind of thing—and if she did, I hadn't the slightest idea of it. She said she wanted to talk to me, and why not travel up together, and I said, 'Righty ho.' And I give you my word that was absolutely all."

When they had let him go Crisp said with gloom,

"If he thought all that up on the spur of the moment he's a lot cleverer than you'd take him for."

CHAPTER 31

Miss Silver was in her bedroom when Eliza came up to say that the Chief Constable would be glad to see her if she could spare the time.

As she crossed the landing with her knitting-bag on her arm, Cyril Felton was coming up from the hall. They passed near the top of the stair, and as she continued on her way she heard him go across to his wife's room and knock on the door. Since she was now out of sight, she remained as she was for a moment, and heard him say insistently,

"Ina—for God's sake let me in! I've got to speak to you."

After a lagging pause the key was turned. The door opened and shut again.

Miss Silver went on her way to the study, where Randal March was waiting. He wore a look which she was able to interpret as one of concern. When she was settled in the chair which she preferred, a low armless affair which very closely resembled one of those in her own flat, he said,

"I thought I'd like to tell you the latest. Not that there's much to tell." With which preliminary he gave her the substance of his interview with Cyril Felton. "And I'd like to know how he strikes you, if you think you have had time to form an opinion."

Miss Silver was knitting in a leisurely manner. She said,

"He is most at ease when he is playing a part. I do not believe that this is anything new. If he can see himself in any role he plays it with facility. For the rest, he is an idle, pleasure-loving young man who would, I think, always do the easiest thing. I cannot believe that he would plan a murder, but he might, as you suggest, have given Miss Adrian a push, after which, I agree, the rest might have followed. He could have brought the raincoat down and hung up the scarf in the hall again."

March said, "Yes."

After a short pause she coughed.

"It might be helpful at this juncture to consider very carefully the whole question of motive. It seems to me that we have to decide to what class of motive this murder was due. Was it a crime of passion and jealousy, or a crime committed for the sake of money? In the case of Cyril Felton it would fall into the latter category, but the motive is a very weak one. She may have threatened to go to the police, but I think he knew her well enough to feel sure that she would not do so unless he drove her to it. She meant to offer him ten pounds, and was quite sure that he would take it. There was no need for him to do murder. Do you agree?"

"Yes, I do."

"In Felix Brand's case the motive would, of course, be the passionate jealousy which he was not attempting to disguise. He could have killed Miss Adrian, but he could not

203

have taken the raincoat or put back the scarf."

"No."

"But, Randal, there are a number of other people in the two houses. I think that most of them have some kind of motive, and that an examination of those motives might be of use. I do not wish you to understand that I suspect anyone in particular, but I think we shall find that most of them had a reason for wishing that Miss Adrian was out of the way. There is, for instance, Penny Halliday."

"My dear Miss Silver!"

She continued placidly.

"A motive for murder does not imply that murder would be committed. Penny had a very strong motive. Mr. Felix Brand was being subjected to an influence which was having a disastrous effect upon his character, his health, and his career. But she had no access to Miss Brand's raincoat, and she could not have replaced the scarf."

He raised his eyebrows, smiled, and said,

"Deadlock."

Miss Silver coughed in a deprecating manner.

"There is the same difficulty in the case of Mrs. Brand and of Miss Remington. They had no access to the raincoat or to the scarf, nor had either of them any discernible motive for getting rid of Miss Adrian. It is obvious that they have no affection for Felix Brand, and in any case his connection with Helen Adrian was about to be broken." She paused, and added thoughtfully, "They had no motive for murdering her."

"Well, that disposes of their side of the house. Who will you have next?"

She said in her prim, serious voice, "Eliza Cotton," and saw him smile.

"Well, well—"

"She has as strong a motive as anyone, Randal. She is

extremely devoted both to Felix Brand and to Penny Halliday. You may say that she has brought them up. I think that Mrs. Brand and Miss Remington must have known of the breach between Mr. Felix and Miss Adrian, but it is doubtful if Eliza did. She certainly had a motive. And of course, like everyone else on this side of the house, she had access to the coat and the scarf."

"But no motive for incriminating Marian Brand."

"Oh, yes, Randal. There is a money motive there. Not for herself, but for Mr. Felix, who would come in for a share of his uncle's money if Marian Brand were out of the way."

"You have an ingenious mind."

She shook her head.

"Ingenuity is not required in a statement of fact. Let us pass to Miss Marian Brand. The only possible motive in her case is an extremely slight one, and need not, I think, be taken at all seriously. Her brother-in-law was carrying on a light bantering flirtation with Miss Adrian during the picnic, and his wife was certainly in very low spirits. But everything else apart, I think we must give Miss Marian credit for more sense than to leave her raincoat where it was found and to hang up a bloodstained scarf in the passage instead of washing it out."

"I couldn't agree more."

He had not learned this phrase in her school-room, but she let it pass.

"Ina Felton's motive would be a little stronger than that of her sister, but I do not think that it need detain us for more than a moment. She is a gentle, affectionate girl whose feelings have been wounded, not, I think, so much by any casual flirtation on her husband's part as by the money demands he was making on her sister. It is true that she appears to be more under the influence of shock than anyone else in the two houses, but she is not very strong, and it is the first time that she has been brought into contact with a violent crime. I think it is possible that she suspects her husband. She shrinks from him in quite a noticeable manner, and this was not the case when I happened to overhear their conversation in the library at Farne. I thought then that there had been some disagreement between them. He had been pressing her sister for money, and Miss Marian was standing firm. But, taking this into consideration, her manner to him was normal, and she went off quite willingly to have lunch with him."

He was standing by the old-fashioned hearth, an arm upon the mantelshelf, looking down upon Miss Silver in her olive-green cashmere with the little net vest and high boned collar, her bog-oak beads, and the brooch which matched them, her small competent hands busy with the four steel needles which were shaping the foot of Derek's stocking.

"You say her manner to her husband was normal then. It is not normal now?"

"By no means, Randal. I think that there is something which she is keeping back even from her sister, and I think that this something concerns her husband. It may, or may not, be connected with Miss Adrian's death. As I came down just now, Cyril Felton knocked on his wife's door and urged her to let him in. His words were, 'Ina—for God's sake let me in. I must speak to you.'"

"Did she let him in?"

"Yes, she did. And I must confess that I should like to know what they are saying to one another at this moment."

He said with a quizzical look,

"Oh, well, even you have your limitations."

Miss Silver coughed in a reproving manner.

"We will now consider the case of Mr. Richard Cunningham."

March straightened up in surprise.

"Cunningham? But he wasn't in the house."

"I do not think that need exclude him from our list of hypothetical murderers, if I may use such an expression. We are, you know, merely considering possibilities. With this premise, it is, I think, legitimate to say that Mr. Cunningham should be considered. He left the house at half past ten, but even if he returned to his hotel in Farne, there was nothing to prevent him from coming back. He could have made an appointment with Miss Adrian whilst the picnic was in progress. He was actually sitting next to her for part of the time. He could have met her on the terrace, and he could have killed her."

March said, "Why?"

"I do not know. But they were at least old acquaintances. She was at some pains to intimate that their relationship had been closer than that. She wished, of course, to annoy Mr. Felix, and possibly Miss Marian. She certainly did annoy Mr. Cunningham."

There was a tinge of exasperation in his voice as he said,

"You're not by any chance setting out to make a serious case against Cunningham?"

She continued to knit.

"I am merely showing you that he may have had a motive, and that he certainly had the opportunity both to make an appointment with Miss Adrian and to keep it. I do not wish to go any farther than that. He would not, of course, have had access to the raincoat and scarf, and certainly could not have brought the scarf back into the house after the murder. And that concludes our survey of all those who may have desired Miss Adrian's death, and who had the opportunity of bringing it about."

He had his broad shoulders against the mantelpiece now, his hands in his pockets. He was reflecting that it was all very well, but it got them exactly nowhere. He put the thought into words.

"You know, this isn't getting us anywhere."

She looked up at him with a smile.

"It has at least cleared the ground, I think. Of the eight people in the two houses, Mrs. Brand and Miss Remington have no discernible motive for desiring Miss Adrian's death, Mr. Cunningham, Marian Brand, and Ina Felton may be said to have a possible but shadowy motive, Eliza Cotton and Penny Halliday have a motive of affection and the desire to protect someone they love, Felix Brand has a motive of passion and jealousy, and Cyril Felton a motive of fear. The persons who could have taken the raincoat down to the place where it was found and have brought the scarf back again are Eliza Cotton, Marian Brand, Ina Felton, and Cyril Felton. It is, of course, possible that it was not the murderer who did this. It may have been done by someone who wished to lay a false trail in order to screen the murderer."

He looked startled.

"Is that what you had up your sleeve?"

"My dear Randal!"

"Do you think I don't know when you're holding something up? If anyone over here did what you suggest, it would be Eliza Cotton. She would cover up for Felix Brand, or for Penny Halliday. But why lay a trail that points to Marian Brand?"

He broke off because Miss Silver had put down her knitting and was looking up at him with an expression which he recognized as portentous. He had the conviction that she was about, not so much to take something out of her sleeve, as to touch off quite a sizable bomb.

She began, "My dear Randal, have you considered—"

CHAPTER 32

Ina Felton came slowly to her bedroom door and turned back the key. She had to see Cyril, because she must tell him that she knew, and that he must go away and never come back. She wouldn't tell the police or anybody else, but she must tell Cyril, and he must go away. And then it wouldn't be he who would be in prison, but herself—shut away from everyone with what she knew and couldn't tell. She couldn't tell anyone, not even Marian, only Cyril, so that he would go away and never come back.

She drew aside from the opening door and saw him come in and lock it behind him. Even in the midst of her wretchedness that frightened her. She backed away from him till she came up against the foot of the bed. It was a wide, old-fashioned bed with brass knobs upon the footrail, a big one at each corner and little ones in between. She took hold of the big knob at the side nearest the window and edged round the corner until she could sit down on the side of the bed. She had to sit because her knees were shaking so.

Cyril sat too. There was a comfortable chair over by the window, and he flung himself into it. For once he really wasn't thinking about acting, but he was so used to the gestures of the stage that they came unbidden. He groaned, ran a hand through his hair, and said,

"They think I killed her."

Ina felt nothing at all. She had said it to herself so often that it didn't seem possible to have any more feeling about it. She had used it all up, there wasn't any left. She held on to the brass ball at the corner of the bed and said,

"Didn't you?"

"Ina!"

Virtuous indignation rang in his voice. He had started forward in his chair, a hand on either arm, his eyes wide with fear and reproach.

A breath of surprise just ruffled the surface of her misery. She said,

"You did, didn't you?" And then, "I saw you."

"Ina—are you mad?"

She shook her head.

"I saw you."

"You couldn't possibly have seen me. What did you think you saw?"

It was a relief to speak. She said in a gentle, toneless voice,

"I couldn't sleep on Thursday night, I haven't been sleeping—very much. I heard the board creak when you came out of your room. I got up, because I was afraid you were coming here. But you went downstairs. I looked over into the hall. You went along the passage and opened the door from the other house and let Helen Adrian through."

"Ina!"

"You took down Marian's raincoat, and she put it on. The scarf fell on the floor. You had a torch—it showed the colours. You oughtn't to have let her take Marian's scarf—" Her voice just petered out.

He was leaning forward, his face ghastly, his eyes fixed on her.

"You don't understand. I had to see her alone. They say I was blackmailing her. What damned nonsense! We'd been friends for ages, and all I wanted was something to tide me over. She was going to marry Fred Mount, wasn't she? Fifty pounds wasn't going to mean anything to her—nothing at all. And Fred wouldn't have married her if he had known she was having an affair with Felix. Why, fifty pounds was dirt cheap, if you ask me. And she had the nerve to offer me ten!''

Ina said in that gentle voice,

"You were blackmailing her?''

He made an exasperated movement.

"Oh, call it anything you like! You and Marian seem to think one can live without money. Mount is simply rolling. What's fifty pounds? She'd never have missed it. But I had to see her alone. Felix never took his eyes off her, so we fixed it up at the picnic. I was to let her through, and we could thresh things out. Mind you, she simply had to come to terms, because Mount wouldn't have stood for the way she'd been carrying on, and she knew it. I'd got her cold. I'll say that for Helen, she could see reason. She knew she was up against it. I'd have got my fifty pounds all right. But I had to see her—we had to talk. And as soon as I let her through I knew it wasn't going to be safe in the house. There was all that about you not sleeping, and the devil of a fuss if you had come down and found us together in the middle of the night.'' He gave an angry laugh. "You'd have been pleased, wouldn't you!''

She said without any expression at all,

"I did come down and find you together.''

"Nothing to be jealous about—you can take my word for that.''

A physical sickness rose in Ina. Her hand still clung to the brass knob. The cold of the metal numbed her palm. She could feel the chill of it right up to her shoulder and down all that side of her body. She said,

"Go on.''

"Well, I had a brainwave. I said, 'Look here, let's go down on to the beach. Ina's not been sleeping—you don't want to start another scandal.' I made her take Marian's raincoat and tie the scarf over her hair, just in case of anyone looking out of a window—that light hair shows up so, and I wasn't sure if there was going to be a moon—and we went out through the study and down as far as the bottom terrace."

"I saw you."

He shook his head reprovingly.

"Well, you shouldn't have been spying. There wasn't anything for you to mind, and it simply wasn't your business."

"I wasn't spying. I went back to my room. You had a torch. You put it on when you came to the steps going down from the lawn. She had Marian's scarf on over her head. The light shone on it as she went down the steps. I saw the colours. You oughtn't to have let her take Marian's scarf."

"What rubbish! It just shows what a sensible precaution it was. We had to have the torch for those steps—we didn't want to break a leg in the dark. As it was, I missed a step. I expect that was when the torch threw high and you saw the scarf. Well, if anyone else had been looking out of a window they would have seen Helen's fair hair—if I hadn't thought about covering it up, I mean. Marian's scarf indeed!" He gave that angry laugh again. "Really, Ina, you do think of the most idiotic things to say!"

She said, "Go on."

"Well, you keep interrupting. There's a seat on the terrace there, so we sat down. It was warm, and she took off the coat—there wasn't anyone to see us. We talked, and she was frightfully unreasonable—I mean *frightfully*. She actually threatened to go to the police. She didn't mean it of course. I just laughed at her. 'All right,' I said—'if that's the way you want it. Let's have a showdown, and everything in the papers, and see what Fred Mount has to say about it.' Well, there was a bit of a scene and some hard words flying. Didn't hurt me—I knew she was just getting it off her chest. So I let her say her piece, and when she finished up with, 'Ten pounds is my last word, and you can take it or leave it,' I said, 'Nothing doing,' and I came along up to the house."

Ina said,

"You killed her."

Cyril produced a look of angry innocence.

"I did nothing of the kind! Why on earth should I? I was going to travel up to town with her next day, and if she didn't come across with the fifty pounds, I was going to see Mount. More in sorrow than in anger, you know. Thought he ought to be told what was going on behind his back—all that sort of thing. I can do it quite well. Of course I didn't kill her. I just left her there and came in. I knew she'd see reason when she'd had time to think things over, so I came away and left her to it."

Ina's eyes were fixed upon him—dark, hopeless eyes.

"Someone brought the scarf in after she was killed."

"Well, it wasn't me. I came in, and I went to bed and I went to sleep, and I didn't know she'd been killed until the morning."

She sat there in silence for a minute. There was a little more life in her voice when she said,

"Who shut the study door?"

He looked sulky.

"I left it open for her to come in that way."

Ina said, "It was shut in the morning. And the scarf was hanging in the passage. How did it get there?"

"I don't know." His tone was impatient. "Stop thinking about it!"

"I can't. It goes round and round in my head. The door into the other house was shut too. The bolts were fastened. Who fastened them?"

He said easily, "Oh, I did that. As soon as it was light I woke up, and I thought about the doors. I left them open for her to come through, and of course I thought

213

she had, so I just went down and shut them."

"You shut both the doors?"

"I'm telling you I did."

She said, "The scarf—was it there when you bolted the door?"

"I don't know—I didn't notice. Don't you understand? It was dark in the passage. It was only just getting light outside. I wasn't thinking about scarves. I just wanted to bolt the door and get back to bed again."

The fear which had been holding her in a cold, rigid grip relaxed. When she breathed her lungs opened to take in the air. She could draw it right down, instead of feeling that everything had gone stiff and tight.

The relief must have been gradual, but suddenly she was aware of it. She didn't know just when or how she began to believe that it was not Cyril who had killed Helen Adrian, but she did believe it. The unendurable burden which she had carried since Friday morning was lifted. He wasn't any of the things which she had once thought him. All the borrowed garments of romance had fallen away. He was mean, selfish, and lazy. He didn't love her, and had probably never been faithful to her. He didn't love anyone but Cyril Felton. He would sponge on her and on Marian, grumble at what they gave him, and come back for more. He was a blackmailer, and he wasn't even ashamed of it. But he hadn't killed Helen Adrian. She could see him quite clearly and know just how worthless he was, but the deep, dreadful shuddering at his presence was gone.

She leaned forward and said in almost a surprised tone, "You didn't kill her—"

Cyril threw up his head and laughed.

"Only just tumbled to that? Of course I didn't, but I know who did."

CHAPTER 33

Every moment of that long fine afternoon was to come under the microscope. Everyone in the two houses would be asked, "Where were you between the hours of three and five? Were you alone? Who was with you? How long were you together? If you were out, when did you return to the house?"

At three o'clock Cyril Felton was still talking to his wife. Eliza Cotton had stepped out into the garden to look for Mactavish, and the sound of their voices reached her from Ina Felton's bedroom. The window was open, and she heard Cyril Felton say, "Don't be a fool! It's nothing." And she heard Ina answer, "No, no, I won't. It's no use your wanting me to, because I won't." Eliza called out to Mactavish, and the voices stopped. She thought to herself, "Just as well they should know someone can hear them," and after standing for a few minutes at the top of the steps going down to the next terrace and seeing no sign of Mactavish she went back into the house. Later she had a bath.

Felix and Penny were up on the cliffs. They had found a place where there was a wide grassy ledge sheltered from the wind. Felix lay full length on the grass, his forehead on his crossed arms, his face hidden. The sun was warm on his back. His mind was as nearly as possible blank. He had feelings, but not thoughts. He felt as a man feels who has had a long illness and knows that the tide has turned, and that he is going to get well. He felt as if he had had a feverish dream and was waking from it. Consciousness was swept clean. He felt the sun, and a light air that came and went.

The new grass smelt sweet where his arms were bruising it. The tide was going out. There was no sound from the sea. Helen Adrian was a long time ago—a long, long time ago. When he began to think again he would know that she was dead. He hadn't begun to think—he only felt. He had no feelings about Helen Adrian.

Penny was sitting beside him. The wall of the cliff rose between six and ten feet at the back of their ledge, following a broken line. She sat leaning against the wall with her hands locked about her knees. Felix was so close to her that she would have touched him if she moved. But she didn't move. She had sat like that, quite still, for nearly an hour, looking out over the sea and saying the kind of prayers which haven't any words. The nearest that they came to it were the old familiar ones which have come down through so many generations. She would never be able to hear them again without feeling just this quivering ecstasy of the heart. "This my son was dead, and is alive again; he was lost, and is found."

She did not speak, and Felix did not speak. The sun shone on them. The light air moved. The tide went down.

Miss Silver was in the study with the Chief Constable until a little before half past three, when he bade her an affectionate farewell and went home to participate in a tea-party arranged by his wife. At the time that she went through the hall with him and let him out there was no sound anywhere in all the house. She locked the front door after him and returned to the study. After which she may or may not have closed her eyes and drifted into a light nap. The room was warm, the sofa corner comfortable. It is certain that she was not knitting when Eliza came in with the tea-tray at a few minutes before five. Derek's stocking, with only an inch or two to go, lay coiled on her lap with the needles sticking up brightly like pins on a pin-cushion. Miss Silver's hands rested upon the grey wool. Miss Silver's eyes were closed. It may have been only for the moment, because at the sound of Eliza's voice they were immediately opened.

"Just on five o'clock, and those that don't come back to tea will have to go without, so I'll give a knock on Mrs. Felton's door and see if I can't get her to come down."

"Is Miss Brand not in?"

Eliza opened her mouth to say, "No," and shut it again, because at just that moment she saw Marian Brand crossing the lawn with Richard Cunningham beside her. The clock struck five as they came up the two shallow steps into the study.

Marian said, "I'm so dreadfully sorry we're late. We've been down on the beach, and I went to sleep, and Richard went for a walk. And we found Mactavish catching sand-hoppers as we came up."

Eliza said gloomily, "He does," and went up to knock on Ina Felton's door.

In the house on the other side of the wall a Sabbath afternoon quiet had set in with the departure of the Chief Constable and Inspector Crisp. Neither of the two dailies came on Sunday. Mrs. Woolley cooked a meal and left it ready, and they could have it cold, or they could heat it themselves. She didn't mind working double time on Saturday morning, but she wasn't working on Saturday afternoon nor Sunday, not to please anyone—they could do for themselves. It was a cause of deep resentment to Florence Brand, even though it was Penny who did the Sunday work. Cassy Remington helped occasionally—if you could call it helping to fidget to and fro and criticize what somebody else was doing. But Florence never put a hand to anything. By three o'clock on Sunday afternoon she had two cushions at her back and her feet up on a footstool in the sitting-room which she shared with her sister. There was always a book on her lap, but it was very seldom opened. It was always a very dull book. On this particular afternoon it was *Some Chapters of my Life* by A Wessex Parson. At five o'clock Mrs. Brand, the footstool, and the Wessex Parson occupied the same respective positions which they had done at three.

Miss Remington's Sunday afternoon programme was different from her sister's, but just as immutable. She always made herself a large strong cup of coffee, which she took up to her bedroom. When she had drunk it she ate a chocolate and occupied herself in going through her clothes, experimenting with face-creams, powders, and even, very tentatively, with lipstick. She had never felt sure enough about the lipstick to be seen wearing it outside her own room. She did not like the feeling or the taste of it, but its possibilities fascinated her. At some period she generally removed her Sunday dress, put on a dressing-gown, and lay down upon her bed. At five o'clock on this particular Sunday afternoon she was fastening her brooch and slipping her amethyst chain over her head. They did not have tea until five o'clock on Sunday, a habit formed so long ago that no one now remembered that when Mrs. Martin Brand taught a Sunday afternoon class in Farne this hour had been fixed in order that she might get home in time to pour out tea.

Miss Cassy, looking at herself in the glass with her head a little on one side, hoped that Penny had remembered to come home and put the kettle on. She was apt to be sadly forgetful when her mind was taken up with Felix. Really the way she ran after him was quite ridiculous. Girls nowadays simply didn't care what anything looked like—no proper pride, no self-restraint. Felix would think more of her if she were not always at his beck and call.

She went downstairs, and met Penny coming through from the kitchen with the tea-tray. They were having tea in the parlour—they always had it there on Sunday. As Cassy Remington opened the door and Penny and the tray went in,

Florence Brand sat up with a jerk and the Wessex Parson fell off her lap.

Cassy said, "Where's Felix?" and Penny answered her.

"He said he didn't want any tea. It's lovely up on the cliff. I said I'd go back."

It was at this moment that Eliza Cotton came out of the study on the other side of the house and went up the stair to knock on Ina Felton's door. There was a little pause before the key turned in the lock, long enough to give Eliza time to disapprove. She didn't hold with people locking themselves into their bedrooms, and she considered that Mrs. Felton did ought to rouse herself and go out with her sister and Mr. Cunningham. And not their fault if she didn't, because she had heard them ask her. All the same, when Ina opened the door Eliza thought she was looking better—not what you would call hearty, but less like something that had been kept too long on ice. She said, "Oh, thank you, Eliza," in quite a human voice, and they went back down the stairs together.

It was Miss Silver who enquired after Cyril Felton. Ina was stretching out her hand to take the cup of tea which Marian had just poured out for her. She stopped like that to look at Miss Silver.

"He said he was going to lie down in his room. He had a headache. He was up very late last night. He said he wanted a good sleep."

Marian said, "He might like some tea. Richard, perhaps you wouldn't mind seeing if he is awake. It's the little room on the left of the front door as you come in."

He said, "Of course," put down his cup, and went out.

There was some talk between Miss Silver and Marian about Eliza's tea-cake and Eliza's superlative raspberry jam.

"Such a light hand. You may have the best recipe and the best materials, but there is a lightness of touch which, I believe, cannot be taught. My housekeeper, Hannah Meadows, has it, and I feel I am indeed fortunate. So much good food is wasted by bad cooking."

Richard Cunningham opened the door and stood there.

"Miss Silver, someone wants to speak to you for a moment. Could you come?"

But when she reached the hall and the door was shut again he drew her away from it and said,

"I'm afraid I'm the person who wants to speak to you. Can you stand a shock?"

"What has happened?"

"Someone has stuck a knife into Cyril Felton. He's dead."

CHAPTER 34

Randal March was called to the telephone in the middle of his wife's tea-party. As he had been buttonholed by old Lady Halbert who knew more people who had undergone operations than anyone else in England and loved to rehearse the particulars of each case with a terrifying command of detail, he was not really sorry to disengage himself.

The voice which met his ear when he took up the receiver was that of Inspector Crisp. It said in an exasperated tone,

"We've just had a call from Cove House. There's been another death."

"What!"

"That young fellow Felton. They've just found him dead in his bed. Stabbed. No weapon."

"Who found him?"

"Mr. Richard Cunningham. Says he went to call him to tea and found him like that."

"It was he who telephoned?"

"Yes, sir. I'm just off out there now. I thought I'd better let you know."

March said, "Right—I'll be along," and hung up.

He found Crisp at Cove House, getting going with the business of looking for the weapon, taking fingerprints, taking preliminary statements. Not that the Inspector himself was personally concerned with anything but the statements, having brought with him two underlings and the police surgeon whom he had snatched from his Sunday tea. He had questioned Richard Cunningham, Miss Silver, and Eliza Cotton, but so far it had been possible to induce him to give Ina Felton a little more time.

Coming through the hall March encountered Miss Silver. Since it was impossible to believe that the meeting was accidental, he stopped and spoke to her.

"What has been happening? You did not ring me up yourself."

"No. I thought it would be better to give Inspector Crisp the opportunity. I am very glad to see you. Randal, that poor girl Ina Felton—Inspector Crisp has not seen her yet. I have been hoping that he would wait until you came."

"Where is she?"

"In her room, and her sister with her. I was going to ask you if I might be present when you see her."

"Oh, yes—there should be someone there. And I'd like your opinion. I don't pretend to know as much about girls as you do. But I'll have to see Crisp first, and the surgeon."

She went back into the dining-room, from which she had emerged to meet him. With the door just ajar, she sat there, her hands busy with her knitting, her ears attentive to every sound in the house beyond. Men's feet tramping across the hall to the little room on the other side of the front door where Cyril Felton lay on his bed with a sheet thrown over

221

him. She knew what they would see when the sheet was lifted, for she had stood there and seen how he lay on his right side with his knees a little drawn up, as a man lies when he is asleep. He had taken off his coat and hung it over a chair. He had pulled up the light coverlet of the bed as far as his waist. There was a rent in his blue shirt just below the left shoulder-blade where a knife had been driven home. The shirt, and the coverlet, and the blanket were soaked and red. But there was no knife. The head of the bed stood against the front wall of the house, fitting in awkwardly amongst furniture not intended for a bedroom. It was a light truckle bed, old-fashioned but serviceable, and easy to handle. A tall mahogany bookcase occupied the whole of the left-hand wall. A Victorian overmantel reached from the mantelpiece to the ceiling. A pedestal table in figured walnut had been pushed into a corner. There were chairs. There was a Brussels carpet. There was a whatnot with pampas grass in a Japanese jar. There was a wallpaper with what had been a bright pattern of roses, but was now a drab background for the photographs, watercolours, etchings, and engravings which did their best to cover it. An ugly, haphazard room, with a murdered man in it, and the warm May air coming in through the open casement window.

The tramp of feet went back again across the hall. There was presently a knock on the dining-room door. At Miss Silver's "Come in!" it opened and disclosed a fresh-faced young constable.

"If you please, miss, the Chief Constable would be glad if you would come to the study."

Miss Silver was, perhaps, inclined to describe quite small things as providential. The fact that during this time of waiting she had been able to finish off the second stocking of the pair she was making for Derek Burkett did undoubtedly present itself in this light. She put the completed stocking away in her knitting-bag and followed the young constable to the study, where she found the police surgeon just about to take his leave of Randal March. "Any kitchen knife—" he was saying as she came into the room. They had met before, and he broke off to greet her.

"How are you, Miss Silver? I was just telling the Chief Constable that I didn't think they'd find the weapon. It might have been any kitchen knife, and if you want my guess, that's what it was. Used, cleaned, and put back—that's about the size of it. Well, as you were probably just going to say, it's not my business to guess, and I'll be getting along."

He went out, and Crisp went with him to the front door, where they stood talking for a minute.

March turned to Miss Silver.

"He puts the time of death not earlier than three o'clock, and not later than five. Well, we know he was alive just after three, because Eliza Cotton heard him talking to his wife in her room about that time. Mrs. Felton will be able to tell us when he left her. Cunningham says he found him dead just after five, so there's very nearly two hours for him to have been murdered in, with a probability that it was somewhere about the middle of that time—say between four and half past. But of course that's guesswork. Doctors don't like committing themselves, and it's a hot afternoon. Now look here, we've got to see Mrs. Felton. She's the last person known to have seen him alive. I want to see her, and I want to see her without the sister. It's easy to see she has always taken the lead, and I don't want anyone prompting Mrs. Felton or answering for her. Do you think you could go up and persuade her to come down? Or if she isn't equal to that, we will come up. But you'll have to get rid of Marian Brand."

"I will do my best, Randal."

"It is a very efficient best. Just give me a call from the top of the stairs if we are to come up. I will wait in the hall."

As he stood there and waited he could hear Miss Silver's light tap on the bedroom door and the sound of her voice speaking with cheerful authority. He could not distinguish the words, but there was definitely a flavour of the "Come along now, dear, and say your lesson!" of schoolroom days.

There was a delay of a few minutes, during which Inspector Crisp shut and locked the front door and came to stand beside him. Then Miss Silver came to the head of the stairs and said with her little preliminary cough,

"I think it would be best if you will come up."

They were no more than half way, when Marian Brand came out of her sister's room and passed the bathroom door to go to her own. Before she could reach it Richard Cunningham called her name. He had been waiting there in the room across the landing for her to emerge. They stood for a moment. Some words passed, too low to be overheard, and then as March and Crisp came up on to the landing, they passed them and went down.

Ina Felton's door was standing open. Crisp allowed the Chief Constable to precede him and shut it behind them.

Ina was sitting in the chintz-covered chair by the window. It was evident that she had been weeping bitterly. The pale skin was blotched, the eyes swimming, the lids swollen and reddened. She made a soft helpless movement as they came in. There could be no greater contrast to the white, frozen girl whom they had interviewed before. Whatever she felt about her husband's death, it had shattered her control. March thought, "If she knows anything, it will come out now." He said in his pleasant voice,

"I am so sorry to trouble you, Mrs. Felton, but you will realize that we have our duty to do. No one has a greater interest in clearing this matter up than you have."

There was a little broken sob in her voice as she said,

"Yes."

Miss Silver had been efficient in the matter of chairs. There was one for herself at Ina Felton's side. One of those long, narrow Victorian couches had been moved from the foot of the bed and set at a convenient angle for the two men. When they had seated themselves March said,

"Your husband had a conversation with you in this room at about three o'clock. I am sure you must understand that everything which happened this afternoon is important. He came here to talk to you. Will you tell us what you talked about?"

She said in a trembling voice, "We talked—"

"Yes? What did you talk about?"

She looked at Miss Silver.

"Must I say?"

"You are not legally obliged to do so, but you would be well advised to give the police all the help you can. You have nothing to be afraid of if you have done nothing wrong."

Ina turned her dark eyes on March.

"I haven't—really. I'll tell you. It won't hurt him, because nobody can possibly think he did it now."

"Go on, Mrs. Felton."

She had a damp, crushed handkerchief in her right hand. She rubbed it now across her eyes like a child impatient of its tears. Then she said,

"On Thursday night I couldn't sleep. I was unhappy— about Cyril. He thought I ought to have had half the money. Uncle Martin left it all to Marian, you know—he thought Cyril would spend it. And Cyril was angry. He wanted Marian to give me half, but she wouldn't. He would have spent it, you know."

"Yes, Mrs. Felton?"

She was twisting the handkerchief with shaking fingers.

"I was very unhappy. And then I found he knew Helen Adrian—rather well. He didn't tell me, but I could see—they knew each other. They were flirting and talking at the picnic. I was dreadfully unhappy. It wasn't just that, you know—it was everything. I thought he didn't care any longer—I thought our marriage was breaking up. I couldn't sleep."

· The brown eyes were fixed on March's face. They were full of tears, but the tears had ceased to fall. It was no longer difficult to speak—it was a relief. And nothing she said could hurt Cyril any more.

"Yes, Mrs. Felton?"

She said, "I heard the floor-board creak. It does, you know—just outside the room Cyril had."

"What time was this?"

"It had struck one. The big clock in the hall strikes the hours. I was thinking what a lot of the night there was to come. Then I heard the floor-board creak. I went to the door and listened. I thought—I thought—" Her voice stopped for a moment, then went on again. "I waited a little, then I opened the door. Cyril was going down the stairs. He had a torch. I thought he was going to meet Helen Adrian. I went out on to the landing and listened. He went into the passage and opened the door through into the other house. The bolt at the bottom made a creaking noise. Helen Adrian came through. They were whispering there. He took down Marian's raincoat, and she put it on. They went into the study. Then I went back to my room. They came out through the study into the garden and went down the steps on the other side of the lawn. Cyril put his torch on when they came to the steps. Helen had the raincoat on, and the blue and yellow scarf over her head. The light shone on it when she went down the steps. He oughtn't to have let her take Marian's scarf." She was speaking in a quiet, exhausted voice. She stopped.

March said,

"Yes, Mrs. Felton?"

"Nothing seemed to matter any more. I didn't want to go on looking out the window. I didn't want to know any more. I went and lay down on my bed. I felt very giddy and faint. I don't know whether I fainted, or whether I went to sleep—I really don't know. I didn't hear the board creak when Cyril came back. I didn't hear anything at all until the clock struck five. I think I must have been asleep, because I didn't hear Cyril come back when he went down to bolt the door."

"He went down again after he had come in? How do you know?"

She said, "He told me," and took a long sighing breath.

"When?"

"This afternoon."

March leaned forward.

"He told you what happened on Thursday night?"

"Yes."

"Will you tell us just what he said."

She told them in the same gentle, expressionless voice. When she had finished March said,

"He told you that he was blackmailing her, that she refused what he was asking and offered him ten pounds, and that he then told her there was nothing doing and came up to the house, leaving her there alive?"

Ina said, "Yes."

"Mrs. Felton—did you think he was speaking the truth?"

She had a faintly startled expression. Her voice changed.

"Not at first—because of the scarf. Someone brought it in, and someone shut the study door and the door through into the other house. He said he didn't know anything about the scarf. He said Helen was wearing it when he came in. He said he left her there on the seat, and he left both the doors so that she could come in and go through to the other house. And then when he woke up in the morning he remembered that she wouldn't have been able to bolt the door after going through, so he went down and did it. He said it was just beginning to get light."

"Was the scarf there when he came down?"

"I asked him that, and he said he didn't notice. It was dark in the passage, and he wasn't thinking about it—he just wanted to bolt the door and get back to bed. After he said all that I believed him. Mr. March, he really was telling the truth. He didn't always, but that part about coming in and leaving the doors open and then going down and shutting them—that was really true. I knew it was when he was saying it. I thought they had had a quarrel and he had killed her. And then I knew he hadn't. I said so, and he said—he said—" All at once she began to tremble—"Mr. March, he said, 'Of course I didn't, but I know who did.'"

There was a brief electric silence.

Miss Silver said, "Dear me!"

Crisp and the Chief Constable both spoke together.

"Mrs. Felton!"

Ina said a little breathlessly, "That's what he said. But he didn't tell me who it was."

"He didn't give you any indication?"

She shook her head.

"He said I'd better not know."

"Do you think he really knew anything?"

Her voice dropped to a whisper.

"Yes, I think he did. I think—he saw—someone. He wouldn't tell me. He said he wanted a good sleep and he was going to go and have it."

"And that was all?"

"Yes."

"You had no further conversation?"

"Not about that."

"Mrs. Felton, I am afraid I must press you. Someone who was in the garden overheard a part of your conversation with your husband. You were heard to say, 'No, no, I won't. It's no use your wanting me to, because I won't.' That does not seem to fit in with what you have just been telling us."

The colour came up into her face. She said,

"No."

"I am afraid I must ask you to explain."

She said, "He wanted me to say that he was here with me on Thursday night."

"I see. But you had already said he wasn't."

"That is what I told him. I said it wouldn't be any good, and if he knew who it was—" Her voice trailed away.

"You went on refusing?"

"I said I wouldn't, and he was angry. He went away angry." She put her hands up to her face and covered it.

Miss Silver directed what might almost be described as a commanding look at the Chief Constable. He got to his feet and said,

"I am very sorry to have distressed you, Mrs. Felton," and retreated, taking Inspector Crisp with him.

As they went down the stairs together, Crisp said in a dogged voice,

"Well, sir, that puts a bit of different complexion on everything, doesn't it? You wouldn't arrest Felix Brand because of this house being shut up from seven in the evening till Jackson got here from Farne in the morning and no possibility of anyone from the other house being able to get in and put the scarf where it was found. And now it seems the house wasn't shut up at all. The study door and the door between the houses, they were both wide open between midnight and, say, five in the morning, when Mr. Felton tells his wife he woke up and went down and shut them. Anyone that had murdered Miss Adrian could have brought that scarf in and hung it up. Felix Brand as well as anyone else. Nothing to stop him—nothing to stop anyone."

CHAPTER 35

A little later, when Crisp had gone back to taking statements, Miss Silver came down to the study, leaving Marian with her sister, and Richard Cunningham in his room across the landing with the door wide open so that he could see everyone who came up or went down. He caught Miss Silver at the top of the stairs and said abruptly,

"I want to get those girls away. They can't stay here another night. There's a homicidal lunatic about and it isn't safe. What did anyone want to kill Felton for?"

She said gravely,

"He knew who the murderer was." And then, "I am going down to speak to the Chief Constable now. I will see what he says about Miss Brand and Mrs. Felton."

She went on down the stairs, and he went back to his room with the open door.

Randal March was standing by the study window looking out. When Miss Silver came in he shut the window and turned. He met a look of intelligence and commendation. She said,

"Ah, I see you have thought of that."

"I don't want to run any risk of being overheard."

"No. You may have noticed that I had shut the window upstairs. It may interest you to know that during his interview with his wife Cyril Felton occupied that armchair by the window, and it was certainly open then, since Eliza heard part of what was said."

"You mean that his remark about knowing who the

murderer was might have been overheard?"

"Yes, Randal."

He waited until she was seated in one of the low armless chairs which she preferred. She was, for once, without her knitting-bag. Her hands lay in her lap. When he had pulled up a chair at a comfortable angle to her own he said,

"Do you think that girl is speaking the truth?"

"Oh, yes, Randal. She had been holding everything back. It was like a sort of cramp. She did not say a word even to her sister. But this second shock broke all her controls. She was no longer capable of holding back anything at all."

"Do you think Felton really knew who the murderer was?"

She gave him the look which would in his schoolroom days have been accompanied by a "Come, Randal, you can do better than that." In their changed circumstances the thought was rather differently expressed.

"Can you give me any other reason why he should have been murdered?"

He nodded.

"It looks that way. But if he really knew anything, why did he not come to the police with it? And why try to get his wife to cook up an alibi for him when she had already said that he was not with her on Thursday night?"

She coughed. Her tone was prim as she said,

"You are not forgetting that he had been endeavouring to blackmail Helen Adrian? I am afraid the answer to your question is that he had no intention of going to the police, because it was in his mind to make a profit out of what he knew. In order to be in a position to do this he required an alibi for himself. He probably felt sure that he could induce his wife to give him one. What he did not take into account was that to blackmail a murderer is the most dangerous form of crime in the world. There is, from the murderer's point of view,

231

only one real chance of survival, the death of the black-mailer.''

"I agree."

"It is impossible to say whether his remark to his wife about knowing the murderer's identity was overheard and his death then and there determined upon, or whether he had already made some blackmailing approach, but from the moment the murderer knew that he or she was discovered Cyril Felton's death became a necessity." She coughed. "I am, of course, taking the murderer's point of view."

At any other moment he might have smiled, but he felt no inclination to do so now. He said,

"Yes—you're right." Then, with an abrupt change of voice and manner, "You see how all this affects Felix Brand's po-sition. I struck out against arresting him because he couldn't have brought that scarf back into the house and locked up— the evidence then being that all doors and windows in this house were shut, locked, or bolted as from seven-fifteen, with the exception of bedroom windows opened after the occupant was ready for bed. Well, that's all gone by the board. The study door was open, the door between the houses was open, from midnight to daybreak when Cyril Felton went down and shut them. Felix Brand could perfectly well have brought that scarf in and put it back on its peg."

Miss Silver coughed.

"And so, Randal, could anyone else."

He said with some bitterness,

"Exactly—the case is wide open again. Any one of the people in these two houses could have killed Helen Adrian. It remains to be seen how many of them could have killed Cyril Felton. Crisp wants me to arrest Felix Brand, and as far as Helen Adrian is concerned he's back at the top of the list. But when it comes to Cyril Felton he's pretty near the bot-tom." He dived into a pocket and took out a folded paper.

"These are just rough notes of what Crisp had got before I came. He's always fancied Felix, so he led off with him. Well, it seems Penny Halliday went up on the cliffs with him as soon as they had washed up lunch. He says they stayed there till getting on for half past four, when she came in to get tea for the old ladies. He said he didn't want any—couldn't face another family meal—and stayed where he was until about half past five, when he came strolling in to see why Penny hadn't come back, and walked into Crisp on the doorstep. Penny Halliday confirms all the first bit. Says it was five-and-twenty past four when she looked at her watch and said she must go in. She says it's about ten minutes fast going, and it may have taken her a quarter of an hour. She boiled a kettle and took the tray into the front sitting-room where Mrs. Brand was having her rest at just after five o'clock, coming up with Miss Remington in the hall. They had hardly begun their tea, when they heard someone scream next door, and she ran over to see what was happening. Now you see, it is just physically possible for Felix to have followed her back to the house, got into that ground-floor room which Felton was using as a bedroom. The window was wide open and no distance from the ground—" He broke off. "It's physically possible, as I say, but looked at from any other point of view, it doesn't make sense. He couldn't have heard what Felton said to his wife about knowing the murderer, because he was up on the cliffs with Penny. If Cyril had already started a blackmailing approach and the murder was planned, is it credible that he would have left it so late in the afternoon? He couldn't have got to the house till a quarter to five, just when everybody would be rousing up and thinking about tea. And how could he know that Cyril would be in his room and asleep? If it wasn't planned, he had to go into the house and get a weapon—probably a knife from the kitchen—whilst Penny was getting tea and Miss Remington was coming downstairs. And then he had to get rid of the weapon—probably by cleaning it and putting it back in the drawer, because both Penny and Eliza say there isn't a knife missing on either side of the house." He made an impatient movement. "I suppose it could just have been done, but nothing will ever persuade me that it was done."

Miss Silver inclined her head.

"I think you are right, Randal. As you know, I have never believed that Felix Brand was the murderer."

He said, "You still think—well, never mind now, let's get on with this. I suppose Penny Halliday could have done it, but everything I've just said about Felix applies, and more strongly, to her. She would have a bare quarter of an hour to boil a kettle and get tea, get in through the window and kill Felton, clean up herself and the knife. That's a point I forgot when we were talking about Felix—the murderer was lucky if he got off without a stain on him somewhere. But to get back to Penny. It would have been pretty good going, wouldn't it? And I may say that even Crisp isn't barking up that particular tree."

"I am glad to hear it. It would not be possible for Penny Halliday to murder anyone."

He looked at her in a quizzical manner.

"Not even to cover up for Felix? Tigress in defence of cub?"

Miss Silver coughed in a reproving manner.

"It would not be possible for her to stab a man in his sleep."

"No—I believe you're right. And, as I say, even Crisp isn't keen on her as a suspect. Of course the person who had all the time in the world to do it is Eliza Cotton. She admits to having heard part of the conversation between Felton and his wife when she was out in the garden, and she could very easily have heard him tell her he knew who the murderer was and then say that he was going to his room to get some sleep. She says she went in and had a bath, but there was

234

most of the afternoon for her to wait until he had dropped off and then go in and kill him. And plenty of time after that to clean the knife, and put it back, and go and have a bath. The motive, of course, would be the same as Penny Halliday's—to protect Felix Brand."

She coughed again, indulgently this time.

"As a hypothetical case you put it well. I do not think that you are very serious about it."

He said, "Perhaps not. Less likely things have happened." Then, after a pause, "I'm rather at a loose end. I brought over a search-warrant for Crisp, and I'm letting him get on with it. He's having a female searcher to do the women and go through their clothes. You see, as I said, whoever knifed Felton would be lucky if he got away without a stain somewhere. I think everyone will have to submit to a personal search."

"I am quite willing to do so, Randal."

"*You?*"

She said in a placid voice,

"I was in the house. I have no alibi. I was quite alone in the study. I could very easily have done it. It would probably make it easier for everyone if no exceptions were made."

He said thoughtfully,

"Yes, that's true. And very good of you to think of it." Then, with a half laugh, "I am expecting hysterics next door."

As he spoke, there was a knock. Inspector Crisp followed it, notebook in hand. On seeing Miss Silver he checked, but was told to come in. To March's "Anything fresh?" he replied, "Not yet, sir. I've left Mrs. Larkin with the ladies. Mrs. Brand is riding a very high horse indeed, and Miss Remington is saying she was never so insulted in her life, so I came away and left them to it. I thought you might like to know what kind of account everyone gives of how they spent the afternoon. Eliza Cotton we've had, Miss Halliday we've had. Miss

235

Brand and Mr. Cunningham say they walked along the beach. She says round about four o'clock she dropped off, and he says he went for a stroll, but never out of sight. Says he wouldn't have left her. Well, he could have, and he could have done the job and got back again—they were only round the next point. But where's the motive? I can't see that either of them has got one."

"As you say. What were the ladies next door doing?"

Crisp did not exactly sniff. He merely gave the impression that he might have done so if he had belonged to the sniffing sex.

"Mrs. Brand says she was in her sitting-room—that's the room corresponding to the one where Mr. Felton was killed. Her sister and Miss Halliday say she puts up her feet and goes to sleep over a book as regular as clockwork every Sunday afternoon. She says she was reading and never closed an eye, and if anyone had gone out of the front door or across in front of the window she'd have known. If you ask me, I should say she was asleep—and she isn't the kind to wake easy."

March nodded.

"And Miss Remington?"

"Says she made herself a cup of coffee in the kitchen, and after that she was up in her room doing this and that. Says she took off her dress and laid down, and she might have dropped off for a bit but she wouldn't swear to it. I asked her if she heard Eliza Cotton in the garden calling the cat, and she says she might have done, she couldn't be sure, Eliza was always calling him. I asked her whether she heard Mr. and Mrs. Felton talking in Mrs. Felton's room, and she said if she did she wouldn't take any notice—the house wasn't their own any longer, and you couldn't expect it to be quiet like it was in Mr. Brand's time. Well, of course I wasn't taking that for an answer. She's a lady that will play up if you give her a chance, so I just let her see I wasn't giving her one. I said, 'Miss Remington, I'm putting it to you straight. Your window and Mrs. Felton's are next door to each other. Did you hear voices coming from Mrs. Felton's room, or did you not? She said yes, she did, and how disturbing it was and people had no consideration for other people's feelings. I asked her could she hear what was said, and she said no, she couldn't, it was just voices. And then she got angry and asked if I thought she didn't hear quite enough of the chatter that went on all day without listening to it more than she could help. I pressed her, but she wouldn't admit to hearing anything more than the voices."

"Have you tried listening in her room whilst someone speaks in the other?"

"I did that next—got her to come up to her room and sent Wilkins in next door. Miss Brand and Mrs. Felton were together in Mrs. Felton's room, and Mrs. Felton showed him where her husband sat when he was talking to her. Well, then Wilkins was to say something like what a fine day it was, and Mrs. Felton was to let him know whether he was speaking about as loud as her husband did."

"How did it come off?"

Crisp frowned.

"Nothing much to go on, if you ask me. Anyone lying down on the bed, well, they wouldn't hear anything but the voices, as Miss Remington said. The nearer you got to the window, the more you'd hear. But only in the way of sound. I didn't get the words of what Wilkins was saying until I went right up to the window and leaned out. So that's what it comes to—if she'd gone and hung right out of that window she could have heard what Felton said, but if she was moving about the room or lying on the bed she couldn't. At least I couldn't." He stooped, pushed the notebook down into his pocket, and said, "Well, I'll be getting back."

When he had gone Miss Silver said,

"A zealous and responsible officer, but perhaps a little inclined to measure everything by his personal standards."

Since this was his own opinion, March made no demur. He merely smiled in a rather non-committal manner and enquired,

"Now what exactly do you mean by that? It wasn't just said to pass the time—was it?"

She said in a thoughtful voice,

"No, Randal. I was reflecting that Cyril Felton was an actor, and that an actor is trained to enunciate more clearly than, shall we say, Constable Wilkins. You will have noticed yourself that Mr. Felton had a very clear and pleasant speaking voice. I was also reflecting that acuteness of hearing varies considerably in quite normal individuals. I seem to have heard that Miss Remington rather prides herself on this quality. Was there not something about her having heard a cry in the night and saying that it might have been a bat?"

"Yes—Crisp said there was something like that. She exasperated him a good deal, I believe."

Miss Silver said gravely,

"Only the most acute hearing is aware of a bat's cry, Randal."

CHAPTER 36

March received Richard Cunningham's demand that Marian Brand and her sister should on no account be expected to spend another night at Cove House with gravity. Impatient of the passing of what he regarded as precious time, Richard had interrupted the Chief Constable's interview with Miss Silver by walking into the room and putting his point.

"Two people have been murdered here, and I want to get those girls away."

He got a very serious look.

"Quite apart from the question of accommodation, which I believe you would find very difficult, I think you must realize that until all the possible evidence has been obtained and gone through no one who was in the house at the time can be considered to be entirely beyond suspicion."

"Good heavens—you can't suspect that poor girl Mrs. Felton!"

"I did not say I suspected her. She was the last person to see her husband alive, and her evidence is of the first importance. There is every likelihood that we may want to question her again, and she should be available for this. We shall, of course, take every precaution for her safety and that of her sister."

"What precaution do you propose to take?"

"I would suggest that Mrs. Felton shares her sister's room tonight. The arrangement had better not be talked about. I also suggest that the two girls keep together, or with yourself or Miss Silver. I will put a man on the bedroom landing with instructions that if he leaves his post for any purpose at all he is to knock on your door so that you may relieve him. Does that satisfy you?"

"I think so. My door will be open anyhow."

March nodded.

"You wouldn't have got rooms anywhere in the neighbourhood. This fine weather has filled the hotels. And the case is bound to be very much discussed—they wouldn't find the notoriety pleasant. Besides, I notice you haven't said a word about their wanting to go. Do they?"

Richard maintained a perfectly inexpressive countenance.

"As a matter of fact Miss Brand rather takes the point of view that this is her house, and that she is responsible for it. I was hoping to induce her to change her mind."

March said, "I think she's right. And you needn't worry. We shall be taking every precaution."

On the other side of the house Mrs. Larkin was going about the business of the search in a very efficient and orderly manner—Penny and her clothes—Mrs. Alfred Brand and Miss Remington and their respective wardrobes. Net result a scratch on Penny's bare brown arm and a smear of blood on her cotton frock, the blood in just the place where it would have been if it had come from the scratch—that is, on the front of the dress and a little to the right. But also just where it might have been if she had handled a blood-stained knife. No other marks either on Penny Halliday or on her clothes.

Mrs. Alfred Brand's dress was not of a colour and pattern to make it easy to see whether it was stained or not, the ground being black with a design of brown and red. Held up to the light, the front breadth disclosed a long dry stain crossing the black background and two bits of red pattern before it petered out against a brown one. At this point, and at this point only, it was possible to discern that the colour of the stain was also red. Mrs. Brand, speaking in a deep angry

240

voice, called her sister and Penny Halliday to witness that they had a red currant and raspberry tart for lunch, and that she had spilt some of the juice on her dress. In spite of which and of a good deal of corroborative detail as to the desirability of bottling your own fruit and the advantage of being able to have raspberries out of season, the garment was set aside with Penny's frock for police inspection, Mrs. Larkin merely replying in a very civil manner that fruit juice was worse than anything to get out, but there were very good cleaners in Ledlington, only the police would have to have the dress first.

Miss Remington's lilac cardigan, her white silk blouse, and her pale grey skirt were spotless. A search of the rest of her wardrobe did bring to light an old navy cotton dress which had been washed out, Miss Cassy declared, on Saturday and rolled down for ironing.

"I shouldn't dream of washing anything out on a Sunday, but if it had been very hot after tea and we were going down on the beach, I might have just run the iron over it and put it on. One gets one's things so dirty on the sands. I am afraid I have never lost a rather childish love of poking into pools, and really the weather has been so warm, I thought this old cotton dress—"

Mrs. Larkin said in her quiet way that the weather was very seasonable indeed, and put the rolled-up dress with the other things to be handed over to the police.

When she had finished she went round to the front door of the other house and rang the bell. Admitted by Eliza, who had reached a state of disapproval which gave her the appearance of being by far the likeliest person in either house to have committed a murder, she was handed over to Miss Silver, who immediately offered herself as the first subject for search.

They had quite a pleasant little conversation whilst this

was going on in Miss Silver's bedroom. Mrs. Larkin, being passionately addicted to crochet, became quite warm in her admiration of the edging which decorated Miss Silver's high-necked spencer and serviceable flannelette knickers, which had three rows on each leg, each row being a little wider than the last. On being informed that the design was original she was emboldened to ask for the pattern, which Miss Silver promised to write down for her. After which they parted on very friendly terms.

Since Miss Silver had submitted to being searched, even Eliza could not manage to feel that she was being singled out for insult. Her demeanour was, however, that of a martyr about to be put to the question. In a voice of awful indignation she invited Miss Silver to be present, observing darkly that there were those she wouldn't name but she wouldn't put it past them to make up something against you if there wasn't anything without they did. After which she stalked up to her room and gave Mrs. Larkin and even Miss Silver the surprise of their lives when the removal of her black afternoon dress displayed pink silk cami-knickers with French legs. Nothing more compromising than this came to light.

Marian Brand also asked Miss Silver to be present. She went through the unpleasant business with dignity and simplicity, and was glad when it was over.

Ina Felton was last on the list. She undressed, and afterwards dressed again as if she hardly noticed what she was doing. There was no stain on any of her things. But in the bathroom between her room and her sister's a pale blue dress had been washed out and hung up to dry. It was the one she had worn at the picnic. She declared that she had not worn it again. Marian Brand said that it was she who had washed it out before lunch, and Miss Silver was able to confirm that it had been hanging there when she came home from church. She was a little vexed when the Chief Constable remarked later on that if Mrs. Felton had intended to kill her husband she could very easily have slipped on the still damp dress, and after stabbing him have rinsed it out again and put it back on its hanger to dry. He was perhaps not unwilling to get some of his own back, since she had once more been advancing with earnestness a theory which he could not help regarding as being farfetched, and for which he could see no evidence at all. As a result, she became a little remote and addressed herself to casting on the requisite number of stitches for the first of another pair of stockings in the sadly uninteresting grey wool which is the schoolboy's universal wear.

CHAPTER 37

There was an eventual departure of the police, with the exception of Constable Wilkins, who remained behind to clutter Eliza's kitchen until such time as the family repaired to their rooms for the night, when he had instructions to be on duty on the bedroom landing and on no account to allow himself to be overtaken by sleep. Everyone was only too anxious for the day to be over. Violent events have much the same effect upon the day in which they fall as a bomb has upon the surrounding country. The bomb itself may provide a brief excitement, but it reduces all about it to a condition of arid dullness. As the dust settles, everything within its reach is blighted.

Eliza served a cold supper out of a tin—one of the more depressing so-called lunch loaves, with a marmoreal cornflour shape and some rather grey apple to follow. In the kitchen Constable Wilkins partook of herrings and cocoa under the watchful eye of Mactavish, who exasperated Eliza by repeating his almost soundless mew until she left off her own supper to bone a nice piece of herring for him, and then intimated that it wasn't good enough by backing away from it and continued to mew. Eliza said "Drat!" but she fetched shredded meat and breadcrumbs from the larder and warmed up the gravy that had been left from lunch. After which Mactavish condescended to partake and Eliza was able to go on with her own supper.

By the time that Constable Wilkins was well away with his third herring and his second cup of cocoa she was preparing him for his night's vigil by narrating the really horrid tale of her grandfather's experience in a haunted house. It had so many uncomfortable similarities to the present situation that Joe Wilkins wasn't really able to relish that last herring. Like himself, Eliza's grandfather had been obliged to sit up all night on the landing of a house where there'd been murder done. It was an old house and it creaked something dreadful, and right in the middle of the night there was a footstep where no lawful footstep ought to be. Down in the hall, and all the family upstairs and abed. It was Eliza's best story, and she told it very well, dwelling with loving care on how her grandfather could feel the short hairs on the back of his neck prickling. When she came to the bit about his taking the candle and coming down to the turn of the stair, Joe Wilkins found himself very resolute that he would do no such thing. Asking for trouble, that was what it was, and why couldn't her grandfather stay where he was, the silly old fool?

Eliza dropped her voice to a frightening whisper.

"And round the turn of the stair the candle came out of the socket and went rolling down afront of him. There was my grandfather, and there was his shadow on the plaster,

244

and the last thing he saw when the candle went rolling down was his own shadow come off of the wall and standing there on the mat at the foot of the stair looking up. And the candle went out."

"Wh-what happened?"

Eliza's voice became brisk.

"What should happen? My grandfather come back and got another candle, and when he went down again there wasn't anything there."

When supper was over in the dining-room Miss Silver announced her intention of stepping in next door.

"Poor Penny—a trying experience for a young girl, being searched. And Mrs. Brand and Miss Remington—really most unpleasant and disturbing. I think it would console them to know that we have all been subjected to the same ordeal. But I shall not stay long."

Penny opened the door. She was pale under her tan, but she had lost what Eliza called her heart-rendering look. She was tired, and everything was dreadful, but Felix had gone off to the drawing-room with the score of his quartet, laid aside for months. Upon the blank of thought images and combinations had begun to take shape. Every now and then he touched the keys of the piano, every now and then he wrote. Penny was so thankful to see him working again that nothing else really mattered.

She took Miss Silver into the parlour, and listened to the aunts animadverting on a system which allowed the police to penetrate into private houses and search the occupants.

Miss Silver was most sympathetic. She herself had been searched.

"Oh, yes, indeed, Mrs. Brand. Not at all pleasant—most distasteful in fact. But I felt it my duty. It is, after all, for our protection. We shall none of us feel safe till this dreadful business is cleared up. I am sure you must feel that."

Florence Brand said heavily,

"I have lived here for nearly twenty years. Nothing happened until my brother-in-law made that unjust will."

Cassy Remington tossed her head.

"Miss Silver won't be interested in Martin's will," she said in an acid voice. "And really, Florence, I can't see how you can make out that it has anything to do with Helen Adrian or Cyril Felton, neither of whom came in for a penny or ever expected to."

Miss Silver said, "Indeed?"

Cassy Remington jingled her chain.

"I don't know why we go on talking about it. It is all extremely unpleasant. Think what the headlines in the papers are going to be, to go no farther than that. Eliza and Mrs. Bell were sending away reporters most of Friday and all Saturday. At least Mrs. Bell would have if she had been here on Saturday afternoon, but she wasn't, so we just kept everything shut. And of course they'll be a great deal worse tomorrow." There was a sparkle in her eyes as she fixed them on her sister and repeated with energy, "A great deal worse!"

Florence Brand pressed her rather thick pale lips together and said nothing. Miss Cassy continued to talk.

"And it's not as if that would be the worst of it. I shouldn't be at all surprised if we didn't have bus-loads of trippers! And have to cook for ourselves! I shouldn't think Mrs. Bell and Mrs. Woolley would come—not after they hear about Cyril Felton. And it's quite extraordinary how things get round. Of course everyone in England will know by the time the papers are out tomorrow."

Mrs. Brand gave her sister a slow, cold look of dislike.

"I can see no good in making out that things are worse than they are. Mrs. Bell wouldn't miss the reporters for anything, and I don't suppose Mrs. Woolley would either?" Her voice went down into depths of disapproval. "They are enjoying themselves." She did not say, "And so are you," but it was in her tone.

Cassy Remington tossed her head.

"Oh, well, I suppose we shall all have our pictures in the papers," she said.

Miss Silver did not stay very long. When she got up to go she asked if she might go round by the garden, as it would save Eliza coming to the front door.

"There is so much extra to do, and I feel that I am adding quite enough to her work by being in the house."

Penny took her out through the kitchen. But when they were there, and the door to the hall had been shut, Miss Silver paused and said,

"Are you still sleeping in the attic?"

Penny looked a little surprised, a little reluctant.

"No, I've come back to my own room. I had to move out for Helen Adrian, but they thought I had better come back. They thought it would be better for us all to be on the same floor." After a pause she added, "It's silly to mind."

Miss Silver smiled at her very kindly indeed.

"The room is your own. You will soon overcome any other associations. And the sooner the step is taken, the more quickly this will be done."

Penny nodded.

"Eliza knew someone whose daughter died, and she kept the room just as it was, and hot water put there, and her nightgown laid out—" A little shudder went over her.

Miss Silver gave a gentle cough.

"Very morbid indeed, and not at all in keeping with Christian hope and faith." Then, with a slight access of briskness, "I am going to ask you if you will do something for me."

Penny had the strangest feeling, a sense that she was going to be asked something important. And of course what nonsense! Because what could Miss Silver possibly want her to do that would matter twopence one way or the other? It was dreadfully silly to think it could, and dreadfully silly to find her voice shaking as she said,

"Oh—yes—what is it?"

Miss Silver's air of kind concern persisted, but it was backed up by a certain firmness.

"It may sound strange to you, my dear, but I hope you will do what I ask."

Penny said, "What is it?" again, and this time her voice didn't shake, because she held it steady.

"I want you to turn back the key of the door between the houses on the bedroom floor."

Penny said very slowly and stiffly, "The door is bolted on the other side."

Miss Silver coughed and said, "Yes."

Penny's eyes were fixed on her—wide brown eyes the colour of peat-water.

"You mean—you might want—to come through?"

"There is no need to look too far ahead. Constable Wilkins is spending the night on our side of the house. He will be on the bedroom landing. Without anticipating any need for his help, I should prefer to feel that there was a possibility of access."

Penny did not ask her what she meant. She kept that wide, fixed gaze and said,

"I don't know—if I ought to—"

"I think so."

"Very well."

Miss Silver said, "Go and do it now, my dear."

Unspoken between them was the thought that there would at this moment be no one on the bedroom floor.

They stepped out into the garden. The smell of the wall-flower came up. The fruit trees against the wall were shedding their blossom. The sea showed blue and calm. Miss

Silver, looking round upon the scene, admired its beauty and remarked that it reminded her of Lord Tennyson's description of the island-valley of Avilion—"fair with orchard lawns, and bowery hollows crown'd with summer sea." After which she proceeded along the flagged path to Eliza's kitchen door and Penny went back into her own side of the house.

As she passed the drawing-room, Felix struck a soft full chord. She hesitated for a moment, and then turned the handle slowly and stood there looking in. He was at the piano, leaning forward and scribbling on one of the tossed pages which littered the polished top. His pencil drove furiously. His face was turned in her direction, but he did not see her. He had gone through into his own country, and as far as Cove House and its problems were concerned he had ceased to be aware of it or of them.

Penny watched him for a little while. Then she closed the door and went away.

She went up on to the bedroom landing and along the little bit of passage which led to the dividing wall between the houses. When she came to the door she turned back the key, and left it there and came away.

CHAPTER 38

By a quarter past ten the ground floor on Marian Brand's side of the house had been deserted by everyone except Constable Wilkins, who had orders from Eliza to stay where he was in the kitchen until the ladies were ready for bed, and then Mr. Cunningham would let him know and he would go up and sit on the landing. As by this time he was a good deal more frightened of Eliza than he was of Crisp and the Chief Constable put together, he said, "Yes, Miss Cotton," and remained where he was in a very amenable manner, whereupon she departed to her attic, where she locked the door and wedged a chair under the handle in approved country fashion.

It was dusk outside, but not quite dark. In the house it was dark enough. As Miss Silver crossed the landing she stood by the bathroom door for a moment and heard on her right the sound of voices coming from the room which Ina Felton was sharing with Marian Brand. On her left Ina's own room lay dark and empty. She turned the handle gently and went in. The window was shut, but the curtains had not been drawn. She could see a pale breadth of sky.

She went over to the window, opened the right half of the casement, and leaned out. On one side the two windows of Marian's room showed chinks of light. On the other, beyond the dividing wall between the houses, everything was dark. The drawing-room windows had been shut. The occasional sounds from the piano had ceased. There was no light in Cassy Remington's room, nor in the one beyond it, which had been Helen Adrian's and was now Penny Halliday's again. The evening was very warm, and the windows of both these rooms were open. Miss Silver closed and latched the casement which she had opened and returned across the landing to her own room. She did not put the light on, but went over to the window and looked out.

The ground floor of the next-door house was dark on this side, as it had been on the other. Over the parlour she could see that Felix Brand's window was open and the room quite dark. But in the room next to hers, which was Florence Brand's, just on the other side of the dividing wall, though the casement window stood wide, there was a light behind the chintz curtains, throwing up a rather heavy pattern of red and purple rhododendrons. Miss Silver had not been in the house for two days without hearing all about those curtains. There had been good thick ones with linings, ageing a little in '39, when of course owing to the outbreak of war it had not been possible to replace them. Seven years later, when they actually fell to pieces, the best that could be achieved was a chintz, and linings were not to be thought of.

As she leaned from the window and became aware of voices from behind the rhododendrons she reflected that this was indeed a fortunate circumstance. Lined damask curtains such as had once obscured the light and prevented the air from entering Mrs. Brand's room would have had a sadly deadening effect upon sound. As a gentle-woman, Miss Silver would not have dreamed of listening to a private conversation. As a private investigator, she had often conceived it her duty to do so. She was very near that open window. The chintz, although so darkly patterned, presented hardly any obstacle to sound. The voices were those of Mrs. Alfred Brand and her sister. Miss Silver conceived it her duty to listen.

She was not the only person to do so. Penny was the last to come upstairs. Since Eliza had moved over to the other side of the house it was she who made a round of the down-stairs rooms to make sure that the doors were locked and the windows latched. She picked up the *Some Chapters of my Life* from where it had once more slipped to the floor, plumped up the cushions and straightened the chairs in the parlour, and then passed on to the drawing-room. Felix, of course, had forgotten to shut the garden door. It stood wide, and the warm air came in with that peculiar sweetness which is never felt by day.

She latched the door and stood for a moment looking at the scrawled, untidy sheets with which the piano top was strewn. The room was full of Felix. He might have been standing there beside her. She came away no more than a minute or two before Miss Silver looked out of Ina Felton's window and found the drawing-room dark.

Penny had finished her round. She went upstairs. The landing was dark. A streak of light on the far side showed that Florence Brand was in her room with the door ajar, and the moment Penny heard Cassy Remington's voice it wasn't hard to guess why Aunt Cassy never could shut a door properly. She kept tight hold of the handle and turned it, and went on keeping hold of it so that it turned back again when she let go. It was one of a lot of little things which had always made it difficult to be fond of Aunt Cassy however hard you tried, and it exasperated Felix to swearing-point. But then, of course, it wasn't at all difficult to do that.

The light-switch was over by the bedroom door. It ought, of course, to have been at the head of the stairs, but Florence Brand's motto was, and always had been, "Put it near me and it will be quite convenient for everyone." There had been raging rows about that light-switch. Penny remembered them quite well in the year before the war when Martin Brand made up his mind to link up with the grid and have electric light put in. It still shook her a little to remember them—rows do something really horrid to children. In the end Florence Brand got her own way. The switch was on the wall just outside her door. It was on the wall not six inches away from where the strip of light showed at the door's edge.

As Penny lifted her hand to it she heard Cassy Remington say in her light, high voice,

"I shall say Felix did it."

CHAPTER 39

The hand which Penny had lifted stayed where it was, just short of the switch. It did not seem to belong to her any more. There was a streak of light in front of her eyes along the edge of the door, and there was Cassy Remington's voice saying, "I shall say Felix did it." She saw the light, she heard the words. She felt nothing. She stood quite still and waited for what would come next.

Florence Brand made a sound of some kind. Cassy Remington's voice went higher.

"I shall say he did it, and the police will take him away, and then we shall have a little peace."

This time Florence spoke. Her voice had the same sound as before, an odd heavy tone that might have been disapproval. She said,

"They don't believe everything you tell them."

Cassy laughed angrily.

"They'll believe this. Because it's only reasonable. Who else had any reason to kill Helen Adrian—answer me that! You can't, can you? Nobody can. He was crazy about her—crazy with jealousy. He saw the light on that blue and yellow scarf she was wearing over her head, and he followed her down to the terrace and pushed her over the edge after Cyril Felton had come in. And then of course Cyril guessed and tried to blackmail him, and he killed him too."

Florence Brand said,

"How do you know?"

There was that high, excited laugh again.

253

"I saw him come in at the gate."

"When did you see him?"

"I was looking for Penny out of this window. She is always so forgetful when she is with Felix—I wanted to know whether she would be back to get the tea. I came in here, and I looked out of the window. I'm going to tell the police what I did, and I'm going to tell them I saw Felix come in off the road."

"And did you?"

"Really, Florence—what a thing to say! Of course I did!"

"He didn't come in till after the police got here."

Cassy Remington said with enjoyment,

"Oh, yes, he did. I looked out of the window, and I saw him. He came in at twenty to five. I saw him, but he didn't see me, because I stood behind the curtain."

Florence Brand said slowly,

"He couldn't have got here. Penny left him up on the cliff at five-and-twenty to five."

"And you believe her! She would lie her head off for Felix, and you know it! Besides, her watch might be wrong, or anything. And he could have run after her and got here very nearly as soon as she did, couldn't he? The police won't take any notice of what Penny says. They won't have any opportunity—I can promise you that!" She laughed.

There was a sound in the room as if Florence Brand was getting to her feet with one of her ponderous movements. Penny heard her say,

"You had better be careful, Cassy. You had better sleep on it. I don't think—"

"You never do," said Cassy Remington in a spiteful voice. "You haven't enough brain, and you are too indolent. But you had better do what you can to back me up. They've taken that dress of yours away, you know, and when they find there's a bloodstain all down the front—"

254

Florence Brand said, "A bloodstain!" Her voice had a shocked sound. Then she seemed to pull herself together.

"Really, Cassy, I don't know what you are thinking about! You know as well as I do that it was the juice out of the tart at lunch."

"Are you sure about that? Are you really quite sure? I wouldn't be too sure if I were you."

"You were there—you saw me spill the juice."

"Did I? Do you know, I wouldn't like to have to swear to it."

"Penny saw—"

"I don't think we need bother about Penny."

"It was fruit juice. They can tell that by testing it."

Cassy laughed, high up and shrill.

"Oh, my dear Florence, I have a feeling that they will find something much more interesting than currant juice! That is one of the reasons I am going to tell the police about Felix. He could have come in, you know, and wiped the knife on your skirt whilst you were reading about the Wessex Parson. Or perhaps better let the Parson go, and stick to it that you were fast asleep and snoring. I don't mind saying you were. After all, I am your sister."

She was coming towards the door, but before she reached it she turned to say something more. What it was, Penny didn't know. Her hand dropped to her side, her feet took her quickly, silently across the landing. She hesitated for a moment, and then went into Cassy Remington's room and shut the door.

It was at this point that Miss Silver drew back from the sill upon which she had been leaning. The conversation which she had overheard alarmed her very much. She considered that the time had come to take a step of which the Chief Constable could not possibly approve, a fact which she deplored without allowing this in any way to deflect her.

As she emerged upon the landing she observed that Richard Cunningham's door was ajar. On the impulse, she turned and knocked. It was opened immediately, and showed him to be fully dressed. When he had joined her on the landing she said, in a low tone,

"Mr. Cunningham, I am not easy. Will you do just what I ask you?"

"What do you want me to do?"

"I am going through into the other house. The door has been unlocked, and I have taken the precaution of oiling the bolts. If I call you, come at once. If I do not, stay in the passage on this side of the door."

"Do you want me to call Wilkins?"

"No—there must be no noise. If there should be any disturbance, you can call to him. I think you had better take off your shoes."

A low-powered bulb afforded enough light for him to see that she had not neglected this precaution herself, and that even in black woollen stockings her feet were remarkably neat. They carried her without any sound at all past Ina Felton's empty room to the door between the houses. When he joined her there the bolts were drawn back and she was turning the handle. The passage and the landing beyond were dark, a circumstance which she considered providential.

Leaving the door ajar behind her, she went forward along the passage and disappeared from Richard Cunningham's view.

CHAPTER 40

Cassy Remington came across the landing from her sister's room. She did not put on the light, because she had lived nearly twenty years in the house and could have walked about it blindfold either by day or by night. As she opened her bedroom door, someone moved over by the window.

On the instant her hand was at the switch. The light showed Penny very pale. She had been leaning out filling her lungs with the fresh salt-tasting air. She stood up now and fixed her eyes upon Cassy Remington.

"Good gracious me—what a fright you gave me, Penny! What are you doing in the dark? And what do you want?"

"I want to speak to you."

"Well, I'm here, aren't I? And half the insects in the cove will be here too, with the windows open and the light drawing them." She came across the room at a run as she spoke, pulled the casements to, drew the curtains across them, and said sharply, "Well, what is it?"

As she came back into the middle of the room, Penny's eyes followed her. It was a crowded place. There was a big old-fashioned bed, a monumental wardrobe, a tallboy, a double wash-stand with a marble top, a pedestal table in polished walnut covered with knick-knacks, photograph-frames and odds and ends. A steaming cup of coffee rested upon the latest book from Miss Cassy's library list. In the middle of everything else Penny found room to wonder about the coffee, because Cassy never took it at night—she said it kept her awake. At a second impatient "Well?" she said,

"I want to speak to you. I must."

Cassy Remington had not shut the door behind her when she came in. She did not shut it now. Why should she? Felix was in his room across the landing, and Florence in hers. If either of them opened a door, she would hear it at once—she was very proud of her quick hearing. They were both behind shut doors, and there was no one else in the house. She left the door as it was, and said softly,

"What do you want, Penny?"

Penny was dreadfully pale. She said,

"I want to speak to you. I want to tell you I heard what you said just now—in Aunt Florence's room."

Cassy made one of her jerky movements.

"I should think you would be ashamed of listening at a door. Like a spy!"

Penny shook her head.

"No, I am not ashamed. You said you were going to tell the police it was Felix. You said you were going to say that you saw him come in from the road at twenty to five."

Cassy nodded.

"It will be my duty. I ought to have told them at once."

Penny said, "But it isn't true. I left him up on the cliff. I got here at a quarter to five. He wasn't here until a great deal later than that. Inspector Crisp had come."

Cassy Remington laughed.

"That is your story! Mine is different. I shall say he came in by the gate at twenty to five. I shall be asked about it at the inquest, and that is what I shall say. On oath!"

"Why?"

"Really, Penny!"

"I can tell you why. I can tell the police. They took away that dress you washed, didn't they? You told them you washed it on Saturday and rolled it down for ironing in case you went down on the beach after tea today. But you didn't

258

wash it on Saturday. The door of your wardrobe was open this morning when I came in to help you make your bed, and that navy blue dress was hanging there. It hadn't been washed then."

"What does it matter when it was washed?"

"It wasn't washed at lunch-time."

"I suppose you went and looked in my cupboard!"

Penny said, "No—why should I? But I washed my hands in the bathroom just before lunch, and the basin was clean. After I came in from the cliff I went to wash again, and there were blue stains. Navy always runs. So I knew you had washed something that ran blue."

There was a silence in the room. Outside on the dark landing Miss Silver waited for it to break. She could see no more than the handsbreadth of the open door had to show—a section of wallpaper, curtains, coverlet, carpet. Nothing to inform her of where Penny was, or Cassy Remington. But her ears served her better. They told her that Penny was over by the window, and Miss Remington a good deal nearer the door. She had already made up her mind that if the distance between them were materially lessened, she must be prepared to enter the room. Meanwhile it was in the highest degree desirable that she should be able to see what was going on. She reflected that Cassy Remington would be facing in the direction of the window, and consequently would have her back to the door. She decided to take the risk of widening the handsbreadth and applied a gentle pressure.

The edge of the pedestal table came into view, with the cup of coffee standing on Miss Cassy's library book. A little more, and she could see Miss Cassy's shoulder, arm, and hand. The arm hung straight. The hand gripped on a fold of her grey skirt. If it had been clenched like that upon anything which would have served as a missile or a weapon, Miss Silver would have gone in at once, but all that it clutched was a piece of grey flannel. But with what energy, what a fury of bloodless knuckles, strained muscles, and digging nails!

The door moved a very little more. Cassy Remington's head came into the picture. It was turned towards the window. The silence was broken by a light, high laugh.

"Really! My dear Penny, how ridiculous you are! If you want to know, I rinsed out some handkerchiefs with blue. What a grand discovery! What a marvellous piece of news for the police! Are you sure you wouldn't like to ring them up about it at once?"

Penny said quietly and steadily, "There isn't any blue in the house. I finished the last a week ago."

The hand remained at its dreadful tension, but the light laugh came again.

"Oh, my *dear* Penny! It doesn't occur to you that I might have a store of my own? Really, you know, this is all too absurd! You've let yourself get worked up about nothing! And I'm going to send you to bed with a nice hot drink and one of Florence's sleeping tablets."

"No!" The word came on a quick uneven breath.

Cassy Remington said,

"Oh, yes, my dear, I think so. Little girls who are all worked up and fancying things had better have a good long sleep and forget all the nonsense they have been frightening them- selves with. You can have my coffee. I shouldn't really take it at night—it keeps me awake. I had a fancy for it, but I won't take it now. Florence let me have two of her tablets last night, and I only took one. I've got the other, over by the bed." As she spoke she moved away and out of sight. "I expect you will find one quite enough. I am sure you need a good sleep. You can't swallow tablets, can you? I remember how tiresome you always were as a child." She came back into sight again, reaching forward over the table. "Here you

260

are—just one tablet. You can dissolve it in the coffee yourself. And I'd like to see you take it, because you really do need a nice long sleep."

The hand with the tablet remained stretched out. Penny made no move. She said,

"It's no good. I know."

The tablet was set down on a photograph album. Cassy Remington's voice went sharp.

"Do you want me to go to the telephone and ring up the police *now*? I am going to unless you take that tablet and go off to bed. I shall tell them that I saw Felix come in off the road at twenty to five. I shall tell them I know my watch was right because I set it by the wireless at one o'clock. I was looking out of Florence's window, you know, and I saw him. But if you will take that tablet and go off to bed, we can talk about it again in the morning. When you are calmer."

"No!"

Cassy Remington struck her hands together.

"You want me to telephone to the police? Really, Penny, you are the most unreasonable creature! Do you suppose I am anxious to bring disgrace on the family? After all, Felix is my nephew."

"You were very careful to tell Inspector Crisp that he wasn't."

Cassy stamped her foot.

"The papers will say that he is! And everybody knows we brought him up. Come along—take your coffee and the tablet, and we'll talk in the morning. You don't want to force me to do anything that you'll be sorry for all your life. Because once I've told the police—once I've told them, Penny—there'll be an end of it. I can't say it and take it back again!" She laughed suddenly. "Dear me, I don't know what all the fuss is about. I used to think you would do anything for Felix. But if you won't—well, I can't make you,

261

can I? I'll just go down and ring up the police."

Penny said, "No—no!"

Miss Silver could see her now. Her eyes were wide and dark, her hands pressed together under her chin. She took a slow step forward, and another, and another, and came to the table. One of the clasped hands moved, released itself, and came down towards the tablet. But it did not take it up. It caught at the table edge. She said in a very low voice,

"If I wasn't here—there would be nothing to stop you."

"There isn't anything to stop me now," said Cassy Remington.

CHAPTER 41

Miss Silver pushed the door open and came into the room. Cassy Remington whisked round. For a moment those rather bright blue eyes of hers stared. Then she gave a little affected cry.

"Oh! You gave me quite a fright! What is it? How in the world did you come here? What do you want?" With each of the short sentences her voice was higher and angrier.

Miss Silver said very composedly,

"I want to make sure that Penny does not drink that coffee or take that tablet which you have laid out for her."

Cassy Remington laughed, high and shrill.

"The tablet! Dear me—you must forgive me if I laugh! You can have it analysed if you like! And what a fool you will be making of yourself! I can show you the bottle it came out of. They are perfectly harmless tablets. My sister has taken them for years."

262

Miss Silver coughed gently.

"How full was the bottle when you took it from Mrs. Brand's room, and how empty is it now? It is that cup of coffee which should be analysed. I think I will take charge of it."

She came up to the table as she spoke. But she had hardly lifted the cup before Cassy caught her by the wrist and dashed it from her hand. The cup fell, the coffee spilled upon the carpet. The blue eyes blazed in triumph.

"Now get it analysed!"

Miss Silver raised her voice and called, "Mr. Cunningham!"

It was plain that he had not remained on the far side of the door between the houses, since he was in the room before she had finished saying his name. Miss Silver addressed him immediately and without any sign of disturbance.

"Will you be so kind as to pick up that coffee-cup? The contents will have to be analysed." Then, as he did so, "There should, I think, be enough of the coffee left to show whether it has been tampered with."

He stood there with the cup in his hand, tilting it.

"There is about a third left, and a considerable white sediment."

Penny had not moved, except to lift her eyes to Miss Silver's face. They had a wide, fixed look. Cassy Remington stood beside the table, rigid with anger, her colour high. At Richard's last word she made a sudden spring, catching at his hand and at the cup. But the attempt failed. The hand was lifted and the cup held high above her reach. In a kind of whirlwind of fury she ran out of the room and down the stairs.

Richard Cunningham said, "What now?" He brought his hand down and gave Miss Silver the cup. She said gravely,

"I think you should go after her, and I think you should be quick."

She set down the cup, went over to the window, and opened it. The sound of running feet came to them, stumbling in their haste. She said gravely,

"You had better go through the other house and take Constable Wilkins with you. I will call up the police."

She had a start of them. Richard Cunningham had to put his shoes on, lay hands on a torch, and collect Joe Wilkins from the kitchen. They went out of the back door and stood listening at the edge of the lawn where the steps went down towards the beach. She could have reached it, knowing every step of the way. But the tide was up, there was no sand to muffle her footsteps. If she moved upon the shingle, they would hear her. They heard nothing.

Descending from terrace to terrace, each was found to be empty. They came down the last steps and stood where the body of Helen Adrian had lain. The water did not come up so far. Even the highest tide with the wind behind it would not come up as far as the steps.

Richard spoke his thought aloud.

"She couldn't get around the point."

"Not either way—not for getting on for three hours, I should say."

"Could she get away up the cove?"

Joe shook his head in the dark.

"Not likely—not her. I've done it when I was a boy, but I wouldn't say I could do it now—not in the dark."

They did what they could. Joe tramped in the shingle, making a circuit of the upper end of the cove, throwing the torchlight before him, whilst Richard stood on guard at the bottom of the steps. Listening to the noise which his boots made on the shingle, magnified by an echo from the steep sides of the cove, Richard considered that Cassy Remington had very little chance of getting away unheard. He began to wonder if they had missed her in the dark somewhere on

264

one of the terraces, a supposition which brought a host of unwelcome fears in its train. Suppose she had doubled back into the house. If she was the murderer they had been looking for she might be insane, and was certainly dangerous. He endured some of the longest and most uncomfortable minutes of his life until the arrival of the police set him free to go back to the house. He had not imagined that he would ever greet Crisp with so much relief.

He found everyone up in both houses, and a state of furious activity prevailing, with Crisp at his most belligerent directing it. Everyone, of course, had done everything they shouldn't. It was inexcusable that the coffee should have been spilt. It was inexcusable that Miss Remington should have been allowed to leave the house. For his part, he could not see why she had done so. He knew what he would call evidence, but apparently Miss Silver had different ideas about it. Admitting that the two-thirds-empty coffee-cup contained a sediment, it wasn't for him to say what it was. All this in front of everyone in the drawing-room.

Miss Silver coughed with dignity.

"I have told you of the conversation which I was able to overhear between Miss Remington and Mrs. Brand, Inspector. This is confirmed by Mrs. Brand herself, and by Miss Penny Halliday who also overheard it. To all three of us it was, I think, evidence that Miss Remington intended to accuse Mr. Felix Brand. I do not think that any one of us believed that she would be telling the truth. When she told her sister she intended to tell the police that she had seen Mr. Felix come in off the road at twenty to five, Mrs. Brand replied, 'And did you?' After which Miss Remington attempted to frighten her sister into acquiescence by asserting that her dress would be found to be stained down the front with blood, as well as with the fruit juice spilled on it at lunch. If this proves to be the case, both Mr. Felix and Miss Penny, as well as Eliza Cotton, will tell you that Mrs. Brand sleeps heavily in the afternoon, and that it would be perfectly possible for the murderer to have wiped the knife on her dress without waking her up. I believe you will find that that is what Miss Remington did."

Florence Brand stared between resentment and relief. To be told that she slept heavily—and in front of all those people! But to have Cassy make her out a murderess! She came down on the side of relief. She said in a dull voice,

"She was always spiteful from a child!"

The search for Cassy Remington went on. Lights flashed on the beach, and the sound of men's voices came up. Nobody went to bed. Eliza made tea and brought it in. By an unspoken consensus of opinion no one suggested coffee.

It was during her second cup of tea that Florence Brand said in an affronted manner,

"I really cannot think where Cassy can be. We are all being kept out of our beds. It is most uncomfortable."

Miss Silver coughed, and supplied the *mot juste*.

"Crime is an excessively uncomfortable thing, Mrs. Brand."

CHAPTER 42

During the short time which elapsed before the arrival of the police Miss Silver witnessed a curious little scene. The telephone was in the dining-room, and she had perforce to leave Penny in order to ring up the station at Ledlington. She did so with reluctance, and made what haste she could to return. She had a tenderness for young girls, and was concerned for the shock which had been suffered.

As she came up the stairs, Felix Brand's door was thrown open and he came out on to the landing, a pair of trousers hastily pulled on, his pyjama jacket open at the throat, his black hair standing on end like the crest on a helmet. Seeing Miss Silver, who had by then arrived upon the top step, he checked, stared, and called out,

"What's happening?"

Miss Silver coughed.

"Miss Remington has, I believe, just made an attempt upon Penny's life."

His face worked. He said, "Penny—" in a stunned voice. And, as if it had been a call to her, she came running out of Cassy Remington's room, stumbling and weeping, to fling herself into his arms. They closed round her. The dark dishevelled head was bent. They murmured incoherences which were meant for each other and for no one else.

Miss Silver took the opportunity of returning to her room and resuming her shoes, a very neat pair with little beaded bows reserved for evening wear. Competent as she was to confront any situation with dignity, she would not have wished to meet Inspector Crisp in her stocking feet. The loss of an inch in height alone—to say nothing of the distaste which a gentlewoman feels for appearing in public with her toilet incomplete!

When she had put on her shoes she went up the steep attic stair to knock upon Eliza's door and acquaint her with what had happened. It appeared that Eliza was not surprised.

"A spiteful little toad if there ever was one. Always wanting what she hadn't got, and the sharp end of her tongue for those that had it. Mr. Brand couldn't abide her, and that's a fact. But Penny that never harmed a soul!" Eliza reached for a formidable flannel dressing-gown. "She'll take it hard. You shouldn't have left her."

Miss Silver smiled in a perfectly amiable manner and advised her to dress.

"Penny is with Mr. Felix, and I believe he is comforting her better than anyone else could. Perhaps you would put a kettle on. I expect we shall all be glad of a cup of tea presently. I am afraid that it may be very late indeed before we get to bed."

It was very late indeed. But in the end the search was given up and the police departed, to return again with the first of the daylight. The tide was out, and in the light before the sunrise the wet sands and the rocks which ran out across them on either side of the cove had something of the look of a silverpoint drawing. There was no colour yet. Sky and sea, rock, sand and shingle, waited for it. With the first touch of the sun there would be blue shoaling to green and amethyst in the water, and pale forget-me-not blue in the sky. The rocks would have their olive and purple shadows, and sand and shingle would shine in all the shades from gold to brown. But the sun had not yet risen, and everything was grey and chill when the two constables whom Crisp had sent to resume the search came on the body of Cassy Remington in one of the rocky pools. Just how she got there, no one would ever know. In the panic fear which had sent her running from the house she may have forgotten that the tide was up and stumbled into deep water before she could check herself. There was a sudden drop not far from the high tide mark, and she could not swim. Or the sea may have held less terror for her than having to face exposure and the sentence of the law. Nobody would ever know. The verdict at the inquest would be death by misadventure.

There were two other inquests. Penny had to give her evidence, and Miss Silver to give hers. Analysis of the tablet which Miss Remington had offered Penny showed it to be quite harmless by itself, but the coffee in which it was to have

268

been dissolved already contained so much of the same drug as to make it highly improbable that she would ever have waked again. Mrs. Brand deposed to having a bottle of these tablets. It had been three-quarters full, and was now empty.

The verdict was a foregone conclusion. Nobody could leave the court with any doubt that the cove murders had been committed by Cassy Remington, and that she had met her death after attempting yet another.

Miss Silver bade a gracious farewell to Inspector Crisp. It was their third encounter, and there still existed considerable irritation on his side. There was nothing on hers but a cordial appreciation of his zeal and devotion to duty. This ceremony over, she returned to Cove House for tea, after which meal she intended to rejoin her niece Ethel at Farne. Ina Felton, who had also had to give evidence, went straight to her room, where Eliza brought her a tray. The party in the study consisting only of Marian Brand and Richard Cunningham, Miss Silver felt able, now that the inquests were over, to respond quite frankly when questioned as to what had made her suspect Cassy Remington.

Marian said, "She appeared to have no motive."

Miss Silver coughed.

"For murdering Helen Adrian—no. But after talking to Mr. Cunningham I immediately began to wonder whether Helen Adrian was the person whom the murderer had intended to kill. There was someone else in the house who might have been aimed at—someone for whose death envy, malice, and stupidity might have supplied a motive. I began, in short, to think whether Helen Adrian had not been killed in mistake for the person whose scarf she had been wearing. That blue and yellow head-scarf—the colours were bright and conspicuous—everyone in both houses had seen her wearing it. If someone had looked out of a window on the beach side of the house on Thursday night and had seen the beam of an electric torch flicker over the colours of that scarf, would that person not have taken the wearer to be Marian Brand? It seemed to me the most likely thing in the world. When Mrs. Felton broke her silence and told us what she had seen that night I found that the torchlight had, in fact, picked up the scarf in the way I surmised—Mr. Felton having stumbled on the steps, with the result that the beam threw high. I had from the first considered that it might be Marian Brand whose death was intended. I now became convinced of it. I had to consider who had a motive and an opportunity. Only Penny's and Miss Remington's rooms look out towards the beach. Mrs. Brand or Mr. Felix might have seen the scarf from the bathroom window. Mrs. Brand is not a pleasant character. She appears to be as nearly without natural affection as anyone I have ever encountered. But she is heavy in mind and body, and indolent to the point of sloth. I could not bring myself to believe that she would without any immediate provocation leave the house at night and go down those steps to the beach with the intention of murdering someone. I felt tolerably sure that she would think of a number of excellent reasons for not doing anything that would involve so much effort."

Richard Cunningham permitted himself an appreciative smile.

"How right you are! Do you always see through people just like that? It is rather shattering, you know."

Miss Silver returned the smile.

"It is sometimes useful. Let me continue. Mr. Felix Brand might have killed Helen Adrian in a fit of passionate jealousy, or he might conceivably have killed Miss Marian because the money which would come to him at her death might induce Miss Adrian to marry him, but I could not in either case believe that he would have brought that bloodstained scarf up to the house and hung it on the peg from which it had been taken. If he knew that it was Helen Adrian whom he had killed, it was incredible. Everything pointed to the fact that he was overwhelmed with shock and horror and intent on suicide. He would not have any room in his thought for the scarf, or any care for its disposal. This would apply equally whether he thought he was attacking Marian Brand and discovered his mistake too late, or whether he knew that he was striking Helen Adrian down. With the body of the woman for whom he felt a jealous passion at his feet, I could not bring myself to believe that he would have troubled about the scarf. If, on the other hand, he remained under the impression that he had in fact killed Miss Marian, where was his motive for suicide? Or, supposing him to be overcome by remorse, what possible significance had the return of the scarf? I found myself unable to believe in Felix Brand as the murderer."

Marian said in a voice not perfectly steady,

"You did not think it was someone on this side of the house?"

Miss Silver looked at her very kindly indeed.

"No, my dear. Murder is like a plant. It must have roots, and a certain soil in which to grow. I saw nothing in you or your sister, in Mr. Cunningham or Eliza Cotton, in which such a plant could propagate. People with the habit of considering others, of weighing their obligations, and of observing a temperate self-control, do not suddenly commit murder. In Mr. Felton's case, he had, of course, no moral scruples where money was concerned, but I did not believe him capable of violent crime. He was of a type to shrink from bloodshed. He had no motive strong enough to make him murder Helen Adrian. She was prepared to pay him ten pounds down, and he would, I think, have believed that he would be able to extract further sums from her. As to any question of a mistake of identity, this would have been impossible, since he let Helen Adrian through from the other house and accompanied her to the terrace from which she fell."

Marian was very pale. Richard Cunningham's hand came out and covered hers. Miss Silver coughed with indulgence and resumed her exposition.

"Let us now return to the next-door house. Penny I did not consider at all. She is a good child. In theory she had a motive for wishing Helen Adrian dead, but in practice she was quite incapable of injuring her. That brought me to Miss Remington, whose window looked toward the beach, whose abnormally quick hearing made her the most likely of all the inmates to have heard the glass door in the study open, and whose restless and inquisitive nature might so readily prompt her to investigate. Looking from her window, she would see two people come out of the study and go down toward the beach, one of them a man, the other a woman. She would see what Mrs. Felton saw, the beam of a torch picking up the blue and yellow of that noticeable head-scarf when Mr. Felton stumbled on the steps. That scarf covered Helen Adrian's fair hair. Miss Remington certainly believed that it was worn by its owner, Marian Brand. Her curiosity would be powerfully excited. I think that she remained at her window for some time, and then went into the garden to find out what was going on. She could have gone out through the kitchen, or by the glass door in the drawing-room. I do not think that she was aware of the fact that the door between the houses had been unlocked. From the garden she saw Mr. Felton come up the steps and go into the house. But where was his companion? Full of curiosity, she goes down towards the beach. On the lowest terrace she is aware of someone standing just above the steep drop to the shingle. We have no proof of this of course, but there is the evidence of a great many small things for which there is no other explanation. We do know that Mr. Felton had quarrelled with Miss Adrian

272

and gone up to the house alone. She waited, perhaps because she did not wish to resume the argument at that time. The tide was nearly full. The place from which she fell is one where there is a good view of the sea. Dark water moving at night has an attraction for many people. I think we may suppose that she stood there for a little to watch it before going in. The night was fine and warm. The sound of the water was in her ears. It would be quite easy for Miss Remington to come up behind her and push her over the edge."

Even after all that had happened Marian could still shudder at the picture this brought up. She said, "Horrible!" and felt the pressure of Richard's hand upon her own.

Miss Silver inclined her head.

"We do not know at what moment Miss Remington realized that she had made a mistake, and that the person whom she had pushed over that steep drop was Helen Adrian and not Marian Brand. Miss Adrian may have cried out as she fell. I think she did so, because Miss Remington was at some pains to mention that she had heard a cry, and then to explain it away."

Marian said,

"I think there was a cry—I think it woke me."

"Just so. It must have startled Miss Remington very much. She may have recognized her mistake then, or later. I think myself it would have been later, when she went down to make sure that her victim was dead. Before she did so I believe she put on the raincoat which Miss Adrian had left upon the seat."

Richard Cunningham said,

"How did she know it was there?"

Miss Silver coughed with a shade of reproof.

"You cannot doubt that she would have provided herself with a torch. Eliza informs me that she possessed one. She put on the raincoat to protect her dress, went down the steps, and completed the murder. She could not risk the chance of her victim's survival. She may have been aware of some circumstance which might have betrayed her identity. She would put on the torch in order to ascertain the extent of the injuries, and it was then, I think, that she recognized Helen Adrian. Instead of feeling any remorse, she thinks only of safeguarding herself and transferring suspicion to Miss Marian. She removes the head-scarf, completes her dreadful work, and returns, leaving the raincoat with its smear of blood on the seat and bringing the scarf back to the house. She had passed close to the study window on the way down, and we may suppose her to have been aware that Mr. Felton had left it open. This, of course, was done in order to allow of Miss Adrian's return. Since Miss Remington must have been very much on the alert when he went back into the house, her keen hearing would have informed her that the door had not been shut. She had only to go in, hang up the scarf, and then return to her own side of the house by whatever door she had left unlatched. It would not occur to her that she could possibly be suspected. Since she had no interest in Helen Adrian's death, the quick, resentful brain which had on the spur of the moment caught at and used the raincoat and scarf to cast suspicion on Miss Marian was, I believe, already busy with further plans. It is all over now, and we need not conjecture as to their exact form, but that they were cunning and malicious, and that they would have been directed against Miss Marian, I do not doubt."

"And then Felton cropped up!"

"As you say. He must have seen or heard something which enabled him to identify her. We do not know what it was. He may have been in the bathroom and looked out of the window and seen her either going or returning. His eyes would by then be tolerably well accustomed to the darkness, and without being able to see more than a moving shadow he could have made a fair guess at her identity, since she is some inches shorter than Penny and there could be no possible confusion between her and Mrs. Brand. It may not have been an absolute identification, but it would be a good enough guess, and if he took his evidence to the police, she would be in very great danger."

Marian steadied her voice with an effort.

"How did she know that he was a danger? Did she hear what he said to Ina?"

"I think so. I have no doubt that he intended to blackmail her. But I think it improbable that he had had either the time or the opportunity to approach her, since he left immediately after Inspector Crisp had taken his statement on Friday, and had only returned on the Sunday morning. There may have been some approach of which we do not know, but I should doubt it. We know that she was in her bedroom on Sunday afternoon. The window of Mrs. Felton's room is very near to hers, and both were open. I have no doubt she would do her best to overhear any conversation between Mr. and Mrs. Felton, and I have no doubt whatever she did hear him tell his wife that he knew who the murderer was. And that she afterwards heard him express his intention of going to his room to lie down and have a good sleep. After that she had only to allow a little time to go by and choose her opportunity. Penny and Felix Brand were out. Mrs. Brand could be relied on to sleep until tea-time. She had that side of the house to herself. On the other side, you two had gone out, Mrs. Felton was in her room, and Eliza would be in the kitchen, her bedroom, or the bathroom. The windows of all these rooms look out upon the beach. The window of Mr. Felton's ground-floor room faces the other way. Miss Remington had only to stroll out to the gate and look up and down the road to feel perfectly secure that no one would see her climb in over that low sill. She had put on the dark blue cotton dress described by Penny, and had provided herself with a sharp knife from the kitchen. No moral scruples restrained her. She had plenty of time to clean the knife and put it back, wash out the navy cotton dress, and roll it down. We know now that she was only attempting to frighten her sister when she spoke of there being a bloodstain on the front of her dress. She need not have troubled. Mrs. Brand might suspect her—and I am quite sure she did—but she would never have opened her lips. She is without energy or principle, and in addition to an inclination towards the line of least resistance she was, I suspect, more than a little afraid of her sister."

Richard Cunningham said,

"A horrible woman! Thank God she is taking herself off! A boardinghouse on the south coast—probably Brighton. She will change her name, establish her right to the best armchair, and sink heavily into coma. Penny and Felix will be well rid of her. They owe you something for that, as well as for all the rest." Then, with a change of voice and manner, "Now just what put it into your head that Penny was in danger?"

She met his look with a thoughtful one.

"I really do not know. I feared there might be some further development. The bias against Felix Brand had been so marked. He would be so convenient a scapegoat for this second murder. But Penny gave him an alibi. I thought an attempt might be made to implicate her. It even occurred to me to wonder whether an attempt might not be made to stage a suicide—" She broke off and said very earnestly, "You must understand, Mr. Cunningham, that it was all very vague— a matter of impression and conjecture. But it was enough to make me feel that I could not acquiesce in those two young people being shut away from the rest of us with a malignant person who had already killed two people in a particularly cold-blooded and shocking manner. I felt that there should be a means of access, and it was with this in my mind that

I asked Penny to unlock the door between the two houses. I really had no plan at that time, only a strong disposition to ensure that the means of access would be available. I knew that by leaning out of Mrs. Felton's window I could keep some check on Miss Remington's movements. When I had ascertained that she was not in her room I went and looked out of my own window and discovered that she was with her sister. As you know, my attention was immediately arrested by the words, 'I shall say Felix did it.' The window was open, and I could hear all that passed. Miss Remington proceeded to elaborate her statement about Felix Brand, and in doing so she gave herself away. When she said, speaking of Felix, 'He saw the light on that blue and yellow handkerchief she was wearing over her head, and he followed her down to the terrace and pushed her over the edge after Cyril Felton had come in, and then of course Cyril guessed, and he killed him too,' she was describing what had actually happened. Only it was not Felix Brand who had seen the light dazzle on that very noticeable head-scarf and followed Helen Adrian to the terrace, but she herself."

Richard said, "There was something about blackmail, wasn't there?"

Miss Silver coughed.

"Miss Remington's exact words were, 'And then, of course, Cyril guessed and tried to blackmail him and he killed him too.'"

"Then it does look as if Felton had actually tried to blackmail her."

"It is impossible to say. You must remember that she was fabricating a case against Felix Brand. As I have already said, I think it is certain that she heard Cyril Felton tell his wife he knew who the murderer was. She had a quick, malicious brain. She was putting together a tissue of lies and making it sound extremely plausible. But when she mentioned the light shining on the head-scarf I suspected that she was describing something which she had seen herself. When, a little later, she said, 'The police won't take any notice of what Penny says—they won't have any opportunity, I can promise you that!' and, later on, 'I don't think we need bother about Penny,' I became very much alarmed. No one who heard Miss Remington pronounce those words could have had any doubt as to their meaning. Cyril Felton was dead. Penny was now the inconvenient witness. But she need not be regarded—there was no need to bother about her. Mrs. Brand was being frightened into submission, and Penny would be silenced. I realized that the danger was immediate. As you now know, Miss Remington had prepared very carefully for this third murder. A fatal dose of Mrs. Brand's sleeping-tablets had been dissolved in the coffee. Eliza tells me that Penny once choked on a tablet as a child and has been nervous about swallowing one ever since. If she took one, it would have to be dissolved. Miss Remington, of course, knew this, and had reserved a single harmless tablet to dissolve in Penny's presence in order to account for the medicated taste. If Penny had drunk that coffee she would have lain down on her bed and never waked again. Miss Remington would have seen to it that the coffee-cup bore no other fingerprints than Penny's. The final wickedness was the scrawled note in a most convincing imitation of Penny's handwriting which was found between the pages of Miss Remington's library book— 'I can't bear it anymore—Felix—' If we had not come in time, that note would have been discovered by Penny's side, and who would have doubted that she had taken her own life under the burden of a knowledge too heavy to be borne? I can never feel sufficiently grateful that my suspicions were aroused, and that we did come in time."

Marian said, "Would she have drunk the coffee?"

Miss Silver coughed.

"It is impossible to say. She was in a dazed and shocked condition. She had been brought up in the habit of obedience. Miss Remington was exerting the utmost pressure of her will. It is indeed providential that we came when we did."

CHAPTER 43

It is easy and dramatic to bring down the curtain at the end of a play, but in human affairs there is no final curtain. If one player leaves the stage, the others still have lives to live and problems to be solved. Marian and Richard found theirs an easy one. In a few days they had come to a mutual trust and understanding which in ordinary circumstances it might have taken weeks and months to reach. Each had seen the other under the pressure of fear and strain, and had found qualities of unselfishness, fortitude, and kindness. The strong attraction which had been between them from the first had brought them so close that neither could now make a plan which did not include the other. Almost without a spoken word, certainly without set question and answer, they found themselves on the footing of lovers. When, on that dreadful night whilst the search for Cassy Remington was still going on, Marian stood for a moment with Richard's arm about her, she had the strangest feeling that they had stepped out of it all into a secret world full of beauty and light, and that this world was their own native country, in which and of which they were, and to which they could always return. In a moment he would go back and take his part in the search and she must go to Ina, but the country was theirs and they would be free of it for all their lives. They did not even kiss. They held each other and were glad, and then went back to all that must be done.

Now, when Miss Silver's farewells had been said, they sat down to talk about plans. Since there was nothing to wait for, and every reason for being together, they would be married at once. And their home would be Ina's—there was no problem there. It was the question of the house which had to be discussed.

Richard said, "Better wait a bit before trying to sell. Even with a housing shortage there won't be much competition. Better wait till the story has died down."

Marian looked out at the sunny garden. Mactavish was playing with a last year's leaf which he had found amongst the wallflower plants. He patted it lazily. His tail was like a banner, his orange coat shone in the sun. She said without turning,

"Does that sort of story die down—just by itself?"

"What do you mean?"

"I was thinking of all the things that happen in houses—people being born, and dying, having good times and bad ones, being good and bad themselves, being miserable or being happy—and the house going on."

"Yes?"

She turned round with colour in her cheeks.

"It's rather like every generation putting in their own furniture—some of it's hideous and some of it's beautiful, and when you come in yourself you keep the good bits and get rid of the bad ones, and you bring what you've got of your own. I was wondering if we couldn't just do that."

"You mean you would like to keep the house—live in it?"

"Yes—I think so. Unless you wouldn't like it. When you said that about the story dying down I thought we could give it a new story—a nice one. A lot of nice people have lived here, you know, as well as some nasty ones. Eliza says Uncle Martin's wife was an angel. I feel as if I sort of owed it to the nice people to get their house clean and tidy again."

He got up, came over to her, and put an arm about her shoulders.

"You're rather a nice person youself—aren't you? I've got a feeling I'm going to like being married to you." They kissed.

After a little he said, "What about Ina?"

"You know, I think she'd like to stay. I think she'd find it easier to be where everybody knows and they're all sorry for her and want to be kind. I think it's easier than going to a new place where one would always be wondering if people did know. Miss Silver has quite a lot of friends in this part of the world. She wants to ask some of them to come and see us. She says Mrs. March will come for one. And there'll be Felix and Penny—"

Felix and Penny were up on the cliff. They had been silent for some time, when Penny said,

"Aunt Florence is going away tomorrow."

He had been staring out over the sea. He turned now, frowning, and repeated her words.

"Going away?"

Penny nodded.

"Directly after the funeral. Didn't you know?"

He shook his head.

"Why should I? She never tells me anything. How long is she going for?"

Penny said as soberly as she could,

"She isn't coming back."

It was difficult to hold on to the lovely light feeling which the words gave her. There must be something wrong about feeling like that when the person who had brought you up and whom you had always called Aunt Florence was going away for good, but the thought of Cove House without that

281

heavy disapproving presence was too much for her. The words very nearly sang themselves.

Felix said, "What!" and she nodded again.

"London first—somewhere Miss Silver told her about. And then I expect it will be a boardinghouse at Brighton. And I think she means to change her name, because letters are all to go to her bank. And anyhow she's more or less said she doesn't want us to write."

Felix gave a harsh laugh.

"The clean cut! Well, that's something to be thankful for. My God—how I have disliked that woman!"

She put her hand down over his for a moment.

"Well, you needn't any more. I tried to love her, but I couldn't. Let her go."

She lifted the hand that had covered his and made a light throwing gesture with it. Let it all go—the hating and the gloom, the trouble which they had brought, the terror and the strain.

Felix watched her with a brooding look. Presently he said, "What are we going to do?"

Penny said, "I don't know."

Her eyes were very clear and bright. They looked at him with a confidence which troubled him. His frown became portentous.

"I can make something out of my music. There was that song cycle for Carrington—I didn't go on with it, but I could. He tried two of the songs, and he was rather all over them—thought they suited his voice. We had a row because I chucked it, but I daresay I could get on to him again. He wanted it for his American tour. There's money in song writing if you make a hit, and I like doing it. I've got plenty of ideas again."

"Yes—"

"My father left me a couple of hundred a year. That woman has the rest of it for her life, and she'll probably live for

282

ever, so it's not good counting on anything from there."

"You'd be all right with what you could make—"

"Yes. I was thinking about you."

"Were you?"

He gave a jerky nod.

"Everything here belongs to Marian."

Penny said softly, "She would let us stay—if you didn't hate it—"

"Why should I? It's always been a good place to work. Some places aren't. I've always been able to work here. You mean you think we could stay on as we are? She's going to marry Cunningham, isn't she? Won't they want the whole house?"

"I don't think so. I think we can have—our bit—if we want it."

All this time she hadn't taken her eyes off him. Now she looked away out over the sea. Her eyes dazzled so that the blue of the water was mixed with the blue of the sky.

Felix said in an odd offhand voice, "I suppose—we couldn't get married—"

"I don't see why not."

"You wouldn't be getting much out of it. There would be very little money."

Still looking away from him, she said,

"I've got some too, you know."

He was so surprised that he sat up and put a hand on her shoulder.

"You! I always thought you hadn't a farthing."

"I hadn't. Uncle Martin gave me some. He settled it on me. I didn't know until he told me last year when I was twenty-one. It's—it's quite a lot. He said not to tell anyone, so I didn't."

"Why?"

"I didn't want to go away, and if they had known it, it would have been very difficult to stay."

"You didn't tell me." His tone accused her.

Her eyelids fell. He saw the lashes wet against her cheek.

"You were away."

He wasn't stupid. He knew very well how far away he had been. He wanted her to know that he had come back, and that he never wanted to go away again. He couldn't find the right words. His grip bruised her shoulder.

"If you've got—enough—without me—"

Penny said in a small, quiet voice,

"I'd never have enough without you."

He said with a groan,

"It would be better for you. When I'm working I shan't even know whether you're there."

"But I'd *be* there—if you wanted me. And you will."

"Penny—" He choked on the name. "I've got a brute of a temper."

The wet lashes lifted. She turned round to him with her hands out, laughing and crying.

"Darling, I've lived with it for twenty years. I expect I can go on."